"Where did it start?" Lenny Bradshaw was studying her carefully.

"Jeez, I don't know." Velvet rolled her bottle between two palms and thought about it. "His chest. Around his chest, I guess."

"Was he smoking?"

"Like a sonofabitch."

"No, I'm sorry, I mean *cigarettes.*"

She shrugged and went back to staring out the window. "I tried to help him, swear to God. Got water, tried to put the fire out, that kind of stuff. Then the alarm went off, and the sprinklers."

Bradshaw made a little *mmm-hmmm* sound, one they probably taught in reporter school. "When you left, was he dead?" he asked.

She snapped back around to look him in the eye. "Of course, he was dead. I wouldn't leave him there like that if he wasn't dead."

He was doodling again. "So, um, what else?"

"What do you mean, what else?"

"Well . . ." He gave her an under-the-lashes look, an aw-shucks-ma'am look of discomfort. "Well, I can't just take this back to my editor. I mean, you know, I need— more. For the amount of money I paid you, I mean. I need— something *great.* Something I can run with."

"Even if I have to make it up?" Velvet asked, and drained the last of her Ginseng Special. He attempted a grin.

"Well, you know, my editor; I really need the story. I'm desperate."

"Okay." She crossed her legs. He crossed his. She leaned forward.

So did he.

"I think," she said, and widened her eyes, "I know who killed him."

PINNACLE BOOKS HAS SOMETHING FOR EVERYONE—

MAGICIANS, EXPLORERS, WITCHES AND CATS

THE HANDYMAN (377-3, $3.95/$4.95)
He is a magician who likes hands. He likes their comfortable shape and weight and size. He likes the portability of the hands once they are severed from the rest of the ponderous body. Detective Lanark must discover who The Handyman is before more handless bodies appear.

PASSAGE TO EDEN (538-5, $4.95/$5.95)
Set in a world of prehistoric beauty, here is the epic story of a courageous seafarer whose wanderings lead him to the ends of the old world—and to the discovery of a new world in the rugged, untamed wilderness of northwestern America.

BLACK BODY (505-9, $5.95/$6.95)
An extraordinary chronicle, this is the diary of a witch, a journal of the secrets of her race kept in return for not being burned for her "sin." It is the story of Alba, that rarest of creatures, a white witch: beautiful and able to walk in the human world undetected.

THE WHITE PUMA (532-6, $4.95/NCR)
The white puma has recognized the men who deprived him of his family. Now, like other predators before him, he has become a man-hater. This story is a fitting tribute to this magnificent animal that stands for all living creatures that have become, through man's carelessness, close to disappearing forever from the face of the earth.

SLOW BURN

ROXANNE LONGSTREET

PINNACLE BOOKS
KENSINGTON PUBLISHING CORP.

PINNACLE BOOKS are published by

Kensington Publishing Corp.
850 Third Avenue
New York, NY 10022

First Pinnacle Books Printing: March, 1996

Printed in the United States of America
10 9 8 7 6 5 4 3 2 1

To J.J. Davis
For years of support, belief, and friendship.

Insanity loves company, eh?
(Or is that the company loves . . . ?)

Acknowledgements

To the good folks who almost literally pulled this book out of me— the Wednesday Weirdos.

Also, to Don Maass— as always, thanks.

Special Thanks

There is nothing more fortunate in life than to have a good spouse. A spouse who knows that when you're staring out the window with your headpones on, you're working. A spouse who has the patience and love to sit patiently through readings of stories he's already heard four or five times.

A spouse who will even talk about spontaneous human combustion over breakfast, lunch and dinner.

Cat, you're the best. Love you.

One

Velvet

God, she hated hallways. This one stretched to her left and right like a pea-green ocean, dimly lit with art deco moons. Velvet Daniels hugged her mink closer and wished she didn't feel so vulnerable out here, so obvious.

I could leave, she thought, and wondered why the hell she was so jumpy. She shook her head and took a quick look at her cheat sheet, discreetly tucked in her eelskin purse.

Burt Everard Marshall. Trojans. Scented banana oil. Likes baby blue. Prefers rich and bossy.

She sucked in a deep breath and gave three sharp commanding raps on the wood.

He was pretty much what she'd expected— overweight, middle-aged, sallow with exhaustion. Bruised bags under eyes that glittered with panic.

"Hello," he began, and from the terror on his face she realized he couldn't figure out what else to say. She put one hand flat against the door and pushed it wide open, swept him aside with it. Walked into the room and gave it her best unforgiving glare.

"What a dump," she said, and thought of imitating Bette Davis too late. "Next time, try to get someplace decent. And don't keep me waiting."

"Hey, that's great, you're— you're in character, aren't you— " He licked his thick lips and swung the door indecisively back and forth. The breeze ruffled her hair. She raised her eyebrows at him.

"Are you going to invite anybody else in?" she asked, and nodded toward the open door. He shut it and stood where he was, fooling nervously with his tie. Velvet resisted the urge to sigh. "Well, don't just stand there, take my coat."

"Ah! Okay." He managed to touch her while he slid the mink from her shoulders, and his fingers felt hot and damp. *Shower,* she reminded herself, as she always did at these moments. *A nice long hot shower.* "Okay, okay."

He hung the coat up and looked panicked again. She lost the battle and sighed.

"Money," she reminded him. He snatched out a thick, bumpy-looking wallet and fanned twenties out on the dresser with shaking fingers. The twenties looked real enough at a distance, and he was too much of a geek to cheat. Having delivered the date money, Burt looked panicked again.

"A drink? Do you think you can spare a drink?"

"Ah. Sure." Burt was going to be stupid, but biddable. She sat down on the edge of the bed and watched him rattle glasses and pour Scotch from tiny hotel bottles. He kept giving her little flicking glances that ricocheted away from her stare.

Velvet took off her shoes and curled up on the bed, legs demurely covered by her dress.

"You look . . ." Burt hesitated, flipping through a mental thesaurus. "Beautiful."

She took the Scotch he held out, and smiled. It was her professional smile. Burt was going to be a lot of work.

"So do you," she purred. "Here. Have a seat. My name's Velvet, Burt."

"I'm Burt," he blurted, and blushed bright red.

He was sweating heavily, dark wet rings under his arms and trickles sliding down his face to drip on his collar. She made sure her smile stayed professional and put several underlines on her mental note to shower. Poor man. If it was such an ordeal for him, why did he do it?

His sweat smelled different than she was used to. Acrid. Was he sick? She didn't like the thought of fucking a sick man, though she'd probably done it often enough. Thank god for rubbers.

Enough foreplay, she thought, and, sipping her Scotch, slowly unbuttoned her silk blouse while he watched. Revealed the baby-blue bra. It had a front hook on it, and she popped it to let the blouse and bra slide slowly down her arms and off, a wave of silk and lace. The air-conditioning felt damp and cold on her skin, like nervous fingers.

She leaned back against the pillows and dribbled a little Scotch on her nipples.

"Lick it off," she commanded. Jesus, he was red. Gasping for air. He started to lean forward to obey her, then sat up and pulled at his tie.

"Can't," he croaked, and fumbled with his shirt buttons. She leaned forward again, genuinely spooked now, as his glass fell out of his hand and tumbled slowly to the carpet, spilling a Scotch rain.

Oh, god, he was going to croak on her. She'd always been afraid of that, had asked Ming what to do, but Ming said it never happened, just in the movies, and now here he was croaking right in front of her—

He clawed at his shirt. She caught a single horrified glimpse of his eyes and they were red, as if they'd filled up with blood. His face was the color of bricks.

"Burt?" she managed to gasp, and smelled something cooking.

His shirt burst into flame. White flame. She felt herself moving and knew that she was crawling away from him, but she couldn't stop watching, and the shirt was *melting* into his skin and burning; she saw polyester blisters sizzle and explode on his skin, raw red muscle peel away and turn lacy black. His chest was burning. His arms. His back.

Water, she thought blankly. *I'd better get some water.*

She didn't remember going in the bathroom, but when she blinked again, she was standing on cold tile in front of the sink. Burt was making noises, awful sounds like creaking bedsprings. Water. She turned the tap on and stared in panic at the gushing stream. Jesus God, what kind of freak scene was this? There was one cup, *goddamnit,* just one wrapped in plastic. She grabbed for it and ripped the shrink-wrap off and the thing came apart in her hands in sharp plastic shards, and from the other room Burt was making those *sounds*.

"I'm coming!" she yelled, and picked up the ice bucket.

The smoke alarm exploded into a scream, drilled into her head like a white-hot needle and pushed at her in waves on her skin. She put her hands over her ears but that didn't help; her throat hurt and she realized she was screaming, too, but she couldn't hear it over the alarm.

I have to get out of here, she thought very clearly. *I'll get the goddamn water and I'm gone. He'll be all right, the ambulance is on the way.*

The ice bucket was too big to fit under the faucet in the sink. Too big for the toilet— no, too small. She ripped the shower curtain away from the tub and stood there panting and clawing at the faucets until a thick stream of water gushed into the ice bucket.

Her chest hurt. She braced herself against the cold tile wall and saw stars.

Right about the time the bucket was halfway full, a cold nasty spray of rusty water came out of the ceiling and drenched her hair. She dropped the bucket and looked up in utter shock at the whirling silver sprinkler.

Okay, okay, it was all over now. She could just get the hell out, he was going to be okay. The sprinklers were on. It couldn't possibly be as bad as it had looked, everybody thought these things were worse than they really were—

She came around the corner into a thin horrible cloud of smoke, and through it she saw the white fire flicker and die on the thing that lay in a tarry mess of melted carpet.

His eyes were white, like boiled eggs. They leaked.

The alarm hiccuped and stopped. There was some other sound, something high and thin—

Velvet put both hands over her mouth to stop screaming. Her ears felt bruised and full of blood.

She stuffed the bra in her purse and threw the blouse over her shoulders, stuffed her feet into her shoes, wrapped the mink around her. Poor little drowned-rat mink.

"Sorry, sorry, sorry," she kept whispering, and found her Scotch glass. It was half full; she gagged the liquor down and wiped the glass with the bedspread. She hesitated over the cash on the dresser, then grabbed the wet bills and shoved them into her panty hose. They felt cold and slimy and used.

She thought that he moved, one strange little twitch out of the corner of her eye as she opened the door. No. He couldn't have.

Jesus. Jesus, she hated hallways.

Two
Robby

Robby MacReady brushed her fingertips across the top of a brown leather wallet and moved on without taking it. She could tell— almost to the nearest dollar— how much was in it, and that one wasn't worth the risk.

While the wallet walked away, oblivious, she eyed the crowd and rubbed her itchy fingers. The weight of other people's money dragged at the lining of her coat— enough money, she thought, but then how much was enough? The hardest part of stealing, like gambling, was knowing when to quit.

Not yet, she promised her itchy fingers. *Soon.*

An overweight young woman with red hair tied back from a round unmemorable face passed close to her, and Robby twitched her finger as if throwing away a cigarette. Kelly— the red-haired woman— forged ahead. Robby fell in behind her.

Kelly had good hands, if not strictly great; she had a limited feel for marks, rarely got called and never got caught. Robby might have liked her except for her generally sour attitude and endless romantic difficulties— the latest was with Sol, their resident Mafia tax collector. Sol dressed as if someone might be filming him for the next movie of the week.

Ah, Robby thought, and felt a distant tingle. Money coming. She let her eyes go blank and watched faces, watched movements. The woman strolling toward them with the red suit and Gucci bag had the walk of wealth.

Kelly eased in and neatly fished a wallet out of the Gucci bag. Robby judged it a seven of possible ten. The mark, busy checking her diamond-studded watch, never even noticed. Kelly made a quick snapping motion with her fingers, and Robby quickened her walk, brushed by and retrieved the wallet from her. It joined about seven other sweet twins in various Velcro pockets in her jacket.

Robby felt sated and relaxed and— at least for the moment— rich. She waved Kelly off from another pinch and slowed to an amble, enjoying the cool sunshine, the fresh breeze. Kelly hurried away down the street.

A block farther down, Robby, in a celebratory mood, entered O'Donnell's.

The crowd never seemed to change— broad Irish faces, a few narrow dark ones that might have been Italian, but could have been Welsh. Hookers, thieves, reporters, morticians, lawyers. Though it was in the financial district, well-connected people didn't find it comfortable to stay in O'Donnell's; the clientele, to put it bluntly, was made up of losers.

It reminded Robby rather strongly of Ireland.

She ordered a whisky and rocks and pulled a stool up to the counter, careful of the drips and stains on the old wood. The zombie-eyed bartender handed her napkins to clean it, and she sat down with a weary fulfilled sigh. She took her first nose-tingling mouthful of Bushmill's, paused to crunch a stale pretzel between her teeth. An older man with defeated alcoholic eyes fed quarters into the jukebox,

and a Chieftains ballad began to wail. Two stools
away, a gentleman in a correctly tailored blue suit
sipped canned beer and smiled when he caught her
eye; Robby gave him a good long look and smiled
back. There was an empty stool next to her. She patted it and raised her eyebrows.

The man— obviously in the wrong place, since one
did not come to O'Donnell's to drink canned domes-
tic beer— had the tingle. No doubt he'd put it down
to sex appeal. Her smile warmed as he stood up and
started over.

Some days, she just couldn't stop.

Someone darted in ahead of her mark— a young
woman, blond, wearing a pale blue dress and a mink
that looked as if it had been drowned, not skinned.
She smelled like a wet dog, and her blue eyes had a
dribble of mascara at the edges, like kite tails. She
sat down heavily on the stool next to Robby and
slumped over the bar, staring blankly ahead at her
dim reflection in the mirror. A pretty face, too sharp
at the chin, a shade too wide at the cheeks to be a
model. Something fox-clever about her face. Her eyes
were wide and as blue as a Texas summer sky.

"Scotch," the hooker snapped at the bartender; he
reached for a bottle in slow motion. "Double. Snap
it up."

Robby, about to give her a frosty send-off, closed
her mouth and watched with morbid attention. She
had no patience with hookers, none at all— counted
them, in fact, one step below the homeless who
smeared greasy rags on windshields— but this one
was nevertheless interesting. Swimming with a mink?
She supposed some— clients— might be perverse
enough to request that, but she couldn't imagine a
hooker being accommodating enough to agree.

More than that, hookers never, ever bought their own drinks on duty. And hookers were *never* off duty.

Her mark, the gentleman in the business suit, leaned over Robby's shoulder; she turned her head to smile at him, but he wasn't looking at her anymore. The hooker. Of course. Where else?

"What's a nice girl—" he began. Robby ran her fingertips over the bulge of his wallet.

"Buzz off," the hooker said without even looking at him. "We're closed."

Robby was only dimly aware of the man withdrawing, nursing his wounds; the hooker had an eelskin purse on a thin gold chain, and the catch was not quite closed. Robby cocked her head and stared at it, interested. The woman's Scotch arrived, doubled, and she tipped it back into her mouth and swallowed until it was dry. She coughed like a cat with a hairball. "Oh, Jesus, it tastes like smoke. Uh— vodka. Double."

Robby sipped her drink and watched. The hooker opened the eelskin purse and peeled a twenty off a wad of bills that looked as wet as the mink dripping on her shoulders. "Hit me until I don't care, okay?"

"Whatever," the bartender shrugged. The hooker fumbled her glass and sent vodka spilling over the bar toward Robby, who scooted her stool away from the danger. The woman's face was flushed.

"Sorry," the hooker mumbled. " 'M having a crisis."

Robby nodded noncommittally and returned to sipping at her Bushmill's, and watched the hooker down vodkas, one after another, a masochist getting slaps in the face. After a while, the woman took another twenty out and waved it at the bartender, in case her tab was running down; the drinks kept coming.

Robby sat, relaxed, and chewed a straw while she waited for her chance.

All in all, it was shaping up to be a great day.

* * *

"Same again," Velvet ordered, and wrestled with the mink. It clung like sweat. Before the bartender could turn away, she grabbed his white sleeve. "Hey. No cheap stuff, goddamn it. I'm paying for the real thing. Russian shit."

She had to admit, she couldn't tell the difference between Russian vodka and Mexican vodka, but it sounded good. He shrugged and tilted a bottle over her glass for the sixth time, or the twentieth, she'd given up counting. She almost spilled the drink in her haste to get it to her lips, and took in a long spicy sip of cold mist, a swallow of fire and ice.

Fire. She choked and coughed and burst into tears. Goddamn *freaks.* She dabbed frantically at her eyes with a cocktail napkin, tried to tilt her head back, but all that did was make cold snail-trails down the side of her face. The tight-assed woman in the business suit on her left leaned forward for a handful of pretzels and pretended not to notice. After another minute the suit finished her drink and disappeared toward the neon-lit hallway that said things like PHONE and RESTROOMS and POOL. Thinking about the bathroom made Velvet remember that she really ought to throw up.

"Pretty lady like you shouldn't cry," said the cowboy sitting on her right. The sticker on his carry-on bag read HOU. He thought he was the Marlboro Man, in his big belt buckle and plastic-heeled boots. She snuffled and took a drink of vodka that tasted like salt and mascara.

"Yeah, what do you know about it?" she muttered around the glass.

"I know you got to kiss the girls to make them cry. That it, sweetie? Somebody kiss you and make you cry?" He had yellow-brown skin he'd bought in a blue-tubed tanning salon, and eyes green enough to have come out of a contact lens case. His hat was new and made of straw and had a feather hatband dyed bright purple.

"You asshole," she whispered, and giggled and choked and swallowed all at the same time. He leaned closer and cupped his ear, a polite cheerful expression on his face.

"Sorry?" he said, and gave her what was probably his most charming smile, dimples and all. Velvet swallowed the rest of her drink in one gulp.

"You're an asshole!" she shouted into his ear, and giggled helplessly as he slid right off the stool and onto his ass on the floor, face gone childishly slack with shock. "The world'sh— word's— full of goddamn assholes!"

She gagged down one more slug of vodka and groped blindly for her purse. She narrowly missed putting her stiletto heel in the cowboy's crotch as she stepped over him to weave toward the door.

Ming was supposed to be here, goddamnit. Where the hell was she? Velvet leaned against a wall that seemed to be moving and looked out at the late afternoon street; too many people, too many colors, too many voices talking about too many things— some of them were talking about her. She swallowed hard and shut her eyes, but that was worse. Her head was starting to pound.

Mom would be so disappointed in her if she threw up in public. She imagined her mother standing in the doorway, shaking her finger. Dad stood behind her in his John Deere cap with a face like a tractor tireprint. She wondered if Burt Everard Marshall had family, a nice little fireplug of a wife, tubby smiling children. He'd looked like a family man. She couldn't remember whether or not he'd been wearing a wedding ring.

Oh, god, she'd throw up if she didn't have another drink. She wavered away from the wall and sank into a creaking wooden chair and, like magic, a gum-smacking waitress in black Lycra pants stretched to light gray appeared at her table. Her laminated name tag said MYRA.

"Get ya something," Myra intoned. She looked about an inch above Velvet's head and tapped her foot.

"Scotch," Velvet said, and then canceled that with a wide uncontrolled wave of her hand. "One for the road. Banana daiquiri."

Myra stuck her finger down her throat and made a gagging sound.

"Seven bucks. Not including gratuity."

Gratuity almost served as a launching pad for the wad of gum in Myra's left cheek. Myra's teeth went back to work, pounding her ammunition into submission.

Velvet opened her purse.

Cleaned out.

She stared in shock, frozen, while Myra tapped her foot in irregular syncopation to the pounding of her heart.

"Sonofabitch," Velvet finally murmured blankly. Had it been the cowboy? She craned her neck and found him, cheerfully gulping down a double at the bar and already laughing with buddies he hadn't had two minutes before. Nah, the cowboy wasn't smart enough. Besides, he'd never gotten close enough. Who else? Anybody— *that prissy-faced, tight-assed suit.* Of course. Goddamn fucking *bitch.* "Ah— forget it."

Myra shrugged and headed off in the direction of the next bubble she blew. Velvet teetered to her feet, wrapped the mink more securely around her, and headed for the bathroom.

The suit was not by the phones. Velvet kept going. In the room on the right a scarred, tilting pool table waited unsuccessfully for suckers. The bathroom was only about five feet farther down, but her balance moved six degrees left and she grabbed a wall. She was still standing there waiting for the floor to get back under her when the bathroom door swung open and a brown-haired woman in blue jeans and an NYU sweatshirt came out carrying a briefcase. Except for the briefcase, there was no resemblance to the suit—this woman had moussed waved hair, round glasses, red lipstick. She had a roundish bland face, no cheekbones to speak of, a button nose, brown eyes smiling under the glasses.

But her eyes went blank when she saw Velvet standing there.

"Excuse me," she murmured, and started to slide by. Velvet's arm came up like a toll barrier. She almost toppled over.

"I want my fushin— fuckin' money."

The woman's eyes grew wide and focused, as if she had just seen her for the first time. Not surprised, though. Even the smile was smooth.

"I'm afraid you've made a mistake," the woman said, and there was a lilt that sounded Irish buried under asphalt-thick layers of Brooklyn. *Great*, Velvet thought. *I don't even get a real American thief. Fucking foreigners.*

"No mishtakes." Velvet concentrated on putting the words together; they kept slipping like wet fish. Her voice kept climbing higher on her, losing its balance. "I'm gonna yell if I don't shee it right now, *now*, you know?"

"You're going to get us both arrested."

"So?"

Slowly, very slowly, the other woman reached in the front pocket of her blue jeans and pulled out two hundred dollars in crisp twenties, not even a little damp. Velvet snatched the money and fanned the bills.

"We're done," the woman said, and started to push by. Velvet grabbed the nearest piece of anatomy— elbow, bony— and hauled her to a stop.

"Buy me a drink," she pleaded mushily. The woman just stared at her. God, she looked so cold, so goddamn cold. "Come on, please. *Please*. I wanna talk to you."

She burst into tears that shook her so hard it hurt. She clung to the other woman for balance, hiding her face in the soggy mink and making loud helpless wails that she tried to gulp down along with bubbling vodka.

The woman's arm went under her shoulders, moved her stumbling across the floor, and sat her down in a chair. Velvet mopped at her eyes with the back of one shaking hand and fumbled for a napkin; the other woman got to it first and used it to wipe her hands fastidiously clean before she sat down. She snapped her fingers over her head and glared at Myra, who started to weave back in their direction.

"Are you all right?" the thief asked. Velvet picked up the crumpled napkin and blew her nose, noisily.

"Shure. Course. Why?"

"Sweet Jesus," the woman sighed. Myra wandered into range, and the thief waved her urgently over.

"Hey, whash your name?" Velvet asked. The other woman glanced at her, then quickly away. She had kind of a squarish face; the lipstick looked all wrong, too red. A pastel face, Velvet decided. Coral lip gloss. Peach eye shadow.

"Robby."

"Like the robot?"

"You could say so." The woman found another

napkin and wiped her fingers again— small hands, stubby fingers, smooth French-manicured nails.

Velvet waved her arms bonelessly in the air and shouted, "Danger! Danger, Will Robinshon!" and giggled when the other woman flinched.

"Quiet!" Robby-the-robot hissed, and leaned forward. She looked as if she might have wanted to slap her, but there weren't any more napkins on the table for her to wipe her fingers on. "Listen, you, you make trouble and they won't serve you any more drinks, is that what you want?"

"You're just worried 'cause of the money in your pockets."

Myra drifted over like a corpse in a current, gave them each fish-eyed stares, and poised a chewed pencil with no eraser over her pad. She blew a pale pink bubble, inhaled it, and pointed her pencil at Robby.

"You," Myra said. It sounded like she was identifying her at a lineup.

"I'm buying for my friend here— give her two vodka doubles, and keep 'em coming."

The pencil swiveled like a machine-gun turret, and Velvet almost crossed her eyes staring at the empty metal socket where the eraser had once been.

"No banana daiquiri?"

"Vodka," Velvet nodded. Myra rolled her eyes and wandered away again. The pencil ended up in her mouth, and Velvet wondered if the eraser had been mistaken for gum.

"Look— you— " Robby said. Velvet broke her pretzel into tiny pretzel particles and mashed them with numb fingertips.

"I have a name, y'know. Velvet." It sounded so good she said it a couple more times. "Velvet. Vel-vet."

"Look, Velvet, why don't I just leave you a twenty to get you going, and you can drink all you— "

"No! No, don't leave, don't— " Velvet felt tears start up again, and she grabbed at Robby's hand, pinning her down. "I just— shit. Shit. Goddamn shit."

Robby blinked. "Excuse me?"

Time did an alcoholic stretch, and suddenly Myra was back, delivering two glasses thick with something that looked like water; Velvet tipped one back fast. Not water. It burned the sticky spiderwebs out of the back of her throat.

"Don't go," she said again. Her head felt thick and light, like styrofoam. "Hey, don't go. Don't."

Robby came up with a dry twenty-dollar bill and passed it to Myra, who popped her gum and swished away toward two guys in gray suits who had the IRS kicked-dog-turned-killer look. They were looking; hell, everybody was staring, every goddamn body.

"What the hell do you *want?*" Robby snapped. "I bought your damned drinks."

Velvet inhaled the second glass of vodka and rubbed her numb cheeks; they felt slick and wet.

"Gotta tell you— he— see— there was this— Burt— and— goddamn— goddamn— shit goddamn you gotta— see I tried to help him, I tried but *whoosh* like a goddamn— goddamn *match*— burned. *Burned.*"

She made helpless circles with her hands, big whooshing motions.

She stopped because she realized Robby was staring at her. Staring *right* at her, no more little holier-than-you quickies. Her eyes were wide and dark.

"What did you say?" Robby asked. Velvet swallowed and tried to look her in the eye.

"Burned. He burned." She added a flap of her hands. "Whoosh. Oopsh. Shorry."

"You were there, and this man burned? Caught on fire?"

Velvet nodded dumbly, happy that she'd gotten the

attention, just plain happy. She'd *said* it. She'd gotten it out, and now it was okay.

" 'Nother drink?" she asked, shaking her glass at Robby. Robby kept staring, a closed expression on the square face, the cool eyes.

"Did he die?" she asked quietly. Velvet lost her grip on the glass, and it tumbled to the table and skittered nervously in circles.

"Died," she said solemnly. "Yeah. Hope sho."

She started crying again, because Burt had been so nice, so goddamn nice, and she hardly even realized Robby was getting up until another twenty hit the table and stuck to scattered drops of vodka.

It hit Velvet late, and hard, that the look in Robby's eyes had been familiar.

Jesus God, she thought through the fog. *She's seen it, too. She's seen it.*

Her ass was just about Velcroed to the chair, but she stumbled up, somehow. Her ankles kept folding over on her. She stripped off the high heels and stuck them in the pockets of the mink and made it to the door, to blinding sunlight and nauseating noise and traffic.

Where the hell—

Ah. There she was. Blue jeans and sweatshirt, walking away down the sidewalk.

Velvet put her left hand on the building and lurched off in pursuit.

Three
Robby

The DON'T WALK sign glared red. Robby glared back at it and bounced the briefcase impatiently on her thigh. Two feet ahead, traffic spilled by in a stream of bright paint and choking exhaust. *Damn* that hooker, it had started out such a good day.

Her neck prickled alarm. She resisted the urge to turn and look, aware of the damning weight of wallets in her briefcase. Probably just a bicycle cop. She'd just ignore it and—

"Hey!" A drunken smear of sound. Robby's neck locked tight. "Hey, wait!"

She stared fixedly ahead at the red DON'T WALK sign, willing it to change. The traffic lights blinked yellow, yellow, yellow—

The sign lazily changed to WALK, and traffic swirled to a disappointed stop. She crossed briskly— not quite running— into the intersection, and made it as far as the left-hand turn lane; the brief blast of warmth from a revving Volvo's front end felt surprisingly good. She hadn't realized how cold the wind had turned.

The WALK sign flickered threateningly, then wavered to a red DON'T, and the lights, never quite on cycle, changed while she was still in the street a few steps from the sidewalk. Close enough. Confidence and relief spread out warm over her body. The curb, a brisk walk to the warehouse— and escape. No more bullshit, thank god.

Brakes squealed behind her with a sound like grating knives. Like Lot's wife, Robby turned to look over her shoulder and saw the hooker frozen a few steps behind her in the middle of the lane, staring white-faced at the oncoming shiny grille of a pickup truck.

No time for thought, no time for anything. Robby leaned back, caught a wet fistful of mink, and pulled as hard as she could. The hooker, overbalanced, pin-wheeled past her, tripped on the curb, and skidded to her hands and knees.

The pickup truck skated by, tires smoking. Robby's sneaker left a kamikaze smear on its blood red side as she jumped for the safety of the sidewalk. The truck fishtailed another thirty feet before straightening. As she caught her balance with one arm around a light pole, the cowboy at the wheel looked back, white-faced, and hit the gas.

Robby gulped deep breaths and looked down at the hooker, who scuffled her bare feet on the concrete and managed to roll to a spread-legged sitting position. The woman stared mournfully at the long dirty skinned patches on her knees, the ruin of her hose. There was a cut on her chin, and it dripped fresh crimson beads on her blue dress.

"Ow," she said. "Shit. Goddamn shit."

Robby had her mouth open to ask where she'd lost her shoes, but the sound of that voice— she took a deep breath to flush the shakes out of her system, turned her back, and started walking. The hell with the hooker *and* her shoes.

She didn't get far before she heard fabric tearing and looked back to see the hooker lurch to her bare feet. The dress hem slouched wearily in the front, dangling strings like jellyfish tentacles.

"Hey!" the hooker yelled again, pointing vaguely at her. "Hey, you— robot— ah— "

Robby flinched and ducked her head, staring determinedly ahead. People stared in her direction— past her toward the hooker, who was probably weaving in pursuit. It seemed so damn undignified to run— not to mention dangerous, if any cops were around. She was only a block from the warehouse and safety, but still—

Ahead, a police car slid greasily around the corner and cruised in her direction. Good. They'd reel in the hooker, dry her out . . . by morning she'd have forgotten all about—

"Hey, stop!" the hooker yelled. Her voice cracked, and it sounded like she was crying. "Hey— please— hey— lady, you gotta— hey, you, *thief,* I'm talkin' to you!"

Robby did not— quite— stop in her tracks. She made a tight circle of steps and walked back in the hooker's direction, thinking calmly, *I can't kill her, if I kill her, they'll arrest me. Maybe I can just hurt her a little.*

She stared at the hooker as she walked toward her, the drowned-cat mink hanging half off her shoulders, the torn dress, the bare feet. Pathetic as a big-eyed drunk clown.

When Robby was within a few steps, the hooker said in a lost quiet voice, "Please don't leave me."

For a second the world tilted, and Robby was back in a Dublin train station, and the words were something she'd said as she'd reached out to her father for the last time. She took Velvet's arm more gently than she'd meant to.

"Okay," she heard herself say. "Okay. Just be *quiet.*"

Behind her she heard car doors slam, and looked

around at an approaching Dallas cop; his face had a wary thousand-yard stare. His partner waited behind the wheel of the cruiser, looking a little too interested. A white flash of panic zigzagged painfully through her body.

Easy. Easy. She found a smile somewhere, shook out the wrinkles, and put it on for him.

No matching smile, no change in his eyes, nothing at all.

"Having some trouble?" he asked. Robby felt the hooker's weight start to drag at her arm and held her up in a grip strong enough to leave bruises.

"Well . . . sir, it's kind of embarrassing— " Robby tried a blush; that seemed to work better than the smile. She avoided his eyes and talked to his name tag, HARTZ. There was a thick fingerprint on its shiny gold surface. "Ah— my friend just had a few too many, officer. I'm walking her home."

"What's your friend's name?" HARTZ asked. The name tag shifted, and she caught a glimpse of her own startled face, brown eyes wide and earnest. *You're trying too hard,* she told herself. *Relax.*

What the *hell* was the hooker's name? Silk?

"Velvet," she heard herself say. "I'm sorry we were causing trouble, sir, but I'm just taking her one more block."

The cop's chest moved calmly, in and out. She risked a look at his face. He was bored. His eyes had already moved on, checking the street.

"One more block to where?"

"Home. Her home."

God, now he'd ask her where home was, and she didn't know, couldn't even find anything that looked like a home. Stores. Parking lots. Warehouses. Oh, god, she couldn't point out the warehouse, not to save her life. Panic tried to rise again; she fought it down and waited, waited. *Please* . . .

The next time she felt the cold touch of the cop's gaze, she raised her chin and met it squarely.

"I'm very sorry for the trouble, officer," she said. He had light blue eyes, tired, cool, suspicious. His smile was tight and unconvincing. He nodded and stepped back.

"Go on, ma'am."

Robby tugged the hooker's arm to get her moving, and they stumbled away. Behind her, she knew he was turning to track them.

Once she heard the door slam and the car pull away, she allowed herself one quiet whispered curse. It sounded shaky. She looked over at Velvet, who was pasty and wide-eyed and very, very quiet. The hooker concentrated on walking, one careful step after another.

Neither of them had anything to say.

"Wow!" The hooker's voice echoed loudly in the silence. "Wow, big. Big. Really— big."

On the whole, Robby had liked her better scared. She let go of the hooker's arm and pulled the door shut behind her with a gritty scrape of rusted hinges. The little sunlight coming through the high dirty windows streaked over the floor, but kept most of the warehouse in shadow. It smelled dirty and stale.

"Why're we here?" the hooker continued. She hugged her mink closer. " 'S cold."

"Quiet." Robby flicked on a row of overhead lights; they made patches of watery gray in the darkness, enough to see by, barely. Acres of concrete floor, pitted and cracked, covered with broad sweating patches of dirty oil, stretched into shadow. "What'd you do with your shoes?"

"Shoes?" Velvet repeated blankly, and looked down. "Oh. Dunno."

They were sticking out of her coat pockets. Robby rescued them and handed them over; Velvet dropped them with a clatter, frowned, and aimed her right foot at her left shoe and kicked it across the grimy floor. She went after it, padding right over a big oily stain. Once she'd captured it, she sat down on the floor to put it on; her face turned tragic when she realized she'd left the right shoe ten feet away.

Robby gave up on her and crossed to a corrugated tin door some nonspeller had spray painted to read NO ADMITENCE, knocked twice, and waited. Psycho Jim opened the door, a wild-haired wino stinking of cheap booze and clothes that had been left to ripen in a landfill. She handed him the briefcase, and his face relaxed.

"Jesus, kid, I was getting worried," he said, his low voice a quiet rumble. He looked over her shoulder, and his face went blank. "Who the hell— "

"She's with me," Robby said. Jim transferred the blank look to her. "I didn't have a choice."

"You— didn't— " He stared at her another few seconds, shook his head, and stepped back. "Come in, if you're coming. Bring her."

The hooker was staring down at her feet; she'd managed to get both shoes on, and was balancing by sheer force of will. Her eyes were Orphan Annie blank. *Maybe*, Robby thought, *if I just go inside and close the door, she won't figure it out.*

Then again, she'd been smart enough to keep her mouth shut around the cops. Robby picked her way around oil stains back to where the hooker waited, and steered her in a zigzag to the door.

A blast of warm air, cinnamon, and nutmeg hit her in the face, thick enough to taste. The hooker hung back in the doorway, staring blearily at the room, the clean carpeted floor, comfortable warm chairs.

"Shthis?" She squinted at a big-screen television set at the far end of the room. "Hey, wow. Cable?"

Robby pulled hard, got her inside, and shut the door with a sense of relief— until she turned and saw Jim staring, and Kelly, and Mark. Mark had come in from the kitchen carrying a plateful of what looked like oatmeal cookies. Kelly half-reclined on the peach-colored sofa, *People* magazine draped forgotten over her chest. They all looked fascinated and horrified, like people passing a car wreck.

Velvet leaned heavily against Robby, batted tear-clumped eyelashes, and said, " 'Lo, folks."

"Not a word," Robby snapped when Kelly opened her mouth; it shut again with a snap. "Ignore her. Ah— Velvet— why don't you go in the bathroom and get cleaned up."

"Bathroom?" Velvet echoed. "Yeah. Good idea."

She pulled free of Robby's grip and wandered off to the left, toward the closet. Jim grabbed her and pushed her in the right direction. Mark leaned over and looked at the oily shoeprints she'd left in the gray carpeting. The silence felt like interrogation.

Robby sank into a floral armchair, closed her eyes, and pressed both hands against her throbbing forehead. After a minute, something cold touched her arm, and she looked up to find Mark holding out a bottle of Perrier, a serious look on his thin delicate face.

"None of my business," he said, "but, honey, I'd be a little choosier if I were you."

She took the bottle and knocked it lightly against the side of his head. He staggered back in mock pain and dropped into a chair on the other side of the couch, near Kelly.

"It's not funny," said Jim. His voice was muffled, because he was in the process of stripping off layers of stinking sweaters and ragged shirts. His tatty raincoat lay in a tired slump on the carpet. "Well? Who is she?"

"Nobody," Robby said, and sipped. The water had a bitter undertaste, or maybe that was just her mood. "A drunk. Look, she tagged me in the bar, then followed me out on the street. I almost got busted before I quieted her down. Just leave her alone. I'll feed her some drinks, and she won't remember her name, much less where she's been."

Jim fought his way free of the sweaters and stood there, hair a leonine bristling mass around his face, glaring at her. He picked up the clothes and began stuffing them into a garbage sack, the better to ferment the odors.

"Stupid," he muttered. "Unbelievable. This is my *home*, Robby, what were you thinking? Oh, forget it."

"You'll feel better after you take a shower," Mark offered kindly. Jim's eyes sleeted over.

"There is a *hooker* in my *bathroom.*"

On cue, there was noise from that direction. Bumps. Knocks. The struggle subsided into ominous silence. Robby sagged deeper into her armchair under the weight of Jim's stare.

"Sorry."

"Let's just get this over with," Jim said with careful precision. "Kelly?"

Kelly, still smirking, sat up and pulled her purse out from under the table. She spilled out wallets and began stripping the contents into neat piles. Identification, credit cards, cash. Mark opened his backpack, searched between textbooks, and added his take to the pile. Robby flicked the latches on her briefcase and pulled cash from under her carefully folded business suit and shoes.

"My Amex guy's out of town," Mark said as he sorted credit cards into stacks—green, silver, gold. He frowned over a couple and put them aside in a reject pile. "Jim, you got anybody for those?"

"Amex? No. I'll take VISA and MasterCard. Oh, and Antoine says he can move all the ID we have."

"That's good, 'cause it looks like I got a lot of it today. Shit, you'd think these SMU assholes would have cash." Mark himself was a sometime-student at Texas Christian University, an arch-rival of Southern Methodist University, and appropriately prejudiced on the subject.

"ATM cards?" Robby asked, and held up one in its suede-paper folder. Kelly beckoned without looking up; Robby slid it over the table toward her.

"Sol will want it."

The name cast a quiet chill over the room. Robby glanced up and saw Jim staring down at the carpet, brow furrowed.

"Yeah, well, I'm sure he does." Jim snatched up his raincoat and raided the hidden inner pockets, finding a steady trickle of cash, wallets, and cards. His hands were the only part of him that didn't fit his homeless image—smooth hands, compact, adept as any stage magician's. The first time she'd met him, Robby had hardly felt the dip that took her watch, and god knew she'd been looking for it.

She smiled at him and saw him look away. The pain took her unexpectedly; it hurt to have him mistrust her, after three years of perfect partnership. Mark, Kelly—she liked them, in a fondly annoyed way. But Jim—

In the bathroom, the shower came on. Jim's eyes

widened, and his mouth opened. Before he could get out whatever damning thing he was thinking, the bathroom door banged open.

"Hey!" The hooker held onto the door and leaned out, naked, barely covered by the angle. "Hey, where'sa soap?"

"In the soapdish," he said wearily. The hooker disappeared back into the bathroom, and the door slammed. More bumps and bangs, the rattle of a shower curtain. "Robby—"

"I know. I'm sorry." She spread her hands helplessly.

He shook his head and counted bills; it was something his fingers did automatically, a machine-quick fanning of paper. Robby began counting her stack, lost track, and had to start again.

By the time she'd finished, everyone else was done. She took a deep breath and handed over her totals.

"Slow day," Kelly said neutrally, as she added on a pocket calculator. "Jim, what you figure on cards?"

"I can get fifty each."

"I'll say forty, in case. Yeah, okay. I'll let you know about the ATM totals. Right now, it's—" She held up the calculator and angled it to get a better look. "Three thousand seven hundred ninety-three. Minus Sol's slice, of course."

"Of course," Jim said. "If he's coming."

"Not today. He said for me to take it for him." Kelly was looking down at her calculator; over her head, Jim looked across at Robby. The doubt was subtle but real, and she knew he read it in her face, too. Sol was a necessary evil—the local wiseguys needed to feel in control—but Kelly had slowly but surely become Mafia-by-marriage, only without the marriage. Nobody liked it.

Nobody had much to say about it, either.

"Ooh, honey, sounds serious," Mark cooed. She

slapped his hand. "Carrying his *money*. More important than carrying his *baby*."

"Shut up," Kelly said, a little too sharply. Her round face colored shell-pink. "He asked me to do it."

"Uh-huh. Sure he did."

"Mark— "

"Heck, honey, I don't care, I was just hoping for a second date with him." Mark batted his eyelashes. Robby saw the malicious gleam in his smile and winced. Kelly didn't tease well. "Those Italians. Spicy sausage."

"Shut *up!*" No pink in those cheeks now, hot little spots of red. "You flaming— "

"Children," Jim said flatly, and reached over Kelly's shoulder to pick up a stack of cash. "Seven-o-five in cash, right?"

"Right," she said; she was still glaring at Mark. "We'll split the credit card and ATM money on Thursday."

"Good. Now. Robby— "

"I know," Robby sighed. "Get the hooker out of your shower."

What the hell was she doing in the rain? The ground underneath her felt cool and smooth. She wiggled a little. Her skin squeaked— oh, god, she'd lost her clothes someplace. What the hell—

Ah. Naked. Shower. Oh, yeah. No wonder the rain was warm. Velvet let her head loll forward, and the warmth beat on the back of her neck with tiny balled fists. Jesus, yes. Just what she needed. Time to relax, to get her head together—

Where the fuck was she?

The shower curtain rattled, and she looked up,

right into the rain. She snorted it out of her nose and tried to focus on the shadow standing there.

A French-manicured hand reached down and turned off the HOT. Velvet blinked, confused, unable to imagine what that meant.

The water turned ice cold and slammed down on her like sleet. She shrieked and covered her head, but that only sent cold water sluicing down her sides. She flailed around and caught hold of the old-lady handhold on the wall and got her feet under her.

It was a mistake. She'd forgotten about the pink soap in the tub, and it made a nice skate. She lost her balance and pitched forward into the tile wall.

"Ow," she said, pitifully. Her chin hurt, and when she swiped at it her fingers came away red. The blood dribbled off in the water, misted pink, and disappeared. She slapped at the COLD knob until the sleet stopped.

The shower curtain rattled back. Velvet turned her head and glared through a wet curtain of hair at the suit— what the hell was her name— who held out a towel.

"Bitch," Velvet said hoarsely. The suit's smile was bone-thin, her brown eyes amused. She wasn't wearing the glasses anymore, probably didn't even need them, more stage dressing.

"Dry off. I'll get you some clothes."

"I don't wear suits," Velvet snapped; her voice sounded almost normal again. "Don't bring me a goddamn Hillary Clinton suit."

The suit shrugged and walked out of the bathroom, shutting the door behind her. Velvet sat down on the toilet and toweled her hair without much enthusiasm.

"Hey, get me a drink while you're out there!" she yelled. That was habit; she wasn't even really thirsty.

She raked her toes through thick gray carpet; her skin looked blue. She shivered and stood up to dry off. When she was done, she turned and looked in the mirror.

Her hair was a curly wet mess. Her chin looked raw where she'd scraped it open. Red patches on her knees, on the palms of her hands— how the hell would she explain it to—

"To Ming," she said aloud to her own pale scared reflection. "Oh, Jesus, I forgot. I *forgot.*"

Ming didn't like girls who forgot. Velvet swallowed and tried a smile; it trembled and looked pasty and unnatural.

"Carpet burns. They're carpet burns. He was— ah— Jesus. Jesus."

She wrapped the towel around her body and sank back on the toilet, knees apart, staring down at the floor. Whosis, the guy with the hair, he was a clean housekeeper. No bugs caught in the carpet. No mold in the corners.

The door swung open, and the suit pushed an armload of clothes at her. Velvet took them to keep from getting hit in the face, and by the time she'd dropped them on the floor, the door was shut again. She picked up the shirt with two fingers and examined it. She'd look like shit in black. Well, at least it had buttons— she could leave it open to the bra line—

Oh, yeah, speaking of that, no way was she wearing a Girl Scout Wonder Bra. She tossed it in the corner and looked at the underwear.

Hopeless. Jesus.

The blue jeans were good; she slipped them on and zipped them up and inspected the results. Okay. A little loose, but not enough to worry about. She tried teasing her hair out but it was just a mass of tangles. No makeup, of course, just guy stuff— she sniffed the bottle of aftershave, dabbed a smear in the hollow of her neck.

The door opened, and the suit looked in. Superior little bitch; Velvet figured the jeans and shirt were from a Salvation Army sack in the back of her closet. She wouldn't give the good stuff to a hooker.

"Drink?" Velvet asked, and leaned toward the mirror to look at her chin. "Ow. Shit."

Cold pressure on her arm. Velvet looked down to find a glass of what was either water or vodka; she took it and sipped.

Not water. She emptied it in a gulp.

When she wandered out, dragging her torn dress and soggy mink, the suit was sitting on a peach-colored sofa, pretending to read a magazine. She had a glass in front of her, too, primly half-full. Velvet saw the bottle of Stoli on the kitchen bar and headed for it, poured herself a tall refill.

"Feeling better?" The suit pretended to care. Velvet just drank. The warmth spread through her and triggered an earthquake in her stomach; she swallowed two or three times.

"Yeah." Her voice sounded softer than she meant it to, smeared by the drinks. "What's it to you?"

"I don't want to haul your dead butt back out to the street." That had the ring of truth. Velvet picked up the Stoli bottle, plopped herself in a big fat chair, and put her feet up on the coffee table. She raised the bottle vaguely in the suit's direction.

"Cheers." She drank, a swallow of liquid ice. "Where's your buddies?"

"Gone." The thief drank a little sip of what looked like Scotch. The taste of smoke shot through Velvet's mouth, and her throat spasmed. "You could at least say thank you."

Velvet stared at her, then looked away. Whoever

the guy with the hair was, he had nice digs; she liked the pictures on the wall. The TV looked like fun.

The vodka picked her up on a big cold wave, and she shut her eyes. The world felt like it was sliding to the right; she leaned left to balance.

"Thanks," she said huskily. "For the— thing on the street. I think."

"You think?" the suit snorted. A picture popped into Velvet's head, a fat metal robot, waving accordion arms.

Robby. The suit's name was Robby. Velvet celebrated with another mouthful of Stoli.

"Been that kind of a day," she said. She looked at the bottle— four inches left in it— and waggled it in Robby's direction. "Gotta friend for this? 'S gonna get lonely."

"You realize that if I keep giving you drinks, you're probably going to pass out." Schoolteacher talk; the brown eyes behind those round glasses looked so damn fucking superior. Velvet flashed a tinsel-bright smile.

"It's a hobby."

She drank in silence, watched inches go down her throat as she thought about Ming. Maybe if she got drunk enough, she wouldn't care about Ming, wouldn't be scared. Maybe.

Robby sipped like a goddamn PTA mom.

"'Y' live here?" Velvet asked. Robby shook her head. " 'S nice. Mean it. Nishe."

"What do you want?" Robby asked. Velvet faltered to a stop. She couldn't quite remember, what with the pickup truck and the skinned patches on her knees and the— Burt—

Burt. Just for a second in the bar, Robby had looked right at her, and there hadn't been any goddamn superior bullshit, there had been understanding. She'd known what Velvet was talking about, all right.

Robby'd *seen* it.

"Burning," Velvet said. Robby's gaze went deep-sea diving to the carpet. "C'mon, don't. You know. Y'do."

Her tongue was thick again, sloshing around in her mouth like a squid— now there was a disgusting thought, enough to make her barf. She'd eaten squid once. The taste came back, and she washed it down with vodka.

"Yeah," Robby said. Velvet leaned forward and had to brace herself with a hand on the coffee table. She dropped the Stoli bottle, but it didn't matter, there wasn't enough left in it to spill. "I've seen it."

"Sho— so you seen it, I seen it— how 'bout that? Kinda strange, huh?"

Robby sipped Scotch. She wouldn't meet her eyes. Velvet hiccuped and covered her mouth. Her fingers felt remote and rubbery and cold.

"Unless it happens alla time," Velvet finished. Robby looked up, eyes wide. "Doesn't. Does it?"

Robby got her another bottle. They shared it.

Incident One:
CHICAGO, ILLINOIS

Kevin Baird Tannery eased back into the bubbles of the Jacuzzi and accepted a fluted glass of champagne; a cheap vintage, biting, but good enough for the present company. Little Sharon Rose was not enormously sophisticated about bubbly, or anything else, but she looked appropriate in a string bikini. Ah, that reminded him— he slipped his free hand under the hot skin of the water and touched cloth. There was a catch at the back— one quick twist of his fingers, and the bright pink top floated off on a cloud of bubbles, and little Sharon Rose giggled nervously and smiled at him. He caressed the small brown nubs of her nipples and leaned in for a kiss, a long one, with tongue.

She was clumsy, open mouth trembling and tasting of salt. He circled her nipples with his thumbs, not quite hard enough to hurt, and ran his hand down her flat smooth stomach to the thin bikini briefs. The curly mass of her pubic hair felt springy through the cloth. She made a squeaky sound of protest. He pinched her nipple harder, and smiled.

"Oh— oh— don't— I— "

"Hush, my dear," he said gently. The gentleness was really automatic; he no more cared what Sharon Rose had to say than he did what the veal thought about being the main course at dinner. What was important about Sharon Rose was that she was seventeen, and gullible, and easily left behind when that became necessary. Young enough to be piquant, old enough to be excusable. He was forced to save his enthusiasm for younger girls for rare trips out of the country, after the embarrassing contretemps in Dallas, which had only gone to prove that there really was no civilization in the western half of the country.

Of course, there'd been that delicious little Asian girl in Los Angeles—fourteen? Wonderful. A juicy, eager mouth. A very pleasant memory.

Sharon Rose was trying to keep her knees together, remembering too late a strict upbringing. He pried them apart with strong fingers and soft meaningless words. She began to cry, which was tiresome; he stripped the bikini briefs away and probed warm moist flesh, sipped champagne, described for Sharon Rose in detail what he wanted from her. Then he wiped her tears away with characteristic blank gentleness, and aroused himself with memories of the Asian girl—exceptional, that one, really. She'd be fifteen now. Not too old to be exciting.

He stepped out of the Jacuzzi and had Sharon Rose wipe him thoroughly dry. He had to brace himself with one hand on the back of a wrought-iron chair against a new wave of dizziness. He'd been drinking most of the night, of course, but the wine had gone to his head in a very strange way, almost disorienting. The scrape of the towel along his erection distracted him back to his pleasure, and he closed his eyes and remembered the Asian's mouth, so muscular, the teeth so fragile.

He opened his eyes and looked at Sharon Rose, whose face had blotched unbecomingly from crying, and decided that one night really would be quite enough of her. Draining the last of his champagne, he put the crystal aside.

"I'll want my robe again," he told her. She recovered his Neiman Marcus robe— rich fluffed cotton, embroidered with his initials— from the chair where he'd discarded it earlier. The familiar lushness of it along his skin made him instantly harder. He left the front open and motioned Sharon Rose inside, to where the bed waited. She ran ahead, holding her towel over her nude body with appealing modesty— little winks of firm buttocks, the barest glimpse of golden pubic hair— and he decided that it might turn out to be a properly amusing evening, after all.

Annoyingly hot, though. He paused at the thermostat and checked it— set at seventy-five, a perfectly acceptable temperature. He flicked a fingertip against it two or three times, and frowned. Perhaps the Jacuzzi had been hotter than usual, or perhaps it was the wine, but he was really quite overheated—

He looked down at himself— curling chest hair, lightly dusted with gray— a firm flat stomach— the bobbing club of his engorged penis, revealed by the open slit of the robe.

How odd that the memory of the Asian girl made him remember the smell of mu-shu pork. But it was more than a memory— it smelled like—

Like flesh cooking.

A feathery curl of smoke threaded through his chest hair, and the first pinpricks of pain flared red along his sides, his flanks, his arms, his back. He plucked at the robe fretfully, but it seemed stuck somehow— glued— Sharon Rose's little joke? If she'd dared, he'd—

The pain sliced into his chest, nerves shrieking. He fought for breath, still thinking clearly about heart attacks and survival rates. He tumbled and caught himself against the wall. More smoke, greasy dark, puffed from his sleeve as his arm exploded in agony.

He saw the fire without believing it, white glowing tongues licking along his skin, searing it black, eating deep into raw muscle. He slapped in panic at his chest, his groin, the smoke burned greasy in his lungs and he coughed and got enough air to scream, a thin sound, hardly anything at all, really. Like a girl's.

He bashed face-first into the wall and hardly felt the impact, left smears of blood and skin and black crust. Pieces of his robe flared and melted on his skin like patches of fur, and he clawed at them with his fingers but the skin was soft and rotten and slick, and his fingers sank deep into it and it sloughed away, still burning. Muscles worked gray beneath, burning black. When he pulled his hands away in horror, his fingernails came off and stuck like guitar picks in the ruin of his chest, and he glimpsed ivory bone where his fingers should have been.

Sharon Rose. It was his one coherent thought. The girl could call for help, do something, do *anything.* He screamed for her, but couldn't hear himself, couldn't really see anything except shadows— thick pressure in his chest, and he couldn't get air. He lurched toward a shadow he thought might have been the girl but his legs faded and suddenly he was lying down and that was all right, the pain was not as bad, distant, going away.

Everything would be all right. Surely, everything would be all right now. He couldn't possibly die like this, so horribly.

The last sound he heard was the cheerful sizzle of bacon.

Four
Martin Grady

Office of Environmental Hazards (OEH)

The air-conditioning was either broken or off—more benefits of government cutbacks, Martin Grady thought, and pulled at his damp collar in frustration. He stalked to the door, yanked it open, and yelled down the hall for a portable fan. There was a scurry of movement in the Secure File area. Beth stuck her head around the corner and nodded, too quickly. Her broad pleasant face had a stunned frightened look. He wondered what she'd been doing. Too much to believe she'd actually been filing.

Martin closed the door just as one of the geeks sitting at the conference table behind him finished up with, "And the frogs are dying all along the river."

"Who the hell gives a shit about frogs?" Martin asked. He couldn't even summon up the energy for a good snarl. The frog deaths were number seventeen on today's agenda, and one through sixteen hadn't been particularly riveting, either. In a Pavlovian response, the geek cringed anyway. "Okay, point taken. We have frogs dying. What's killing them?"

"But— the problems may be— "

"What my colleague is trying to say is that two events may be related." That was Jill Westfield, cer-

tainly no geek. She sat like a knockoff of Marlene
Dietrich, legs crossed, skirt tightly wrapped around
her tanned legs, showing enough thigh to invite
dreams but no touches. Blond waved hair, perfect
skin, round red lips. The only thing she was missing
was a cigarette holder. Martin sat down in his chair
and stared at her gloomily.

"Which two?"

"Numbers seventeen and eighteen. What we're
talking about here is not just pollution, but chemical
reactions among various pollutants. The frogs especially are vulnerable to high chemical concentrations.
There are also indications that fish are becoming
scarce, too, especially bottom-feeders like catfish. I
think we're talking about a widespread infiltration."

Martin opened his file and flipped past red-
stamped pages. He pulled his coffee toward him and
sipped; it tasted gritty, rather oily. Government coffee.

"A water problem."

"Potentially. You'll notice that the men who've been
affected—"

"Christ, what a term," one of the geeks muttered.
The geek nest at that end of the table leaned away
from him; one of them even shrugged in Martin's direction, meaning, *geeks. What can you do?*

"The men who've been *affected*—" Jill leaned on
the word, a hard set to those ruby lips. Her blouse
gaped to show a blush of lace-topped bra. "—have
all been middle-aged, overweight, borderline alcoholic. Liver biopsies have all turned up traces of di-
oxin and dichlorhyradine. Dichlorhyradine has also
turned up in the analysis of tap water in these cities,
in microscopic amounts."

"You're saying you think it's the tap water," Martin
said. His gaze strayed toward his coffee cup, and he
shoved it an inch of two farther away with an out-

stretched fingertip. She shrugged. "Jesus Christ, Jill, do you understand what you're saying?"

"I'm saying—" Dr. Westfield shrugged and lit a thin cigarette; she blew smoke toward the stained yellowed ceiling. "I'm saying the frogs are dying, Marty. You figure it out."

The geeks all nodded.

Of all of them, Martin thought, he was the only one who was scared. It was his name on the big door, after all. And his ticket to Washington.

The Dallas Morning News, **December 14, 1994, page 26A. (shorts)**

ONE DEAD IN HOTEL FIRE

An unidentified man is dead after what firefighters describe as an intense fire in the Adolphus Hotel. The fire was contained in one room of the hotel and apparently involved only the area of the bed, leading to speculation that the victim fell asleep while smoking.

"We see things like this all the time," commented Ralph DeLawrence, spokesman for the Dallas County Volunteer Firefighters Association. "People are careless, and people get killed. They're just lucky that the fire was small, and the hotel's sprinkler system put it out."

The Adolphus issued a statement saying that today's incident is the first fire-related fatality in its sixty-eight-year history, and that the hotel's evacuation and safety procedures worked "like a charm."

The identity of the victim is being withheld pending notification of next of kin.

Big D Gazette, December 14, 1994, page 1.

MAN SPONTANEOUSLY COMBUSTS IN FRONT OF HUNDREDS OF WITNESSES! EXCLUSIVE PHOTOS OF THE EERIE SCENE!

"I never seen nothing like it," wailed Irene Perez, maid at Dallas's historic Adolphus Hotel. "It's just him that's burned, not the room. It's like they say, he just burned up!"

Irene Perez and hundreds of eye witnesses say that Burt Marshall, 47, owner of Marshall Dry Cleaners of Oak Lawn, "just burst into flames" after checking into his hotel room at 3:00 P.M. with a mysterious blond beauty. Hotel security found Mr. Marshall lying mortally wounded in his room, burned over ninety percent of his body, after responding to a fire alarm. He died on the way to Parkland Hospital.

"They're trying to cover this up," say informed sources at the Dallas County Fire Department. "Things like this happen all the time, and they pass it off as bad wiring or cigarettes or arson. That guy spontaneously combusted, and everybody knows it."

Dr. Nils Hansen, noted expert at the Swedish Institute for Combustion Research, agrees.

"Yah, it happens," he responded in an interview with this reporter. "We do not want to cause a panic, but there is no denying it, it happens all the time."

There is no official ongoing investigation, although an unofficial search continues for the mysterious blond woman with Marshall at the time of the combustion. Anyone with information is urged to report it immediately to the Big D Spontaneous Combustion Hotline, at 1-900-555-FIRE.

Five
Velvet

Wherever the hell she was, it was dark, and she had to throw up. Velvet stumbled, fell over something on the floor, and laid there with her face in the still-slightly-damp ruin of her mink until the world stopped bobbing around her.

"Oh, Christ," she moaned. She wasn't sure if she meant it as prayer, but there was a first for anything. One thing she was sure about— she wasn't going to ralph on the mink. Not if she could help it. She got her tingling arms and legs under her, and crab-crawled off of the silky fur and onto ratty coarse carpet. Her hand found a cool smooth wall.

She had to stand to reach the light switch. The sudden glare drove a nail through her head, but at least she could identify the room— hers— the trail of clothes— not hers, but the ones she'd been wearing— and, gloriously, the bathroom.

She was on her way there when a hand fell on her shoulder, a big hand, male. She spun around and flattened herself against the wall, all urge to vomit forgotten in the need to scream. The hand slapped over her mouth hard enough to raise bruises and spark pain in the cut on her chin.

Paolo. Oh Jesus, Jesus, she'd forgotten about Ming

again. She should have called or something. Paolo
was Ming's leg-breaker, the size of a refrigerator; he
had a face like a two-year-old slice of meatloaf, and
the dull glitter of his eyes didn't tell her a thing
about how much trouble she was really in.

"Ming wants to see you," he said, and took his hand
off her mouth to fasten it around her wrist. "Let's
go."

"But— I need to— "

"Later."

Ming Lee Fong had never gotten over being the star
of the Kiss The Whip Club. She still had a fondness
for studs and leather; the outfit today was sleek black,
edged in silver spikes that looked as if they might be
able to slice skin. Her hair was a long waterfall of black
silk, her eyes dead, quiet. Ming accessorized well.

Velvet swallowed hard and waited for Ming to say
something. She radiated cold, like the big room, the
icy wood floor; it made Velvet feel even sicker. The
world was a turntable on 33 1/3, geared down from
the fast 45 it had been in the limousine with Paolo.
She'd managed not to puke all over the expensive
upholstery, at least. He'd allowed her to throw up on
the side of the freeway.

"But I got the money," Velvet said forlornly, and
shifted on her chair. All of Ming's chairs were uncomfortable.

"Yes, I know," Ming said; she had a soothing voice,
low and smooth. Her eyes reminded Velvet of a meat-
eating Bambi. "Tell me how it happened."

"I just— I was just starting, you know, hadn't even
got his clothes off, and he just— " She stopped and
swallowed. Scotch. Jesus, she'd never get the taste of
Scotch out of her mouth again, no matter how much

vodka she drank. *Or the taste of Burt.* The thought almost made her heave. "He just burned up. I don't know how it happened, Ming, swear I don't. It just— happened. *Whoosh.*"

"You know what they'll say." Ming got up and walked over to the window; it looked out on a blank wall. Velvet looked around, saw Paolo leaning in the corner's shadows, next to some leather contraption that looked uncomfortably like a harness. Black and red leather hoods hung on the wall like severed heads, with black tails of whips between. He pulled on something, and the leather swayed uneasily. "They'll blame you. Bad for business."

"Yes ma'am."

"Was he smoking?"

"Well, sure, I mean, you know, he was on fire— "

Ming flicked her black-lacquered, needle-sharp fingernails in Velvet's direction. Velvet shut her mouth with a snap.

"Cigarettes," Ming said. Velvet shook her head.

Ming lapsed into silence, stared out at the blank brick wall. She tapped a cigarette out of a silver case and lit it, dragging the smoke deep, blowing a hot fog out against the windowpane. Velvet watched the glowing tip of the cigarette with complete fascination.

"I'm concerned, Velvet. Take some vacation," Ming said. She turned and smiled. "Two weeks."

Velvet's lips said *yes ma'am*, but she was watching the cigarette. The hair on the back of her neck crawled. The smell was all wrong, not burning tobacco, burning— melting— she swallowed a gag. The cigarette flared bright red as Ming sucked, went ash-gray with masochistic disappointment when she stopped.

It wasn't at all like Ming to be concerned. Not at all. And "vacation" was a word most girls heard right before a "special" job. One that put them in the hospital on a respirator. If they were lucky.

"Don't make trouble."

"No ma'am."

"And don't talk to anybody."

Ming drifted over, and Velvet looked hard at the floor. There was a tuft of red hair near her chair.

Ming's hand felt as cold as ice on her cheek, long nails a sharp pressure near her ear. Velvet didn't want to see her eyes.

"You know," Ming said, very slowly, "I'm thinking of moving you up. No more hotel tricks. Very specialized stuff. What do you think of that?"

Velvet kept staring at the floor.

"That'd be great," she said, and ignored the fluttery feeling in her stomach. "Really great."

The smell of smoke was greasy in the back of her throat, like mucous.

"Now go with Paolo," Ming said, and the icy hand left her face. "He needs a little company."

Me too, Velvet thought, and tried not to think about Paolo too much. She'd never done Paolo; she wasn't really in shape to be creative, either. But she'd fake it.

Like Ming always said: business was always a pleasure for somebody.

Paolo propped himself up with pillows on the king-sized bed of the guest room, and stared straight over her head while she went down on him. Her headache continued to throb, a steady backbeat rhythm. After three or four minutes of industrious licking and sucking, Velvet heard a click and looked up to see Paolo holding the TV remote. Behind her, canned laughter swelled out of the set.

Gilligan's Island, she thought as she went back to

work. *That's the difference between paying customers and freebies.*

Paolo poured himself a glass of Johnny Walker Black Label from a bottle next to him on the night-stand. He drained it in slow controlled gulps, never looking at her. Except for the fact that he still had a rock-hard boner, she might not have even been there. She tried moaning louder, until his heavy face collapsed into a frown and she realized she was in-terfering with the TV. She felt like an X-rated mime.

The oily taste of the condom (plain peach-colored, nothing fancy for Paolo) reminded her unpleasantly of the time she'd sucked a balloon into her windpipe at the age of six. She shut her eyes and tried not to think about suffocating, but then she started thinking about burning, and the smell of smoke, and had a bad few seconds of panic while her mouth kept on mindlessly doing its lonely job.

Right about the time she was considering biting Paolo's dick just to remind him she was there, he came. She only knew that because the reservoir tip of the condom filled up. She performed an obligatory moan-ing orgasm, mostly to keep in practice. He craned to look over her shoulder and turned the volume up.

She had performed solo before, but usually the guy was across the room, not in her mouth. It all seemed pretty damn disheartening. Still, she reminded her-self as she sat up— it could have been worse. Burt—

The thought occurred to her (oh, bad timing for her still-rolling stomach) that Burt could have done his flaming marshmallow impersonation while she'd had his dick in her mouth. Suddenly, Paolo looked like a bargain. She peeled the condom off and wrapped it deftly in a tissue before tossing it— a three-pointer— into the corner wastebasket.

Paolo was completely engrossed in the program.

She sat for a few minutes watching with him. Gilligan picked coconuts. The Professor talked about building a generator. The Skipper complained.

"Maryanne or Ginger?" she asked. It took a second for Paolo to distract himself from the intense drama on the screen enough to notice she'd spoken.

"What?"

"If you were on the island, would you go for Maryanne or Ginger?"

Paolo considered for a full minute, staring at the flickering set with narrowed serious eyes.

"Mrs. Howell," he said.

She realized she'd been staring too long. Time to go. She gathered up her clothes— the mink had managed to fluff out again, there was quality for you— and was turning her panty hose back inside-out, when suddenly the TV went off. She looked up to find Paolo staring at her.

"I love you," he said. There was nothing in his face, nothing in his voice. For a bad second she thought he meant it, until he started laughing. She got dressed and closed the loft door. Somewhere in the distance, she heard the methodical twig-snap of whipcracks. Ming was busy. Velvet squared her shoulders and started down the hall, toward the elevator. A hollow-eyed man dressed in a Metallica T-shirt and crusty gray pants sat at the far end, waiting; she wasn't sure if he was a client or a bum or a killer. As she walked past him, she felt hands on her back, ghost-hands, cold.

Fucking hallways.

She really, really needed a drink or she *would* ralph all over the mink.

Six
Robby

Robby adjusted her jacket and checked her reflection in the mirror one more time— hair neatly styled, makeup minimal, face under control. She felt ever so slightly sick to her stomach— souvenir of her half of a vodka bottle— but the headache was gone, thank god. She needed every brain cell firing.

She touched up her lipstick, a color just a shade darker than her lips, and blotted the excess away on a square of toilet tissue. *Focus,* she told herself. Her fingers were vibrating, and not from the scent of money. She clenched them hard enough to hurt, then relaxed them. The tremble was gone.

She opened the bathroom door and walked out into the garlic-scented dimness of the restaurant, past a stocky-looking waiter singing in a reedy tenor while he poured red wine from a wicker-wrapped bottle. It took a second for her eyes to adjust, and then she spotted Sol Lipsky in the back booth, smiling and nodding at her.

Panic flared white under her skin.

Jim wasn't there. Goddamn him, Jim wasn't in the booth, wasn't anywhere in view, and Sol was making his big round Italian gestures, smile cool and getting colder the longer she paused.

She had to move. Door or booth. Escape or—

There was no escape, not really. She walked toward the booth.

"Robby, Robby, sweetheart, so good to see you. Wine? Good for the heart." Sol never stopped to hear her answer. He didn't pour very well; drops of red splashed on the red-checkered plastic tablecloth. Robby automatically dabbed them up with her thin napkin, then wiped some scattered bread crumbs off the table as well. It didn't really matter; the plastic still felt as sticky as a porn palace floor.

She settled the stained napkin in her lap, fussed until it was square. The fabric had started out red and was now a nappy red-gray, edges fraying, old stains like ghostly Rorshach blots. The large one looked like the shadow of a knife.

"So," Sol said. She looked up to see his eyes on her, dead-man gray behind rimless glasses. The shine in his slicked-back hair looked oily enough to be a fire hazard. "Baby, you look great. Just great."

"Thanks, Sol," she murmured, and sipped wine to keep from having to return the compliment. It was rough and vinegary on her tongue.

"I was just saying the other day to Mario, Mario, that Robby, she's a real classy lady. Class through and through. Right? Hey. Pavarotti." Sol snapped manicured fingers at the waiter. "What's the matter with you? The lady needs a menu. Move."

"Don't you think we should wait until Jim gets here?" Robby asked a little desperately. The waiter scurried over and thrust a plastic-covered menu into her hands. Sol smiled at her and flicked his fingers to make the waiter go away. He leaned toward her across the table, and the red-glassed candlelight flickered hot over the side of his face and made red rainbows in his diamond pinkie ring.

"Sweetheart, I thought you understood, it's just you and me. Just you and me. Business." He didn't bother to give her a choice, just shrugged and topped off her wine another quarter-inch. More red drops on the tablecloth; she resisted the need to wipe them away. She held her menu like a life preserver, a shield, but before she had time to do more than read the title— *Pasta Romana*— she heard Sol saying, "A bowl of minestrone for me and the lady. And two Caesar salads."

His thick fingers pried the menu out of her hand and laid it aside. She looked up and saw that he was smiling, a benign contented smile.

"Something wrong?" he asked. She blinked. "You look worried, sweetheart. I don't like it when you look worried. Gives you wrinkles."

"I'm not worried."

"Not even after the trouble yesterday?"

Oh, Jesus. She had to force herself to keep staring at him.

"Trouble?" she asked neutrally. "What trouble was that?"

"You think I don't know?" He sounded smug instead of mysterious. "This stranger, this woman— "

"It wasn't any big thing, Sol," she said. Did she have an earnest look on her face? She couldn't tell.

Sol chose to give her the reproving silent treatment, staring, and she gave in to nervousness and wiped up the wine droplets on the tablecloth, shook her napkin, folded it carefully in eights.

"You don't decide what's important. I decide what's important. Your job is to tell me everything, you understand?" The comic-opera Italian had dropped out of his voice, a bad sign. She didn't dare look at him, and was happy to catch sight of their waiter approaching with a round tray.

"You're right, of course," she said. "Minestrone, right? My favorite. Really."

The waiter delivered a steaming bowl. She fished her spoon around in it and pretended to be fascinated by what she discovered; it smelled like old dishwater, and the pieces of vegetables looked wasted and transparent. She looked over at the limp disheartened Caesar salad and kept stirring the minestrone.

Sol spooned his soup with slurping relish. One good thing about his mulberry sharkskin suit, it wouldn't show any stains. The shirt was about a half-shade off, the tie scrawny and black. The jacket was big enough to hide a gun; she figured him for a flash piece, something silver and mother-of-pearl, tucked in a custom shoulder holster. All the fucking wiseguys in this town, and she had to get one who thought he was an extra in *The Godfather.* He was stupid, he was cheesy, he was good for a laugh at a slow party.

And every once in a while— like now— he scared the living shit out of her.

She hated, *hated* being alone with him.

"Eat," he urged her, caught for a second in the no-man's-land between his Jewish upbringing and his Sicilian pretensions. "Eat, baby, it's good for you."

She dutifully swallowed a mouthful of dishwater, felt something lumpy on her tongue that might have been potato or well-cooked cockroach, reached for her wine, and took a hasty gulp.

The acidic bite reminded her of lemons and cold sores.

"So tell me about this woman, this whore," Sol said. He broke a piece of garlic bread from the loaf and set it afloat in his minestrone.

"Deadhead. A sponge. Honest, she couldn't remember her own name, much less where she was."

Exaggeration, but not by much. By the time Robby
had poured Velvet into the taxi, there had been little
left in the way of functioning brain cells. Robby had
not taken the hooker's remaining cash. It had probably been a mistake.

"I hope you're right," Sol said. He gave it just the
right inflection— worried, threatening, doubting. All
with a smile. Jesus. In spite of her better judgement,
Robby took another sip of wine that blasted through
her sinuses like a nose full of pepper. She sneezed
into her napkin, two or three times, while he looked
on indulgently.

She was still wiping her nose when the waiter returned, bearing a new basket of wine and an aria he
said was from *Tosca*. She listened with her chin resting on her fist, shooting glances at Sol. He looked
enthralled, but his eyes were cool. Not a music fan,
though he had to pretend to be, to fit in with his
fantasy.

She had once allowed a friend to convince her to
lay out three hundred dollars for a leather miniskirt
and halter top. She kept it hanging in the far corner
of her closet, price tags still attached, and took it out
about twice a year to hold it up against her body and
pose for the mirror. For those few guilty moments,
she was somebody else. Somebody dangerous.

She wasn't absolutely sure how much of Sol's
playacting was fantasy, and that scared her.

When the waiter stopped singing, she passed him
a dollar. Before she could order, Sol spread his hand
palm-out to stop her.

"Linguini for myself and the lady. And get rid of
the minestrone, it's cold, what's the matter with you?
Eh?"

The waiter stalked away in search of a more cultured audience. She bit off a desire to tell anybody who might listen that she hated linguini.

"I like you, Robby," Sol said. "You're an artist. You know how rare that is, your kind of game? Kids today, they gank old ladies for a couple dollars and change. No finesse, not like you. You and me, we're old country."

She doubted it. *She* was old country, born in County Meath; he was far too nostalgic to have ever been outside the States.

"So I worry when I see you acting crazy, baby." He leaned over and laid his pinkie-ringed hand over hers. Up close, the ring looked chunky and uncomfortable, the diamond almost feverish in the middle of all that gold. "It isn't good for business."

"I'm okay," she said. She slowly pulled her hand away. His smile faded.

"You better be. I gotta tell you, I got people to answer to. Your little operation down there, it's nice, it's profitable. Very low profile. We like that."

We. She wondered what his bosses would think about the plural.

She thought she'd stepped down hard on her temper, but a little of it got control of her mouth and said, "So glad we're making you happy, Sol." The sarcasm was a little too obvious even for Sol.

While the storm built up in his dead-gray eyes, she looked away at a cheap concrete cherub in the corner. It looked dirty, too many pats from grease-smeared fingers, and the expression on its rough face looked more like indigestion than happiness.

"Attitude, Robby? Now you're giving me attitude?" Sol leaned back against his red leatherette seat and studied her; she felt the pressure of it like hands. "Hey, I don't want trouble. You remember what happened to Annie."

She didn't let him see her flinch, but the knife went deep on that one, right to her heart. She clenched her fingers in her napkin hard enough to hurt, but that was better than letting him see her shake. She didn't dare let him know he scared her. God only knew what he'd be like then.

"You and Jim and Mark and Kelly, you're my high-priced talent," Sol's voice continued smoothly. She moved her stare back to the concrete cherub; it was slightly cross-eyed, missing a thumb. The amputation looked fresh and jagged. "I can't let anything fool around with that. So maybe this woman isn't a problem, maybe that's so, but I got to worry, Robby, that's what you pay me for. I'm your *friend*. So if she comes back again, you let me know. I'll take care of it. Eh? That's what you pay me for."

The waiter was bearing down on them with two steaming platefuls of linguini. The noodles looked like spilled guts, the sauce gore. She felt her throat clench up in protest.

"Hey," he said sharply. She looked up at him, and got a wide smile, sharp as a razor. "Smile."

She did.

Jim's phone rang six times before he answered. At his snarled, "What?" she said, "Goddamn son of a bitch dago *bastard*, and where the hell were you, you asshole? Shopping?"

Her accent had gone back to Dublin, thick and rolling with anger. In the second or two of silence that followed, some of the suffocating panic bled out of her chest. She adjusted her head on the arm of the couch. Across the room, the TV played silently, its flickering the only light in the room; it gave everything a surreal blue glow, like radiation.

"What the hell are you talking about?"

"Dinner with Sol. Fucking wiseguy wannabe asshole." She hardly ever cursed, but the words just spilled out, natural as blood. Her voice was shaking. She took deep breaths to steady it.

"Tell me everything," Jim said. He sounded calm, dangerously calm. "Did he move on you?"

"No." Better if he had, she thought. It would have been more humanizing. She still heard Irish in her voice, and forced it flat. "Just played daddy. Dammit, where were you?"

"I wasn't invited. So?"

"Linguini and singing waiters. Christ, it was like a bad Italian soap opera." She stopped and wished he were here, with her, close enough to touch. She wouldn't have to tell him then, he'd know, he'd see it in her. "I was scared, Jim. I was really scared."

She rubbed her eyes and opened them to stare at the ceiling. Shadows from the window, leaves rustling like dollars in the dark.

"There's nothing to be scared about, you know that. He's a lowlife. Let him play his little role and strut around, and when he's gone, we'll still be here, working. What did he want? Was he complaining about the take again?"

"No," she said. The apartment felt cold and lonely. She thought for the thousandth time that she needed a dog, something warm and bouncy to come home to. "No, he was bitching about Velvet."

"Who?"

"The hooker."

"Jesus Christ, that was fast. Anyway, it was my god-damn shower, I don't know what he was upset about. You *did* get rid of her."

"Sure I did."

"Then there's nothing to worry about. Nothing at all."

She nodded, chewing the inside of her lip, and rolled over on her side, staring now at the television. The evening news was on, grainy footage of wars in countries she'd never heard of, shell-shocked faces, wailing women. No matter where it was, what they were wearing, it always looked like Dublin to her. She hitched back over on her back to avoid the memories.

"Velvet— the hooker— she saw somebody burn up, Jim. Just like Arnold."

A long silence now, very long. She remembered the look of broken trust.

"I thought we agreed to forget it."

"I tried. Look— Jim— "

"No, Robby, you look. Forget it. Sol's an asshole, but he works for people who are bigger assholes. Stay quiet."

She started to say *I can't do that,* but closed her mouth on it. Instead, she said, "Okay." In the corner of her eye, the news footage shifted to weather reports. Colder temperatures. Winter storm warnings.

"Want to come over?" Jim asked. "I'll let you win a game of chess."

She found herself smiling, which was odd, because she really didn't feel like it. Acting again, even when she didn't mean to.

"No. Think I'll call it a night."

"You know you're welcome." Just the slightest hint of apology in his voice. "Always."

"I know," she said, and after she'd hung up she stayed on the couch, staring at the moving shadows on the ceiling.

She hated being helpless, hated it worse than anything else in the world.

Seven
Velvet

Velvet spat a ropy string of vomit that had the taste of Scotch and bitter sleeping pills into the toilet, and remembered Paolo. She felt hot enough to burst into flames, but tired, so tired. *Great ending to the Velvet Daniels movie of the week*, she thought. *Hooker chokes on her own vomit.*

"Could be worse," she said aloud; her voice sounded raw and thick, and she could almost taste it in her mouth, medicine bitter. "Least I made it through the night."

She decided, after thinking about it for a few minutes, that she wasn't quite sick enough to throw up again, and turned on the shower. Cool water. After she'd been in the stream for about five minutes, she began to shiver, and sat down hard enough in the tub to make her tailbone twinge. She wrapped her arms around her knees and sat huddled in the rain.

Can't stay out here all night, honey, her mother said, a distant whisper. A warm hand on her shoulder, on her cheek. *Come inside. Come get warm.*

"I'm hot."

You're going to catch your death, honey.

"Go away." Velvet covered her face with wet cold hands and rocked back and forth, back and forth. Her heart sounded slow in her chest, like a clock running

down. How many sleeping pills had she taken?
Enough? Too many?

Honey—

Velvet reached out and batted the water off. It was
too hard to get up again and dry off. She pulled a
towel down from the rack and wrapped it tight
around herself, rested her head on the hard cold lip
of the tub, and closed her eyes.

Burt Everard Marshall was standing in her bathroom, fire dripping off of his hands like water, face
melting like warm candle wax. His eyes were her
mother's soft kind eyes.

Dying is easy, he whispered, or she thought he did.
She came upright with a gasp and clawed her way out
of the tub, knelt next to the toilet again, and found
more booze and pills to heave. The bathroom rug was
a better place to lie, soft and warm. She closed her
eyes again and this time Burt was right there, lying
right next to her, warm as a campfire.

Jesus, she couldn't even die comfortable. She got to
her hands and knees and crawled, determined to find
someplace not haunted. Her bed was all the way across
the room, miles away, and the carpet kept rippling and
moving, and now the bed was uphill. She hugged the
rug.

"I'm not going to die," she told Burt, when he
appeared in the bathroom doorway to watch her.
"See? I'm okay."

Hard to tell if he nodded or not. When she closed
her eyes again, she only saw darkness.

The phone woke her out of a warm sweaty silence,
and she squinted against the glare of noon. She was
lying in a thick square of sunlight, still twisted in the
damp towel. Her stomach twinged again, but only as
a reminder, and since the room had leveled out during the night, she stood up and walked to the bed,

picked up the phone before flopping spread-eagled on the wrinkled sheets.

"Speak," she said. God, her mouth tasted terrible. She couldn't remember why.

"Honey, it's your mom. Are you all right?"

Velvet pulled the towel closer and sat up against the cold wrought-iron headboard. Her hair felt slimy and thick on her shoulders; she patted it back with nervous fingers. It was brown when wet, almost the mousy shade she'd been born with.

"Yeah, Mom, I'm fine. How are you?"

"I'm fine. I'm not bothering you, am I?"

"No, of course not." *I was just sleeping off an overdose on the floor, Mom, nothing to be concerned about. Happens all the time.* "So what's happening down on the farm?"

"Your sister's having another baby in October, isn't that nice? And Ron Junior, he's thinking about buying old Ned Armstrong's hardware store and turning it into one of those chain stores. Oh, I don't mean they'd sell chains, I mean— well, you know what I mean. And your Aunt Jane Lee had the flu, but she's better now. Happy birthday, honey."

"It's not my birthday, Mom."

"Oh, sure it is, honey. Your twenty-seventh birthday. Remember?"

Velvet pulled her knees up to her chest and rested her forehead on them, trying to press out the ache, but it kept tunneling deeper. It was somewhere around her stomach again.

"No, Mom, you're talking about Amy." Her voice was patient and not quite steady. Why didn't she remember this would happen? It was the same every year, just the same, and she was always surprised. Maybe that was her part of the agreement, her half of the masochism. "Amy's dead, Mom."

The silence lasted for several seconds before the

crying began, gentle empty sobs. In the middle of one of them the phone went dead, and Velvet listened to the flutter of the line and tried to find the strength to hang up.

Amy's ghost hadn't shown up in the night; it never did. Amy was the forgiving one of the family.

Velvet let the phone fall back into the cradle, and curled up on her side while the sun beat down and tried uselessly to warm her.

When the phone rang again, she ignored it. Three rings. Four. A click, and the answering machine rescued the call.

She didn't recognize the voice.

"Hi, um, Miss Daniels, my name is Lenny Bradshaw and I'm a reporter, um, with the *Big D Gazette*. You know, the one with the color cover? I understand you have some information about the fire at the Adolphus. Give me a call and we'll talk it over. I'll make it worth your while."

He gave a number. As she slowly twisted around to look at the answering machine, he hung up. The tape whirred. The light blinked.

She played the message again, listened to the number, one finger on the erase switch.

Money. *I'll make it worth your while.*

What was it Ming had said? *Don't cause any trouble?*

Velvet tapped the switch with a fingernail, lightly, then again, harder. Not quite enough to erase.

That sonofabitch Paolo had laughed at her.

She moved her finger over and hit play. While his message recited again, she found a scrap of paper and a pen.

Really, it was just another slower way to commit suicide.

* * *

She met him at Fong's Deli on Maple, a dusty little place that even the hungry hordes of downtown workers avoided. A parade of them passed outside, second-rate suits and boring ties and women in ugly skirts and walking shoes. She was on her second Ginseng Special when Bradshaw slid into the booth with her.

She had expected a guy in a hat. In the movies reporters wore hats and leisure suits that had celebrated Nixon's inauguration. It bothered her that Lenny Bradshaw was a clean prep-school kid with short hair and a button-down shirt. He didn't look old enough to be *delivering* papers, much less writing for them.

"Hi," he said, and stuck a hand in her direction, palm sideways. She shook it limply. His smile brought out dimples, not the Kirk Douglas aggressive kind, but suburban ones, inoffensive. "Hope you weren't waiting long. Can I buy you another one of those— uh— "

"Nope."

"Right. Fine. Well, I'll just get a Snapple . . ." His voice trailed off vaguely as he looked around at the bottles in the case. He had a little crisp frown that started right in the center of his forehead. "They don't have Snapple?"

"Here, have the rest of this, I'm not thirsty anyway." She shoved her Ginseng Special over. He eyed it and pushed it back into neutral territory. She smiled. Too good to drink after a hooker, but probably wouldn't turn down a free blow job. "Let's not beat around the bush, okay? So how much?"

"How much for what?"

She stared at him until his dimpled smile faded. "You trying to be funny?"

"Well, no, I— I'm sorry, maybe I didn't understand you. You're asking me . . ." He paused. She didn't help him. "How much I'll pay you for the story?"

"Ooh, you're so smart. Yeah, that's what I'm asking, you think I'm trying to buy your watch or something?"

"I'm sorry. I'm authorized to offer you the standard fee, three-fifty."

She got up and started to slide out of the booth. He reached out to put a hand on her arm, but thought better of it and just waved her to a stop instead.

"Four hundred," he amended, and she sighed and sat back down. "But that's only if you give me some very interesting information."

"Five, and it's the best shit you've ever heard, kid. Let's see cash."

They settled for five hundred, two-fifty up front. She counted the bills and stuffed them in her purse. He took out a pad of paper and a pen and waited expectantly.

And suddenly she had no idea what to say. She looked around at the rice-paper menus glued on the walls, the faded paper dragons fluttering overhead. What did he want to hear? Always give the customer what they want, that was Ming's first rule. Ming's second rule was, always charge more than they intend to pay.

"First of all, you have to understand, I don't normally do this kind of thing. I'm new at it." Velvet tapped long fingernails nervously on the table. The fallen-angel thing was always good with prep-school guys—that and cheerleader outfits. "Used to be a model, you know? But then I got too old. This date thing, this is pretty new to me."

"You like it?" Bradshaw asked. She glanced up at him. His face was innocent and chubby-cheeked. "Just asking."

"I like it okay. Most guys are nice enough."

"How about Burt Marshall? Was he nice enough?"

She fought the urge to look away, because she just

knew that if she did, she'd see Burt out of the corner of her eye, burnt red and black like Fong's barbecued pork ribs. *Oughta tell him he beat me,* she thought. *Oughta tell him about bruises and broken bones. Good copy.* But she couldn't lie like that, not for this little stack of bills.

"He was nice," she said. "Nothing special. Never done him before, but yeah, he seemed pretty nice."

"He has a wife and three kids out in Lakewood, did you know that?"

Time to look away, now. The street was safe, cars a bright smear of speed, a few pedestrians bundled in coats and scarves. Behind her, on the other side of the counter, Fong cursed his cook, a singsong wave of sound. The cook sang harmony.

She smelled something burning and closed her eyes, felt for her abandoned Ginseng Special and sipped half-heartedly. It tasted like old sweaty socks.

"Sex scandals make good copy. Did you have sex with him?"

"No." A glance at his face warned her it was the wrong answer. "Well, yeah, sure. Took my clothes off. I was sucking his dick when it happened. Hey, can you print that? Sucking his dick?"

He looked uncomfortable, tapped his pen on the pad.

"We can call it engaging in oral sex."

Velvet waited for him to break a grin, but he looked serious.

"So I was engaging in oral sex with the guy when he started burning. Poof."

"Where did it start?" Lenny Bradshaw was studying her carefully, maybe wondering why her hair wasn't burned off. She hadn't thought of that. Wig. Yeah, she'd tell him she was wearing a wig, and the wig got burned.

"Jesus, I don't know." She rolled her bottle between two palms and thought about it. "His chest.
Around his chest, I guess."

"Was he smoking?"

"Like a sonofabitch."

"No, I'm sorry, I mean *cigarettes.*"

She shrugged and went back to staring out the window. Traffic was tying itself into a knot; the rumble
of frustration came through the glass like airplane
turbulence.

"I tried to help him, swear to God. Got water, tried
to put it out, that kind of stuff. Then the alarm went
off, and the sprinklers."

Bradshaw made a little *mmm-hmm* sound, one they
probably taught in reporter school. He hadn't made
very many notes, she noticed. Mostly doodles. Did he
think she couldn't read upside down? Probably
thought she couldn't read, period.

"When you left, was he dead?" he asked. She
snapped back around to look him in the eye. Cute
little prep-school asshole, all smiles, just like the ones
back home with their she's-an-easy-lay grins. Some
of it must have shown in her face, because he looked
startled and a little ashamed.

"Of *course* he was dead, I wouldn't leave him there
like that if he wasn't dead. Jesus."

God, she hoped to hell he was dead. He had to
have been dead. Why the hell would he ask something like that— unless Burt hadn't been dead. Unless
she'd left him there melted into the carpet like somebody else's garbage, oh Jesus, no.

She couldn't think about that. She just couldn't.

He was doodling again, but stopped when she
slammed her hand down over the page.

"Listen. I don't know where the hell you got my
name, but don't use it. Don't even use the initials, un-

derstand? You can call me Deep Fucking Throat or whatever you want, I don't give a shit, but I got to protect myself."

"My sources are always confidential," he said, and looked pointedly at her hand covering his pad. She pulled it back. "So, um, what else?"

"What do you mean, what else?"

"Well— " He gave her an under-the-lashes look, an aw-shucks-ma'am look of discomfort. "Well, I can't just take this back to my editor. I mean, you know, he's kind of a hard ass. I need— more. For the amount of money I paid you, I mean."

"I don't— "

Lenny stared at her with eyes as blue as a Disney character. He smiled. Dimples. His expression clearly thought he was adorable.

"Um . . ." He leaned conspiratorially forward over the table and tried for a sexy whisper. "Maybe I could, you know, let it go. For a consideration. Give you the, you know, the rest of the money."

She smiled, a seething lazy smile, and under cover of the table put her foot up and rubbed the toe of her shoe along the inside of his thigh, right up to the crotch. She gave him a slow gentle pressure, just enough, and when she was sure she had his attention, she flicked her toe up. The sharp point of her four-inch stiletto heel dug hard into his balls.

"You know," she said, "come to think of it, there may be a few things I could do to you for a couple hundred. Want me to give you a free sample?"

Lenny's face turned the color of old paper. The plastic bench seat made popping sounds as he tried to press himself back through it. She wiggled her heel deeper and balanced her leg comfortably on the seat, ready to shove hard.

"You're going to be a good boy, aren't you, Lenny?

I would hate to think you were trying to take advantage of me. Reach in your pocket and take the money out and put it on the table. Now."

He licked his pale lips and nodded.

"Um, could you— you know— move your foot first?"

"Nope, sorry, not possible."

He gingerly eased one hip up off the bench and dug in his pocket, until she heard the sound of crackling paper. He slid an envelope over the edge of the table toward her. She counted it slowly; when she felt Lenny getting restless, she jabbed him a little, and he settled down.

"I don't like it when assholes like you try to shake me down, Lenny. Now we're even."

"Well, not quite." His voice wasn't steady, but he was making a good run at it, and she eased the pressure in his crotch a little. Relief spilled over his face like water. "Uh, look, what you gave me is good, sure, but I need more. I need— something *great*. Something I can run with."

"Even if I have to make it up?" she asked, and drained the last of her Ginseng Special, a mouthful of sweat and bubbles. He attempted a grin.

"Well, you know, my editor— I really need the story. I'm desperate."

"Okay." She took her foot completely out of his target area and crossed her legs. He crossed his. She leaned forward.

So did he.

"I think," she said, and widened her eyes, "I know who killed him."

Eight
Velvet

She felt like an alien from outer space at the library. People stared at her with that weird what-the-fuck-is-she-doing-here look, even the shuffling drunks with their paper bags, and the librarians— Jesus, you'd think she'd come in with a spinning chainsaw and a severed head. The cops— there were so many on duty at the doors you would have thought the fucking President was in the Periodicals— eyed her like they were measuring her for mug shots.

Velvet sat down in an orange 1970's chair too ratty for a yard sale, and tried to figure out where to go. Hell, she hadn't been in a library since her sophomore year in high school, when Miss Ardelia Ferguson had made her write a paper on salmonella. A long-haired guy in a ratty old army jacket shuffled toward the magazines— wino, looking for a place to snooze. A yuppie-looking asshole in big-butted Dockers and a ski jacket insulated with shredded twenties asked the librarians about financial statistics— she yawned, on reflex. A guy came by looking for newspapers.

Ah.

She got up and followed him to the elevators, up to the third floor. He sneaked little glances at her lace-inset blue jeans, her high-heeled red shoes, and

gave her a smile small enough to have come off a
chihuahua. She gave him a go-to-hell-you-asshole
look. He shrugged and wandered off to the right.

Newspapers. She looked around at the shelves, the
stacked papers, and started pulling things out at random. The smell of ink and cheap paper was kind of
nice, after a morning of sniffing wino's b.o.— soothing. It reminded her of Dad reading the farm reports
in the morning. There was a very small difference
between soothing and boring.

She found a two-day-old Dallas paper and carried
it over to a chair, checked through it page by page
until she found the article about the unidentified
dead guy at the hotel. She checked the next day's
paper, but there was nothing. He hadn't even been
unusual enough to rate a second notice. They were
calling it some kind of smoking accident, the
assholes— burying it, whatever it was. She stuffed the
paper back haphazardly in the slot and found the
new one, today's paper.

Nothing. She kept turning pages, checking out police reports, the occasional fashion item, dress sales.
She lingered over a three-for-one on shoes.

Obituaries.

*DALLAS— Burt Everard Marshall, co-owner of the
Elegance Dry Cleaners chain, died suddenly Tuesday.
He was 47.*

*Memorial service will be at 2 P.M. Friday at Faith
Baptist Church in Dallas. Eternal Care Services is in
charge of arrangements.*

*Mr. Marshall was born in Dayton, Ohio. He was
a graduate of Texas A&M University.*

*Survivors: Wife, Sherry Marshall of Dallas: three
children, son Tyler, age 17, and daughters Martha,
14, and Evelyn, 13.*

"God," Velvet whispered, and realized there were tears in her eyes. She blotted them away with a twisted old tissue, careful of her mascara. One deep breath, then another, and she folded the paper in the wrong places and put it back. "Sorry, Burt."

A young woman in standard student attire— sweatshirt and jeans, running shoes, hair well-poufed enough to be SMU-standard— was in command of one of the big tables nearby, five or six newspapers spread out in front of her while she made notes. Velvet blew her nose loudly, stuffed the tissue back in her pocket, and walked over to where the kid sat. Even though she must have known she was coming, the kid didn't look up until Velvet said, "Excuse me, hon, but I need to find out about spontaneous combustion."

The kid blinked at her and looked around uneasily; everybody else in the area deliberately didn't look back. She gave up on help and stared back at Velvet with big empty blue eyes.

"Excuse me?" she said.

"You know, where people burst into flames and shit. If you were looking for that shit, where would you look?"

"Um . . ." The woman shifted in her chair, back and forth, like she was working up to making a run for it. "I guess— start in reference?"

"Reference. Right." Velvet gave her a brilliant smile. "Thanks, hon. You have a real nice day."

"Sure." A faint, half-terrified smile. Velvet picked a direction and started walking. When she looked back, the woman was staring at her, but quickly looked away. *What?* Velvet wanted to yell. *I look like a psycho to you?*

Not a psycho. A hooker. Just like the wino looked like a wino.

Over by the elevators a middle-aged guy with a

whining little girl clinging to his pants leg gave her
The Look. She returned a professional smile, then
she remembered she was on vacation, and dimmed
it to something like the librarian's tight little grin.
He kept staring, though. Hungry eyes.

She slowed as she approached him. His expression
perked right up.

"Hey, buddy, where's the reference section?" she
asked. He offered to show her, she refused, the kid
whined, and she ended up in the elevator again, heading down.

It took an hour and two more unwilling strangers
to get what she wanted— mostly crap, hot-brain theo-
ries about fat people and alkies and aliens. She found
pictures. They looked so familiar. Bright white teeth,
black flaking skin, wet muscle.

When she closed her eyes, she could still see him
lying there, melted to the carpet. Her stomach
lurched noisily.

One day to the funeral. Maybe—

Maybe she'd go. Just as a send-off. Hell, she had
nothing else to do.

Incident Two:
EL PASO, TEXAS

Jerry Lintz, still dripping from his shower, shoved hangers around in his closet. Blue jeans, suit pants, shirts. He frowned. Things were always like this after vacation— half his stuff missing forever, or, at best, stuck in the wrong place for six months. The first day back was always the worst, and his desk would be an absolute disaster at work. Probably a long day, a late night.

He needed to burn off stress already.

"Hon, where's my running suit?" he yelled. Brandi stuck her head around the corner and gave him a weary look— her face was still puffy with sleep, her hair matted flat on the side.

"I told you last night, in the hanging bag. I didn't unpack it yet."

He ripped the zipper open and wrestled out his favorite running suit, the one he'd worn in his last six cold-weather marathons. As he was taking it off the hanger he stopped, frowned, and ran the fleece through his fingers.

"Hon?"

"I'm making coffee," Brandi shouted back. Disturbing her at the coffee machine was like interrupting a prayer. He walked through the house holding his sweatpants, still frowning.

"Did you wash this?"

She stood at the counter, scooping brown powder into a filter, and avoided meeting his eyes.

"Oh, sweetie, the whole thing stunk like a dead cat. While we were on vacation I had the hotel send it out."

Jerry stared mournfully at his sweatpants, patted the clean springy cloth, and sighed.

"I liked them the way they were."

Still, it was already six, and no time to worry about it. He pulled the pants on, zipped up the thick fleece jacket, and sat down to lace up his running shoes with the absent skill of a true fanatic. Brandi yawned and waited on her coffee; they didn't discuss breakfast, or anything else. She'd have it ready when he got back, just like always. They'd share the paper and watch a little of the "Today" show and go off to work, then end the day with dinner and dishes and two hours of television. Brandi would go to sleep reading, and he'd lie awake, staring at the ceiling, for another hour or two.

Jerry hated his life in a cordial, contemptuous way. He'd planned on being rich, having a fast red car and a glitzy job and a beautiful model for a wife. He'd compromised, and in the end there was nothing wrong with what he had. The disappointment only got to him once or twice a month, watching the bigwigs chat about golf and tailored suits and the latest vacation extravaganza.

He'd had four days in Dallas, for god's sake. Some vacation.

Brandi waved to him as he went out the door.

In the yard the grass was lightly moist. It hardly ever rained, and Jerry's grass was a neighborhood scandal, since he watered it every night for hours. Water rationing was in force, but he was careful not to turn it on too high and make a telltale puddle on the street. He trotted past the stunted evergreen trees at the back and came out on Lee Trevino Road. Even at six, there were some cars out, though nothing like the traffic he'd seen in L.A. on his last business trip, or even in Dallas. El Paso's cars had a different quality—older, dispirited, rough-running. Even the new ones had a kind of bleached arid quality. It was the water, he was convinced. Nasty water.

Stretching was an automatic thing, accomplished efficiently. He began to trot and found his stride within a block. The sidewalk spilled a thin gray ribbon down the hill; once his feet were on it, it carried him along like a concrete river. His breath burned cold for a few seconds, then began to warm up. His shoes slapped with soothing regularity, and overhead a night-flying bird chirped and passed him with a feathery rush of wings. Headlights from an oncoming car washed him in halogen glare, quickly gone. He felt the muscles in his back loosen and swell, and in the distance the sun was a hint behind faraway sawtoothed mountains. The air was still and clear.

He'd only gone a mile when dizziness hit and he broke stride, caught a light pole for support. He put his head down and sucked air, a little alarmed. So sudden. But he was in condition, he'd never had any kind of trouble before. The disorientation reminded him of the last time he'd gone out bowling with Viola and Greg, of too many beers and blurring lines on the road.

Maybe he was coming down with a bug. Time to go home. He turned and started back up the hill at a slower pace. The dizziness continued and even got worse, a fuzziness in his head, a churning in his stomach. God, maybe he had the flu, wouldn't that be a pisser? Vacation, and sick the first day back—

Funny how fast the day had warmed up. He

thought about taking his fleece jacket off, but his fingers felt clumsy and slow, and he decided to wait until he got home. His legs seemed leaden and uncooperative, but he made it to the top of the hill and home was only three more blocks— a quick shower— maybe a lie-down—

"Oh, Jesus," he whispered when the pain started— heart attack, he'd been afraid all along— God, no—

But it wasn't his heart. He looked down and saw the running suit flaring white. While he was still thinking clearly, he tried to work the zipper, get the damn thing off, but the metal was so hot it burned his fingers and then his skin, and oh God the fire was everywhere, his skin popping and blackening. He clawed at the fabric and dug out handfuls of burning fleece and his own muscle. He screamed rawly into the peaceful silence of the morning.

Insanely, a commercial played in his head, children singing something— stop, drop, roll—

Yes. Yes. He let his legs go limp and fell hard, half on concrete, half on grass; he rolled wildly, back and forth. It didn't stop. It didn't stop. Oh God—

He rolled again and fell six inches, kept rolling. Gritty harsh pavement under him. He saw his hand clearly in front of his face, rotted black, skin gray and smoking— bright, so bright. Halogen-bright.

Something hit him in the back. He heard the sound, bump-bump, bump-bump, bump-bump, bump-bump, strange rattling heartbeats, and then a scream that sounded like metal.

He couldn't move at all now, didn't even feel any pain except twinges from his chest. There were red lights in front of him now, pulling away, slowing—

Taillights. A truck. A tanker truck had run over him.

At least the pain was gone. Blood ran past him in

a thick red stream over the blacktop, down toward the truck where the tires smoked as the driver tried to stop. The tanker twisted sideways and tipped, dragging the cab with it, and the metal tank split open and gushed gold liquid down the hill.

He watched the tires spin. One of them had a piece of his running suit caught on it.

It burst into flames. A drop of fire fell from the tire into the spreading lake of gasoline. He had just enough time to think, *thank you*.

The morning lit up like an early violent sunrise.

Nine
Martin

The meetings were no longer being held in Martin Grady's office building. They'd moved to a numbered marble hall with Classified Areas and a whole new group of geeks with expensive suits. The whole goddamn building was nonsmoking. Martin fished a cigarette out of a pack in his pocket and stood outside on the marble steps, staring out toward a haze of morning fog, and tapped the tobacco end thoughtfully on the back of his lighter. He had only taken two puffs when a young woman in a tweed suit and black leather gloves came out to join him, not really dressed for the chill. She was smoking Marlboros; he lit her cigarette for her and got a nod in return.

Pretty and young. He wasn't sure from the suit if she was office staff or agent, and didn't want to be wrong. They stood in silence, blowing streams of white smoke out toward the city.

"You're Grady," she finally said. He looked over at her in surprise. "OEH. I saw your reports on the water contamination. Good work."

"Thanks." He shrugged, eyeing her. He didn't recognize her, and didn't want to get caught out. In Washington, in bureaucracies, everything was political, even compliments.

"It's all wrong, you know," she finished.

"What makes you think so?"

She just smiled. Cold pink spots burned in her cheeks under smooth makeup. "You know, the administration's buying your report, pork barrel and all. They're committing resources. It's a goddamn waste."

"Look, lady—"

"Adrian Carling."

"Ms. Carling, we should discuss this inside." He gestured vaguely with his cigarette at the city spread out in front of them, the pedestrians hurrying past at the end of the walk, the armed guards at the gates. There was a knot of dispirited protesters waving signs across the street. She gave him a bitter smile and stubbed out her Marlboro with two or three puffs left in it. She was wearing some light lipstick, coral or peach or something; it left a shimmer on the butt.

"They can't keep this thing buttoned up for long," she said, and pulled her arms close over her chest. "You know that. A couple more public occurrences, and we're going to have our faces all over CNN."

Martin finished his cigarette and flicked the butt out into the fog in the general direction of the Pentagon.

"Yeah, well, we've got our orders."

"The Bureau has a possible terrorist connection."

"You're shitting me." There were a lot of bureaucrats, but only one Bureau. The Bureau was always following terrorist threats, like kids chasing balloons in the wind.

Carling turned away. He reached out and grabbed her shoulder.

Agent, not office worker. He slowly removed his hand, as if he'd stuck it into the bars of a tiger cage.

"We're not wrong," he told her. Carling cocked her head and brushed a strand of auburn hair back from her forehead. Under her tweed jacket he caught a glimpse of metal. "It's not terrorists. It's an environmental hazard."

"Well, Marty." She took in a deep breath of foggy air and gave him a cool brilliant smile. "You'd better be right, hadn't you?"

Incident Three:
LAS VEGAS, NEVADA

Ed Julian arranged the newspapers more carefully on the coffee table and stepped back to take a critical look at the arrangement. Casual, yet organized. Plenty of coffee, plenty of cream and sugars, plenty of croissants. He wondered if he ought to order a better assortment of jams, but no, everything looked just fine. Pity he had to use a hotel room, even this spacious suite. It was so— impersonal. He always liked to make a strong personal statement to potential buyers.

Still, he could hardly have this kind of meeting in his own office.

He checked his reflection in the big floor-to-ceiling mirror behind the fully stocked bar, smiled winningly, straightened his Jerry Garcia tie. Was the tie too much, or just the right touch of devil-may-care?

Too late to worry about it. Three strong knocks shook the door.

Showtime. Ed took a deep breath and flexed his shoulders, then grasped the knob and swung the door open.

"Gentlemen," he said warmly. "And lady, of course."

They stared at him with identical expressions of distrust, four men and one woman. The Nordic blond man wore a tailored suit. The greasy-looking dark-haired man wore blue jeans, a plain black T-shirt, and a worn green jacket with tweed patches on the elbows.

"Let's get to it," the dark-haired one said as Ed tried to introduce himself. Ed held on to his smile and closed the door behind them as they entered.

The sole African-American man shoved past the others and, very practically, poured himself a cup of coffee. He sat down in one of the comfortable pastel chairs arranged near the coffee table. The other men silently followed suit, except for the last one, an Arab with cinnamon brown skin and warm dark eyes. A smiler, that one. He gave the woman a little bow and let her go first to the coffee server. She— a small, thin, dark-haired woman— seemed to neither notice nor care.

Ed made sure everyone had been served before he took his seat and made the meeting informal by loosening his tie. The unsmiling faces on the other side of the table failed to take the cue.

"Well, wonderful that you all made it. Anyone visit here before? Always something new to see, every time I come to town."

"Let's get to it," the brunette repeated, with a little more menace. No one else spoke. Ed cleared his throat and smiled.

"Of course. Busy people, I understand. Now, we've agreed to go by neutral names here, so you can call me Mr. Zero."

"How about calling me a cab," said the blond man, rising. "I haven't got time for these games."

"Please, sit down, sir. Please." Thankfully, the man did, though he kept glaring. "You can call me anything you like. Now, I'll call you numbers, all right? You, sir, you're One— sir, you're Two— ma'am, you're Three— Four— and Five.

"Why's he One?" the woman asked immediately.

The African-American man— One— turned to her and said amiably, "Shut up."

"Ms. Three, the numbers don't mean anything at all. Each of you represent organizations that seek to purchase my new breakthrough process. No names of organizations should be mentioned here. No causes. Your religious or political affiliations do not matter. You are just— numbers."

She subsided. Ed looked around at each of them in turn, fixing their identities in his head. IRA, the blond. The Patriot Brotherhood, the other Caucasian. The black man was shopping for a corporate client. The Arab was a broker, not a player. The woman—

He gave her a nervous smile.

"You all received the list of names I sent you via Federal Express ten days ago?" he asked. The heads nodded in various degrees of enthusiasm. "I believe Kevin Baird Tannery was one of them."

Rustles of paper as lists were removed from pockets and examined. Everyone agreed that Tannery was on the list.

Ed pulled a newspaper from the coffee table. *Chicago Tribune*. The below-the-fold story was of a man burned to death in his apartment, apparently by a disgruntled girlfriend.

Kevin Baird Tannery.

The paper passed silently from hand to hand. Each of them noted the date, the circumstances, the time.

"Also on your list, I believe was Jerry Lintz of El Paso, Texas. Yes?"

He passed the second newspaper, watched their expressions change.

"And, of course, Burt Everard Marshall, Dallas, Texas," he continued. The third paper made the rounds.

"How do we know you didn't hire someone to torch

these people and say it was some new chemical process?" Mr. Two asked sensibly. Ed checked his watch.

"Well, as a matter of fact, you can't. I'm not here to sell you snake oil, Mr. Two. I'm a very successful, very busy man. Do you seriously think that I'd take the chance of bilking people in your particular lines of work?"

"You'd have to be insane," Mr. Four agreed unblinkingly. "But that don't change the fact that you could be crazy. We're gonna need a little more proof."

"And you'll get it. In the next ten days, the rest of the names on this list should go up in flames. I'm sure you'll know how to find out the facts of the cases. Believe me or not—" Ed paused to pick some lint from his gray wool pants. His fingers were ever so slightly shaking. "As you like."

"I think we're going to need a little more dramatic proof," said Mr. Five, the Arab. He was still smiling. Ed smiled back, feeling the strain in his facial muscles.

"Of course you are. Could I ask your help in a little demonstration?" Ed stood up. Mr. Five shrugged and stood, hands folded before him. Close to a gun, Ed suspected, and felt a dizzy wave of nervousness. No time for that. He'd come so far—

"Hold her, please," he said, and nodded toward Ms. Three. Her eyes went wide. She went for a weapon hidden somewhere in her jacket, but Mr. Five wrenched her arms behind her and held them cruelly tight. She struggled until they all heard cartilage pop, then subsided into limp surrender, face dirty white with shock.

Ed nodded at Mr. Five. "Take her jacket off, please."

She fought so hard it took Mr. One's help to get her coat off, revealing a shoulder holster and a small deadly-looking .38. They searched her thoroughly for a wire, but found nothing. Ed opened the coat closet next to the door and took out a long black coat— cheap knock-off leather of no particular pedigree. Ms. Three started to struggle in earnest when he came back with it, kicking over the coffee table, sending cups flying. Mr. One drew the .38 from the shoulder holster and held it to her head. She subsided into stillness, except for the labored rise and fall of her chest. A drop of sweat glided down her cheek.

"Sorry about this," Mr. One said, and leaned forward to look into her face with disturbing intimacy. "Nothing personal, dear."

She took a deep breath to scream. Mr. Two jammed a handkerchief in her mouth.

Between One and Five, they got the coat on. Ed provided a length of nylon rope and tied her to the pastel chair, hand and foot. She tossed her head madly from side to side, sweat-slick black hair flying, and the rest of them pulled their chairs away from her. Ed retrieved a red fire extinguisher from the closet and handed it to Mr. Four.

And then he turned the heat up in the room.

"Normally, now, you wouldn't have to do this," he said as the fans kicked on and hot air whispered in around them. He perched on the edge of a table near the windows, eyeing the sweating face of Ms. Three. "Body heat is quite sufficient to build up the reaction, but sweating increases the speed, and, of course, we don't want to spend all day waiting. If you'll watch her face, you'll see the disorientation first— there. It hits two or three times, in waves, and then becomes nausea."

Ten minutes later, she made muffled wretching sounds. Mr. Two leaned forward and said, "She might choke on that gag."

Mr. Four said, "If she's lucky." He gripped the fire extinguisher in white-knuckled hands.

"At this point, she'll begin to feel some pain through the disorientation," Ed said. He'd judged the time perfectly. Ms. Three jerked hard against her bonds, making a high thin squealing noise. The heavy chair jumped and moved sluggishly side to side as she thrashed. He flinched as she thrashed; somehow he hadn't expected that, the terror, the hysteria. It made it all seem so unpleasant.

A thin wisp of smoke came out of the coat.

"Oh my God," said Mr. One, almost reverently.

"Yes, yes, quite right. That's enough. Mr. Four? Ah, Mr. Four?" Ed swallowed hard as the flames blossomed white, bright as magnesium flares. The stink of burning meat made them all flinch, but the sound was worse, sizzle, sizzle, bacon in a pan. Ed kept his seat with an effort and tried again. "Mr. Four, if you wouldn't mind, please, Mr. Four, you have the extinguisher. Sir? Mr. Four— *now*, please— "

"Put her out!" yelled Mr. One. He was on his feet, eyes wide. "Christ, man, you made your fucking point, put her out!"

Mr. Four cradled the fire extinguisher in his arms and rested his chin on the safety-locked valve. Ms. Three's pastel chair jittered and jerked and blackened with heat and the cooking juices of her body. Mr. One took a hesitant step toward him, and Mr. Four turned. He had an unpleasantly gleeful shine in his eyes.

Ed licked his lips and said. "Mr. Four, please. Please." How had things gone so *wrong?* He'd just wanted a simple demonstration, yes, of course, she would have died, but not like *this*, not this ghastly piece of—

Mr. Four popped the pin and sprayed the black corroded thing with white foam. There was surprisingly little smoke, but the smell was hideous, burst bowels, cooked muscle. Mr. One retreated to the windows and stood looking out blindly at the sunshine. The skyline of Las Vegas looked carnival-bright in the glare.

All right, all right. Ed took a deep breath through his mouth, tasting acrid grease, and cleared his throat. He struggled to put his mind back on the business at hand, because business it was, important business. Clearly Mr. One, though laudably conscientious, wouldn't be a reliable repeat customer, and all good business was founded on repeat customers. Equally clearly, he could *not* sell to Mr. Four. The man was a *lunatic*.

Ed built himself a sturdy Scotch and soda, and drank it fast without tasting it.

"Impressive," said Mr. Two, the IRA man. "I'm prepared to buy now. Exclusively, of course. If you're fixing drinks, I'm up for one."

Ed turned in relief, Scotch bottle extended like a welcoming hand.

Mr. Five drew a gun from his coat, a silenced automatic, and coolly shot Mr. Four in the forehead. Blood flecked the wallpaper. As Mr. Two went for his own weapon, Five shot him twice in the heart.

Mr. One didn't even have time to turn away from the window. His head made a dreadful mess on the glass.

Ed was still gaping, shuddering, when Mr. Five holstered his gun and stepped across the bodies to take his hand and shake it firmly.

"My name is Fathi el Haddiz, Mr. Julian," he said. He was still smiling. His eyes were warm and amused. "Terribly sorry about the carpet, but then I don't suppose you were planning on paying for the cleaning, were you?"

His life was teetering on a tiny, tiny edge. Ed thought about his Sales Power Seminars, all his Self-Affirmation classes, and took a deep breath and said, "I'm looking forward to doing business with you, sir."

Ten
Robby

Sol counted bills with a slow math-impaired style that made Robby want to bounce him off a wall. She exchanged a long burning-hot look with Jim and went to the kitchen, looking for something, anything, to kill time. Maybe she'd make Mark's oatmeal cookies— but then again, unless it came pre-mixed in a roll, she was sure to screw it up. She opened the refrigerator and found a bottle of Sprite, poured herself a glass, and searched Jim's cabinets for something to chew on so she wouldn't say anything stupid. Graham crackers. She poured a pile on a plate and carried them back.

Sol had worked his torturous way through six stacks of cash. There was one left. She sat down next to Jim on the couch and shared the crackers. Since this wasn't a work day, he was dressed in a hunter green shirt and faded blue jeans, clean and comfortable. His hair was combed into a gray brown shag around his rough face. She felt a perilous urge to relax against his warmth, knew he'd put his arm around her.

She didn't relax. There was no sense giving Sol more leverage than he already had.

Kelly sat curled up in the armchair, reading a romance novel with a pastel-and-glitter cover. She shot Robby jealous glances from time to time— she'd probably heard about Sol's intimate little dinner and taken exactly the wrong interpretation. Robby remembered to smile.

"You're short," Sol finally said. His head jerked up, and the cold eyes behind the bifocals were hot now, angry. "Jim, Jim, my friend. What, you think I'm too stupid to count?"

Jim, Robby knew, thought exactly that, and he was right. Sol was an idiot, and Jim might be a thief, but he was a goddamn *professional* thief, not a top-skimming amateur. She kept her mouth shut, her eyes down. Nibbled a graham cracker. It tasted like dust and chemicals.

"How much is it short?" Jim asked neutrally. Sol glanced down at the cash as if he'd written the total on top.

"Two-eighty-eight."

Robby risked a look at Jim's face; it didn't tell her anything at all. Across from her Kelly had put down her book and was watching with what looked like dread but Robby suspected was really fascination.

"You know I wouldn't do that, Sol," Jim answered. He sounded a lot calmer than Robby felt; that was why, as they'd always agreed, he did the talking. "Why would I?"

"I trust you, you know that, but the count's the count, and you're short. Hey, maybe it's just a simple mistake." Sol leaned forward. His mustard yellow jacket gaped and showed the silver butt of a pistol. She'd been right, it was a flash gun. "I'm nothing if not fair, you know that. Just make up the difference, and we'll call it even."

Jim sat in silence for a few more seconds, staring at Sol, past him, then stood up and walked away to the bedroom. Robby forced herself to sip Sprite. The fizz tingled the back of her throat like a feather, and she had to fight an urge to sneeze. Maybe she was allergic to Sol.

Jim came back and handed Sol three hundred in cash that Robby knew he couldn't really afford to lose. Sol smiled his shark-smile and stood up to wrap a too-friendly arm around Jim's shoulders. Kelly's face held a look of open relief. Robby felt muscles tighten in her stomach; Kelly had done the original count, after all, had handled the cash. Jim knew it, too. They were all capable of skimming, of course, any good dip was. The question was, which one of them *would*?

It wasn't really much of a question, when it came right down to it.

"I love you like a brother," Sol was saying, which really wasn't a hell of a lot of comfort, since Sol's brother had died of a .45 caliber brainstorm. "You're a good guy, Jimbo, real good. Hey, you too, Robby. You guys working the hockey game this weekend?"

Robby nodded. Sol grinned.

"Yeah, well, make sure you stay away from my Uncle Frank, he's got season tickets. See you on—" Sol checked a black Day Timer. "Tuesday. You guys, you bundle up, keep warm."

Jim hustled him out into the warehouse. Blessedly, Kelly chose to go, too, eager to hang on Sol's arm. Robby waited until Jim was back inside, until the door was safely closed, before going over and putting her arms around him. He felt like coiled wire.

"I told you he was a goddamn sonofabitch dago bastard," she said. Jim's arms wound around her. His hand cupped her hair.

"When you were in Ireland, was it this bad?"

"Sure. Two different payoffs— my Da handled most of them, of course, but I saw it. The IRA bureaucrats took a cut— not the special wings, those bastards would have killed us if they'd caught us—and, of course, the Brits. They wanted to make a little money and make it home alive." She drew back. His face looked seamed and old, the lines deep as knife cuts. "I'll split the damage with you."

"No. Kelly will."

"Ouch. You sure that's wise?"

Jim shrugged. They didn't call him Psycho Jim just because of his costuming. She supposed she'd have to assume he knew what he was doing.

Somebody knocked on the door, timidly. Robby pushed away from Jim, and they both turned to face the door.

"Expecting somebody?"

"I didn't order a pizza."

"Damn." She traded a look with him. "Where's the gun?"

"We don't need the gun."

"Don't be an idiot, of course we need—"

Jim went over and opened the door a crack. For a second he just stared, then swung it wide.

"Well," he said. "Look who's here. Rebecca of Sunnybrook Farm."

The hooker, overbalanced, had to brace herself with one hand on his chest, and gave him a Hollywood smile that was too bright to be real. Her glitter nail polish was a shade hicks put on speedboats. Robby looked at her in disbelief and horror, grabbed her by the elbow, and dragged her inside, slamming the door behind her with unnecessary force. The hooker had cleaned up everything except the hard set of her mouth and the smart-ass eyes. She was wearing a pair of blue jeans that had three-inch slits of white lace running from hip to ankle along the sides, and were tight enough to be body paint. Luckily, her electric blue coat covered up whatever she wore on top. The four-inch fuck-me shoes looked ludicrously uncomfortable.

"What the *hell* are you doing here?" Robby demanded, and resisted the urge to shake her. In fact, she let go of her arm and stepped back, to remove the temptation. Jim, still blank-faced, watched.

"Well, shit, don't make me feel at home or anything. Hey. Robby." The hooker gave her a lower-wattage version of the Hollywood smile. She held out a paper sack, folded over at the top. "Brought your clothes back."

"Are you crazy? Did Sol see you?"

"The fashion victim? Nah. I stayed in the shadows. Hey, who's he? Kind of a babe, ain't he?"

Robby grabbed the sack out of her hands and looked inside. A neatly folded pair of blue jeans, a black shirt. She set it on the floor and looked up to see Velvet watching her with a narrow bitter smile.

"What, you think I was going to steal from you? Jeez." Velvet rolled her eyes. "Anyway, thanks. For the clothes and stuff. It was— nice of you."

"It was goddamn stupid, was what it was," Jim interrupted. "Jesus Christ, Robby—"

"I know, I know. Look, um— Velvet— you got to understand, you can't come here. That guy, the one in the suit, he's looking for you. He doesn't like loose ends. You understand me? You don't know what you're screwing around with here."

"Sure I do," Velvet said indifferently. She walked over to the sofa, prodded it with an experimental finger, and plopped down. She stacked her ankles on the coffee table and admired her shoes. "He looks so much like a wiseguy, he must be fishbelly low on the food chain. Anyway, I pay my dues through Ming, he can't touch me. Sit down. Come on, sit. Let's have a drink."

"No. You're leaving, now." Robby grabbed a slick satin fistful of coat; Velvet yanked free with a glare.

"Hey, watch the merchandise. No way, honey, you and me got things to talk about. See, we had a real nice time drinking your friend's vodka, but you never did tell me about your guy. The one who burned." Her face lost some of its hard edge. "Come on, Robby. Please. I need this, I really do, and then I'm out of here. Out of your hair for good. Please."

"There's nothing to tell."

"Then it won't take too fucking long. Hey— buddy— can I have a beer or something? No hard stuff. Thanks." Velvet patted the armchair and smiled. "Come on, Robby. Spill."

"That's it," Jim growled, and leaned over to muscle the hooker to her feet. She twisted like a cat, slapped him hard, wiggled out of his grip and stood there glaring.

Jim, for just a second, looked like he might go after her. Robby put a hand on his shoulder and felt muscles twitching under his skin. "You want to know so bad, here it is— Deep Ellum. Loft apartment. I was supposed to collect some stuff from the guy and there was this— this smell." She looked over at the hooker, who nodded; she knew it, too. "I just looked in the window. He was on the kitchen floor. Smears of blood and black stuff all over the table, the wall, the refrigerator. His skin was black, and cracked; pink in between. I didn't see it happen. I don't know anything."

"When? When did it happen?"

"Seven months ago."

"This guy, was he, you know, in the trades? Connected?"

Robby looked at Jim and didn't answer. He avoided her eyes. The hooker's gaze skipped from her face to his, then back again.

"Ah, hell, you think the big guys are in it, don't you? Cleaning up, or something."

"You've heard it. Get the hell out," Jim said.

"Never got my beer," she purred, with a laugh somewhere deep down in it. Jim's fists clenched. "What's the matter, lover? You got a thing for smashing women around?"

Jim's head came up with a snap, and his eyes went blank. Robby was afraid for a second that he *would* do it, but he only said, "For you I'd make an exception. Get the hell out of my house."

"Sure," she grinned, and reached in her pocket. She tossed him something hot pink and square. He let it hit his chest and fall to the floor.

It was a condom. There was a square of paper taped on it that said VELVET, 555-7473.

"Be seeing ya," Velvet said. When Robby looked up, she was already at the door, turning the handle. "Hey. Seriously, thanks for the clothes and shit. Really."

She swung the door open and came face-to-face with Sol Lipsky, who blinked dead-gray eyes at her and, when she tried to step back, caught her wrist.

Sol looked absolutely calm, except for the hard set of his lips.

"Let's go have a talk, sweetheart."

Velvet was only still for a second before she smiled and said, "Sure, handsome, where to? Got a place?"

He slapped her, hard enough to make her wobble on her high heels. Robby flinched and saw a red handprint form on Velvet's cheek. The hooker's smile cracked.

"Well, fuck me, everybody's a critic today."

"Put a cork in it and move."

Sol no longer looked stupid, he looked frightening. Robby must have moved in reaction, because Sol's eyes flicked toward her and clung.

"What?" he demanded. "You got something to say, Robby? You going to tell me why the count was short, and who the whore is? You going to *lie* to me?"

"She didn't take it," Robby managed to say, and wished she hadn't. Jim's hand closed around her arm, not quite hard enough to hurt.

"No shit she didn't, and you and me're going to have a little talk about that later. No, Jim, you shut your trap. You and me, Robby. Later." He looked back at Velvet; the hooker was still smiling, but it looked shopworn. "You and me, sweetheart, we talk first."

"Sure, honey. Whatever." Velvet licked her lips. "If talk is what you want."

Sol slapped her again, harder. Robby gasped for breath and shut her eyes. Jim's fingers dug deeper into her arm, holding her still.

When she opened them again, the doorway was empty. She heard shuffling footsteps echoing in the warehouse.

"Oh, god, Jim—"

"Quiet," he said savagely. "Just be *quiet*, for god's sake."

He slammed the door and locked it, leaned his forehead against it. The room felt airless, like a crypt.

"He's going to—"

"No."

"Jim, he's going to—"

"No!" It was a raw yell; he slapped his hands flat on the door. "Shut up, Robby, just shut up. Do you want to get your ass killed?"

"No, but—"

"There's nothing we can do about it!" he snapped and whirled on her. "Dammit, do you think I like it? Do you?"

Sol wouldn't have gone far, she knew it. Maybe he'd only taken her to a corner of the warehouse, maybe he was doing it there, slamming his fist into her over and over, breaking bones, tearing, destroying. Jesus, Jesus, suddenly Dublin was back, thick around her, thick enough to taste and gag.

She couldn't just stand here, not again, never again. She *couldn't*.

She started for the door. Jim intercepted her and wrapped her in a tight bruising bearhug. Close up, the pain in his eyes looked like shame.

"What if it's me next?" she yelled, right in his face. "Are you going to stand there and let it happen? Are you that goddamn scared?"

He didn't answer her. He didn't have to. She stepped back from him, went into the bedroom. In the middle dresser drawer, under his socks, she found the snub-nosed .38 he kept for emergencies, and slipped it in the waistband of her blue jeans, under her sweatshirt.

Jim was a dark shadow behind her.

"They'll kill you," he said, voice like broken glass. "Jesus, kid, please don't do this."

She didn't even bother to tell him why she had to.

It was just ending in the warehouse, meaty thuds, wet sounds that echoed hollow in the dark. Sol's grunt of satisfaction sounded orgasmic. Robby stepped out into shadows, scared and shaking, and pressed her back to the rough concrete wall that hid Jim's apartment. Jim hadn't followed her out. As she stood, petrified, the light from the door shrank and folded in on itself and disappeared with a soft metal sound. The lock whispered closed.

"I guess we understand each other now," Sol said from somewhere across the room; his voice was uneven and breathless. "Don't we, you fucking cunt? Don't we?"

Velvet moaned. Robby felt a sharp stab of relief, or regret.

Footsteps grated on concrete and broken glass. Her eyes weren't adjusted to the darkness yet, but she sensed him moving toward her and fumbled for the gun. *Mary, Mother of God, let me have the guts to do it, please don't let it happen again, please.*

He kept going, his passage a breeze in the dark, and she saw the outside door stretch into a rectangle of dim dying sunlight. For a second Sol was silhouetted, adjusting his collar, checking the shine on his shoes.

She felt the weight of the gun in her hand. An easy shot, if she'd had the guts, but, of course, she didn't, and in a second he was gone into the street, door swinging shut behind him, booming.

She stuck the gun back in her pocket and ran toward the corner, toward the uneven moans, the whisper of skin on concrete. A pale face lifted toward her as she approached. The fast heave of Velvet's breathing sounded like heartbeats.

Robby cautiously squatted down and touched her hand. Velvet's fingers curled around hers. After what seemed like a long time, Velvet said, "Thanks." Her word sounded misshapen and thick. Her nose was bleeding, black ribbons down pale skin. She dabbed at it with her coat sleeve.

"I'm sorry," Robby said; it sounded awkward, horrible, stupid. She wanted to say *I would have shot him to save you, I would have,* but she knew it wasn't really true, and the hooker wouldn't believe it, anyway. "Do you want an ambulance?"

"For this? Fuck it. He's a pussy." Velvet's nails bit and relaxed on her fingers. "Well, maybe a couple of bandaids."

"I'll take care of you," Robby promised. Velvet coughed; it sounded wet.

"What, again?" she asked, and laughed.

Robby felt a tickle of relief and laughed, too, leaned forward and put her arm under Velvet's shoulders. Velvet tried to get up and failed, kicked off her too-high shoes and succeeded. Robby grabbed the shoes and stuck them in her coat pocket.

"Don't know why you wear the damned things," she murmured, and felt the pulse of Velvet's laugh through her shoulders.

"Basketball."

Jim heard them coming and swung the door open before she could knock. Robby stopped and squinted in the sudden light. She couldn't see his face in the glare, only a silhouette like Sol's. She paused and waited. The silence stretched. She thought he might close the door, but then he turned and stepped back. She barely heard his low rough voice say, "I'm not that scared, Robby."

Eleven
Ming

Ming had only been in the office twice—once, in the beginning, to let her know the risks of failure, and now. She had forgotten how dizzingly high it was, views of mist-gray clouds and a dim maze of streets below. The furniture was padded, the carpet lush, the colors warm and comforting.

It should not have frightened her so.

"Do you understand me?" the man on the other side of the desk asked. She nodded. Such a piggish little man, overweight, overdressed—he might have been one of her clients, coming to her for whippings and bootlickings and harnesses strapped cruelly tight. But this was a man who would never release control, never. "Tell me what you understand."

"You want no word of this event on the street. No rumors. No hints of trouble." She was surprised that her voice was so steady, so smooth; so many years of performing had armored her better than she'd suspected.

Another nod of her head, a gesture of respect. The man behind the desk blinked dead-quiet eyes. She thought about extinguishing a cigarette in the dark well of his pupils. The imagined humid smell washed over her.

"And how do we keep her from talking?" he asked. Ming sat completely still, staring over his shoulder at the smoky gray of mist, the deceptive comfort of other offices in facing buildings. No one would see what happened here. No one would know. There were places in the world where the law did not reach— here— a room in Taiwan. A quiet room.

She pulled herself from memory and met his eyes.

"The surest way is to close the girl's mouth," she said. They both understood what was meant. "But if I may, this would be a great loss. She is very beautiful, very skilled. You will have many years of profit from her."

"I don't like the risk."

"With respect, I questioned her myself. If you fear she knows what she should not— it is not so. She knows nothing of the man but the manner of his death. Even if she should talk unwisely, no one will believe her. No one."

The man at the desk studied Ming for a few seconds, then picked up a silver letter opener. As he toyed with it, the edge reflected hot silver, glittered in her eyes. Had he meant to aim it so? Afraid, so afraid— she had left Paolo downstairs, as requested, but, of course, Paolo would not have helped her. He was an animal with a keen survival instinct. If he were here in this room, he would be holding her down for the cuts. She shut her eyes for a brief eternal second and saw herself bleeding, substituted the man in her place, held a knife under his arm where the scars would be nearly invisible.

"How many years?" the man asked. Her eyes flew open.

"Sir?"

"How many years have you worked for us?"

"Seven, sir."

"You run a good business," the man said. He studied the letter opener, the sharp edges. She knew how it would feel to have that edge drawn along her skin. In her mind she ground a sharp metal heel in his soft skin. He opened his mouth to scream, and the stub of his tongue sprayed blood.

"Thank you, sir," she managed to reply. His smile flashed and was gone, like light from the knife's edge.

"I'll take your advice, Ming, for now. But if she makes trouble for me, you'll wish you'd never opened your mouth. Understand?"

The cutting of his tongue was not enough. She stuffed a rubber ball in his mouth and fastened it in place with a strap, picked out her favorite lash. Perhaps, for the occasion, she'd add razor blades. His dark eyes, so wide with terror. Perhaps now the cigarette. Perhaps now—

"I understand perfectly."

She stood up when he did, bowed low in the Oriental fashion she knew he would expect. He was a small man, really, hardly taller than she, with neat hands and small fingers.

She did not know his name, and had never wanted to.

Her fantasy of revenge was sweet enough to drown her fear. She even had the courage to smile at him, and saw he was surprised.

"Perhaps," she said, forcing her voice low in her throat where it purred and vibrated, "you would allow me to do you some service. It would be my pleasure."

Close, so close; she saw it in his eyes. He was aroused and ready to agree.

"A fine offer," he said, and stood aside as he opened the door. "I expect you'd make an exquisite servant."

Her fear returned with the force of a tidal wave, slamming aside her fantasies in favor of red memories, old terrors. She hoped her smile remained enigmatic, and bowed.

As she walked slowly away down the cool paneled hallway, she thought, *no master. Never again. Not at any price*.

If Velvet was the price of retaining her freedom, she would flay the stupid girl and present the man her skin.

Twelve
Velvet

Velvet stared into the mirror and probed a blue green bruise on her cheek, winced when pain spread like waves in a waterbed. The bruise was bad—half her face—but her eye looked worse. She was starring in a movie. Blood Eyes of the Zombie Hooker. A straight-to-video release.

Outside the bathroom, she heard Robby and Jim talking, a smear of quiet hissing voices. He was trying to talk her out of something. Jesus, she'd only been around a couple of times, and she already knew that was the way those two went. Boring as shit.

She probed her teeth with her tongue, found one a little loose, and pushed on it with her finger. She didn't think it would come out, but this seemed like a good time to take advantage of Ming's free dentist. One good shot of novacaine and she'd never feel anything anyway—better to do it when her face was already busted up. More efficient.

Robby had left her an ice pack. She picked up the plastic baggie and weighed it in her palm. The ice cubes slid greasily from one side to the other.

"Now, this will sting a little," she told her reflection, and put the ice pack on her eye. The shock almost made her pass out, and she braced herself

with white knuckles on the counter. "Oh, shit, sonofabitch— oh, *man,* I broke a nail."

Nope, not just one— she spread her scraped fingers
wide and counted three, no four, that were trashed
beyond repair. The pain from her face retreated under pressure of this new disaster. She'd just paid
Mary Ellen Davis fifty goddamn dollars for a mani-
cure, with the special polish, and now—

Now—

She met her own eyes in the mirror and what she
saw there scared the shit out of her— just another
pathetic stupid hooker with glitter nails and neon
bruises and wounded eyes. Wounded eyes.

Same old shit, Velvet.

She sat down on the toilet and tried to let the tears
come, but instead of tears there was only pain, and
under the pain an ache that went way down to her
bones. Pathetic. Totally pathetic. What was she so
proud of? That she'd taken her beating like a pro?
That she'd proved to herself, one more time, that
she was exactly what everybody thought she was?
Who the fuck did that jerk think he was, anyway?
Beating on her like that? She'd show him something— stomp on his balls, snap his kneecaps, watch
him piss his Armani suit and scream—

The tears came suddenly and hard, spilling down
her cheeks, warm under the ice pack.

Somebody knocked on the door— a polite knock,
respectful. Velvet sat up and wiped at her face with
a torn sleeve, cleared her throat, and yelled, "Yeah,
what?"

Robby eased the door open a couple of inches and
looked inside.

"Are you ready to go?"

"Go where?"

After a moment of what looked like second

thought, Robby said, "My apartment. You can stay there until tomorrow."

"No shit?" Velvet gave her a narrow look, or as narrow as she could with one eye swelled shut. "I ain't working, you know."

"What?"

"No freebies."

Robby's face went stiff.

"That's not what I meant," she sputtered. Velvet shrugged. "It's not!"

"Hey, whatever. I'm just laying out the house rules."

"Well, so am I." Robby glared at her for another beat and said, "Are you ready?"

Well, at worst the suit would have a prissy little house with plastic carpet runners and cellophane on the lampshades. A museum house. The bathroom floor would be cleaner than most people's plates. Who says you can't go home again? Maybe Robby would have those stupid collectible salt and pepper shakers Mom loved so much.

"Sounds yummy," Velvet lied, and followed her out to the living room. The guy with the hair— Jim, that was his name— Jim glared at her. Another thief who thought he was better than she was. Jesus, the world was just full of assholes. She paused long enough to bat her eyelids at him, even though it hurt like poking a needle up her nose. "Bye, sweetie. Sorry I can't stick around. Maybe later."

He looked like he wanted to slap the shit out of somebody, and couldn't decide between the two of them. He flopped down on the couch, flicked the remote control on his big-screen TV. Basketball. Robby moved around the room picking up things and jamming them in her purse— a hairbrush, a makeup bag, a wallet. She yanked open the door and glared at Velvet.

"Come on," she barked. Velvet readjusted the ice pack on her face, checked her balance on her high heels, and followed.

Once the door was shut behind them, she heard Robby take a deep painful breath in the dark.

"He ain't worth it," Velvet said helpfully.

"How the hell would you know?"

"Well, shit, none of them are," she shrugged. Robby took her arm and led her across the warehouse, out to the dark deserted street. Nothing moving, not even a wino, just empty yellow pools of streetlights and cold, cold wind. Live music drifted on the air from someplace toward Dallas Alley— a free concert, probably. Velvet liked the Alley— a fun place to work, lots of drunk tourists looking for a little local adventure. She trolled there in between Ming's jobs, sometimes. There was a barbecue place on the corner, closed up tight but breathing sharp tasty mesquite smoke out of its chimney. Her stomach growled.

"Where we going?" Velvet asked as Robby set out down the sidewalk, walking much too fast. Velvet's ribs protested under the sudden impacts, and her face felt like one big blood clot. Thank god for the wind chill. She couldn't have stood it if it had been hot. "Hell— hey— would you slow down? How far is it? Don't you have a *car?*"

Robby, lit gold by the streetlamp they were passing under, shook dark hair out of her eyes and sighed. "No car. Six blocks west, two north."

Velvet stopped dead in her tracks, reached down, and stripped off her shoes. She clutched them in one hand and shivered as her feet absorbed the shock of cold pavement.

"These," she said to Robby's questioning look, "are *not* walking shoes. Get it?"

Robby rolled her eyes, but she slowed down a little.

Velvet concentrated on watching the pavement for bits of broken glass or sharp rocks; whispers of cheering and tatters of guitar riffs blew by. Velvet's stomach growled again.

She wondered how Robby felt about Italian food.

"So what really happened?" she asked. Robby's eyes flashed to her, then away, searching alleys and doorways for surprises. She kept her hands in her coat pockets; for the first time Velvet wondered if she was carrying. She had that paranoid look.

"When?"

"When you found the guy who burned up. What happened?"

"I don't know what you're talking about."

"Oh, god, don't lie. You're a pissy liar. What'd you do, go inside?"

Silence. Robby hunched her shoulders and stared down the street. Velvet avoided a spray of broken glass on the sidewalk and did a jig to catch up.

"Yeah," Robby said. "I went in."

"And?"

Robby's jaw had tightened. The soft brown eyes had a hard glittering look to them.

"He was still alive," she said. "I heard his breath bubbling. He was bleeding from his mouth and nose, bubbling blood."

"Jesus." Velvet watched her face. "What'd you do?"

"Nothing," Robby said. She kicked a sharp-edged piece of metal out of Velvet's way; it shot off into the darkness and whined off a curb. "I took his money and I left. I left him to die."

A car passed them, stirring papers like batwings in the gutter, and left behind an echo of laughter like wind chimes. Velvet wrapped her satin coat closer and looked down at her feet, white as marble in the cold.

"Burt could have been alive," she said. The truth

felt like a chunk of broken glass in her throat. "I didn't check. I ran out on him."

At the next intersection, a yellow DART bus farted black smoke as it passed. Velvet shifted from one numb foot to the other. She stared straight ahead, aware that Robby was looking at her, not wanting to look back.

"You think they knew we left them to die?" Velvet asked at last. Even though Robby was a shitty liar, she wanted her to lie. Robby didn't.

"Yes," Robby said. "Yes, they knew."

Thirteen
Martin

Martin Grady hurried down a concrete-floored hallway toward what was politely referred to as his office. Unlike his colleagues from the more Northern states, he'd ended up with a coat closet down here in what he'd heard somebody refer to as the engine room of the *Titanic*. Which made him, he supposed, the stupid schmuck going down with the ship.

It was two in the morning, and deserted office buildings got his goat, always had. He'd signed in upstairs with the crisp-pressed Marine guard, but supposing he got eaten by the Phantom of the Bureaucracy, would they notice? Not unless it involved cleaning up.

Something clattered in the distance. He froze and listened, but all he heard was his own accelerated breathing. His breath was smoky in the freezing air, which reminded him he hadn't had a cigarette since dinner. Thinking of cigarettes reminded him of Adrian Carling, the she-beast of Washington; he wondered where her offices were. Upstairs, of course, somewhere with two-inch pile carpeting and imported coffee served in thin china cups.

He counted plain gunmetal gray doors. Six, eight, ten, twelve. At sixteen he stopped and fumbled for his keyring.

Christ, it was quiet. Should have brought a radio, that would help. Something to break the silence. He'd buy one tomorrow, maybe a Walkman. No, he couldn't hear people coming with headphones on.

"Mr. Grady?"

He spun around, keys clutched like a weapon in his fist, and saw Adrian Carling standing only about ten feet away. She was shorter than he'd remembered, maybe five-foot-five. He couldn't tell what she was wearing under the calf-length dark-red coat, except that it must have been a skirt because the calves had hose and the feet had medium-heeled pumps.

"Ms. Carling," he remembered to say. "Surprise."

"I think that was my line." She came a few steps closer, and the coat gaped open, showing him a dark brown suit, a cream-colored blouse. "Working late, aren't you?"

"No, I just thought I'd come in and redecorate, maybe spill a little water in the hall and play ice hockey."

"Glad you're keeping your sense of humor." He didn't like the hint of pity in her voice, or the sad smile. "You must have enemies on the Hill."

"You don't?"

"Mine are more subtle. So, are you going inside, or are we waiting for the faceoff?"

He remembered the keys in his hand and used them. The door swung open on an office as dreary as the rest of the hall, gray walls, a battered Vietnam-era desk, a chair that leaned back enough that it might have been second-hand from a dentist. The corkboard on the wall was more holes than cork, but Grady had managed to pin up a photo—just one. It looked lonely and defiant.

Carling, of course, went over to look at it. She raised her eyebrows.

"Your daughter?"

"Yeah."

"What's her name?"

"Sally." He waited for the inevitable comments, the sympathy, but Carling just nodded.

"I assume there's a wife?"

Grady sat down in the chair, which squeaked like bedsprings, and fought the gravitational urge to tip over.

"Was," he said shortly. "What's on your mind, Ms. Carling?"

She continued to stare at Sally's photo, her eyes bright and sharp.

"She's a pretty girl. It's such a pity." The words sounded smooth and social, but they burned through him like acid. Her eyes never moved away from the picture, and he had to fight the urge to lunge up and tear the photo off the wall, hide it face down, protect it. "Suzanne left you in— what?— ninety-one? Left you all alone with Sally to care for. That must have been difficult."

The shock left behind an ache, like arthritis of the soul. He couldn't seem to think of anything to say, not even *Stop*.

She continued the autopsy.

"It really wasn't your fault, you know. Could have happened to anybody. I'm sure you didn't intentionally turn your back on her. It was hot, you were tired . . ."

She let it trail off, without even the courtesy to give him the fatal stab. He sat dumb and hurting while she turned away from the picture and settled herself in the guest chair across from him. Legs crossed with a whisper of nylon, and he stared at the shadowed revelation of her thigh.

"Why are you doing this?" he asked. She raised an eyebrow.

"To show you I can," she answered, as if it were

obvious. "By the way, I had your office swept for bugs
today. There were six."

It took a second or two to sink in, and then he sat
up so suddenly that his chair squeaked in alarm. She
held up a hand to stop him.

"Now there's only one. Mine. I'm being straight
with you, Marty."

"Whose were they?"

"Well, they don't usually label them, so I have to
guess. Other U.S. intelligence organs, the Israelis—
they do it for fun, I think. The fifth, of course, was
mine. It's the sixth one that worries me. I don't know
whose it is." She pulled off her brown leather gloves
and rubbed her hands. She didn't bother with mani-
cures; her nails were blunt-cut, clean but unpolished.
"Why are you here, Marty?"

It sounded like a trick question. He said cautiously,
"To present the— "

"No, *you*, Marty, *you*. Why you? Why not, say, Dr.
Harrison, Dr. Scheider? Why a bureaucrat, when obviously one of the scientific experts would have been
so much more convincing?" She watched his face for
awareness of the answer. "Because you're expend-
able, Marty. Because, frankly, if you get lost in big
bad Washington, nobody cares. Nobody except Sally,
provided she even knows you're alive."

Another surgical strike, one he suffered in silence
because he had no defense to offer. It was all so easy
for her.

"You're down here in the engine room," she continued more softly. "Marty, you're going down with
the *Titanic*, understand? This isn't a game for ama-
teurs. Pack your bags and go home."

"No."

"That's not a suggestion." She sat back, folded her
hands neatly together. "It's a threat."

He met her gaze, and it told him nothing at all; she was as smooth as plastic, as cold as nitrogen. He couldn't imagine her warm.

"I'm right," he said. It sounded feeble and stupid, and he thought he saw a flash of impatience in her eyes. "We're *right,* Agent Carling. We could save lives! Doesn't that mean anything at all?"

"Sure. It means you don't understand the game." She studied him for a few more seconds and said, "Got a cigarette?"

He sat back, staring, and finally pulled out a pack of cigarettes, tapped one out, passed the pack to her. They lit up together in silence. Martin studied the sole government-provided decoration in the room, an unevenly lettered red NO SMOKING sign behind Carling's head.

The heat of the smoke he sucked in was the only warmth in the room.

"Dichlorhyradine," he said. The word came out wreathed in white. "Processed chemical byproduct, but we don't know who's producing it. It's hydrophilic and inserts itself in cellular membranes. It's in the water, Agent Carling. Ordinary tap water."

She stared over his shoulder. Over the sharp tinny smell of burning tobacco, he caught a hint of flowers. Perfume?

"Damn it, are you listening to me?" he demanded. She focused on his face.

"What does it do?"

He watched Carling smoke; to her it was a neat efficient process, no sensuality to it at all. He imagined she ate the same way, mechanically, fueling up.

"Under certain circumstances, dichlorhyradine destabilizes. It has a low ignition threshold and causes an enzymatic reaction, highly exothermic." He thought he caught a flash of interest in her eyes.

Could he convince her? Hell, he'd better. If he couldn't convince Carling, what chance would he have on the Hill? "Uh, just a sec."

He flicked the latches on his briefcase and sorted through papers, found a folder and laid out a chart, traced a jagged red line with his thumb.

"See? Oxidization. Self-fueling. From the moment of ignition to irreparable damage is a matter of minutes, maybe less." He fumbled through his papers and pulled out another chart, this one in green and blue. "We think it's facilitated by high mineral concentrations. Some water samples are dense with it, some are clean. Anyway, once it ignites, the victim is certainly dead from shock and release of toxins. I don't know how you'd save one, provided you caught him in time to try."

She leaned forward to study the chart, but suddenly it looked to him like a parent dutifully examining a third-grader's drawing. *Oh, honey, it's lovely. Let's put it on the refrigerator.*

"I understand you found traces in liver samples," she said. Did she mean it? Was it just a soft-soap? God, how could he tell anything at all about her?

She might have lied about the bugs, just to throw him off. He glanced around the room. Six bugs? Where would they have hidden them? Behind the corkboard? Under the desk?

"Minute traces. Not enough to prove anything— but it does raise suspicions. It's possible the stuff could be ingested, or absorbed through the skin."

"And once in the body . . ."

"Once in the body, it causes a violent chemical re-action that starts a self-fueling fire," he continued. Was it under the desk? He had to resist the urge to lean over and look, couldn't resist running his fingers under the drawer in front of him. Something bumpy there. It felt like an ancient wad of chewing gum. "Spontaneous combustion."

She waved away a white veil of smoke. Her smile looked predatory.

"Fantasy," she said. "Nicely done, though. I like the charts, very colorful. I'll bet you even have overheads, don't you? Maybe, if you're really ingenious, you'll have a multimedia presentation. They'll love that."

She stubbed out her cigarette on the corner of his desk, leaving a bubble in the abused walnut varnish, and dropped the butt in his battered trash can.

"Crap," she finished quietly. "It's scientific crap. Listen, Marty, you're right, but you're wrong. Right about the method, wrong about the delivery system."

"Are we back to your terrorists again?" He chuckled, stopped when he saw the quiet frightening look on her face. "Oh, Jesus, you've got to be kidding me."

"You're wrong about the delivery system. It's not in the water, and they're going to buy your theory because it's something environmental, something they can appoint a blue ribbon panel and study. They'll waste years, Marty. They'll waste lives." She cocked her head to one side, studying him like a bug on a pin. "I can't let that happen. I can't let you go in there and give them an easy out. It's nothing personal, I want you to understand that. I like you."

"Gee, that makes everything swell." His sarcasm was feeble, but it was all he had. She'd left him with nothing else.

She leaned across the desk, put her face very close to his. He smelled a rich perfume, whispery-sweet. Her eyes were dark teal green, almost blue, as reflective as mirrors.

"This time tomorrow, you're going to want to use my head for a football," she said. "I thought I ought to give you an even shot. That's all."

She straightened and walked to the door. He stood up, not quite sure whether or not to follow her, and watched her close the door. She took her guest chair and jammed it up under the handle with a squeal of wood on concrete.

His heart squeezed into a hard knot. So easy to make him disappear. One more missing crewmember on the *Titanic*.

She reached under her coat. He watched the gun come out in little freeze frames of alarm, cold matte metal, long lethal barrel.

Somebody might hear him if he screamed.

"I told you, I'm sorry," she said, and walked toward him. She raised the gun and put it down on one corner of his desk. When her hand left it, he continued to stare at it, as stunned as if she'd dropped a body part.

She took her coat off and draped it over his chair. He didn't move as her hands pushed his own coat off his shoulders. "Tomorrow you'll hate me, Marty. So there's only tonight. No more time."

Her lips were cherry-sweet, warm, soft. The feel of her hair on his fingers was like cold silk. His erection caught him by surprise because it was instant, as if it had been lurking for the opportunity, and he couldn't remember needing anybody so badly, not his wife, not the occasional date, not anybody. He pressed her against the desk and fumbled at her suit buttons, got her coat off, her blouse. Her skirt slid down and tangled with his pants on the floor.

She had a condom ready, and she was expert with it, rolling it on with quick sensual strokes of her fingers. He had just enough time to think dazedly, *I don't know anything about her,* and then it was too late, he knew everything, everything.

He wondered, too late, if her bug was recording it.

Fourteen

Velvet

Robby had a paranoid's weight of locks. Velvet watched her open the second deadbolt— bottom of the door— and fumble for the key to the knob. When the door opened on darkness, something gave a sharp beep. Robby stepped around the corner and, in the dark, punched in a code.

"Make yourself at home," Robby said, and flicked on an overhead light. Velvet hobbled a couple of steps inside and hardly noticed Robby pressing past to shut the door and reset all her locks; she was busy absorbing details.

Hardwood floors— well, it was a downtown loft, so she'd expected that. High industrial ceilings, girders painted garish red and blue. Windows, lots of them, wrapping all the way around the big room; the vertical blinds were open, letting in the neon glow of downtown.

No plastic carpet runners. What carpet there was wouldn't have been caught dead in Mom's house— wild carpet, black with sharp slashes of blue and yellow and purple. The couch was black, the chairs mint green and an unbelievable magenta. The TV, compared to Jim's big-screen altar to the networks, was puny, the stereo correspondingly huge. The CD tower

rack next to it was so full it leaned like the Tower of
Pisa.

There was only one thing on the one un-windowed
wall. Velvet couldn't imagine how Robby had gotten
a billboard up here, but there it was, stretching from
floor to ceiling, corner to corner. It was a bright yellow ad for Ringling Brothers and Barnum and Bailey,
with a big red SOLD OUT sign taped over the date.

"Jesus," Velvet said blankly. Robby had finished
with the locks and gone off somewhere around the
corner— God, there was *more*. She wasn't sure her
eyes could take the strain. "Jesus Christ, Robby— "

"Yeah, shocking, isn't it?"

"It's— " Velvet took a step forward and got a stab
of protest from her feet. She kicked her shoes off
and walked over to the couch, tentatively fingered a
thick purple throw pillow. "It's— *cool*."

"You don't have to sound so surprised," Robby answered. "Want coffee?"

All this and a kitchen, too— or at least a coffeemaker, which was the same thing. She followed the
sound of Robby's voice and came around the corner
to find a big shiny room tiled in alternating white and
red.

"Wow. The Purina kitchen," Velvet blurted. Robby
laughed and spooned coffee powder into a machine
that looked space-age enough to make coffee on "Star
Trek." "Hey, you got any snacks? Like, chips or pretzels or something? I'm kind of hungry."

"There's soup. You probably don't need to do a
lot of chewing."

"Oh. Right." So much for her pizza fantasies. "Uh,
Robby? This is— real nice of you. Really."

Robby finished pouring water and switched on the
machine; it hissed and bubbled like a flattening tire.

She opened a cabinet and pulled down two mugs, contemplated them with a frown.

"Bugs or Taz?" she asked. Velvet blinked.

"Sorry?"

"Bugs Bunny or the Tasmanian Devil?"

"Uh, Taz, I guess." Velvet accepted the mug and looked at the cartoon on the side. "Cute. Anyway, uh, thanks. Really."

Robby looked up at her.

"I stood there," she said quietly, "and let Sol pound the living hell out of you. Why are you thanking me?"

She didn't wait for an answer. By the time Velvet closed her mouth, Robby had walked around the corner. Velvet stared at the Tasmanian Devil's grinning toothy mouth.

"You," she growled. "Wipe that smile off your face."

Robby was in the living room, sitting on the couch, flipping through a pile of mail that looked like sales circulars and HAVE YOU SEEN ME cards. Velvet walked over to the windows and looked west, toward a tangle of neon and streetlights.

The windows were wired with intrusion alarms. Shit, who was she afraid of? Spiderman?

"Wasn't your fault," she said to the city, and to Robby's reflection. "And anyway, shit, he didn't break much. It's not like I'm a virgin in that area, either."

"I thought you said you were protected."

"Well, sure. It's kind of like a union. I mean, my shop steward'll complain to the local, and the local'll complain to management, and somebody'll apologize." Velvet shrugged. "Bureaucracy, you know?"

"The curse of the working class."

"Yeah, that and cellulite."

Robby laughed. Velvet decided that she might be okay after all.

In the kitchen, the coffeemaker dinged. Velvet went back and poured Bugs and Taz full, and carried Bugs back across the room to Robby, who murmured a distracted thanks and sipped while she flipped through a Christmas sale circular.

"What's with the circus?"

"Hmm?" Robby glanced up. "Oh. I saw them in Ireland when I was ten, been going ever since. It started out to be a useful place to practice—"

"Practice what? Oh. Stealing."

"Dipping," Robby corrected primly. "I liked it so much I kept going just for the spectacle. Haven't worked there in years."

"What was it like?" Velvet sat down in the mint green armchair; it felt surprisingly comfortable. "Ireland, I mean, not the circus."

Robby stared at her. Didn't answer.

"Okay, obviously, this is not the right time. Excuse the fuck out of me. Hey, what about that soup, anyway?"

"Do you know how to use a can opener?" Robby asked.

"Of course, I—"

"Read the directions." Robby pretended to be fascinated by the prices of garage door openers in her circular. "This is not the Hilton. I am not room service."

Velvet opened her mouth, closed it, and went meekly to figure out the microwave.

She made chicken noodle soup and drank it straight out of the microwave bowl. As she was rinsing up, she heard Robby say from behind her, "Ireland was beautiful and I loved it. My Da was blown up on a train by the IRA. Collateral damage. Come on and I'll show you your bedroom."

Velvet decided she liked the bedroom, in a masochistic sort of way. The comforter on the bed was neon blue, the dresser the same mint green as the armchair in the living room. A full-length mirrored closet spanned one wall.

"My room is the next one over. Call me if you need anything." Robby opened the closet and took out an armload of bright green sheets. "I suppose you can look through my closet if you like, see if there's something you could stand to wear."

"Uh . . ." Velvet accepted the sheets and hugged them close, felt bruises twinge in protest. She took a deep breath of fabric softener. "Okay."

After an awkward moment, Robby nodded back and left, shutting the door behind her.

Velvet sank down on the bed, felt the mattress with professional expertise. Not bad. Not bad at all. She held onto the sheets and stared at her reflection in the closet door for a long time. She matched the room, blue green bruises. She hadn't expected this, didn't want it, hadn't expected to understand Robby even a little, or like her.

It made her want to break something.

The phone on the bedstand was round and squatty and lit up with blue neon. When she picked up the receiver, the light went out. A quick fumble in her wallet and she came up with the scribbled number.

Five rings. She got his answering machine.

"Hey, Lenny, listen, this is Velvet. You know, Velvet? Anyway, I got some good shit for you." She curled up on the neon blue bed, pulled her head down and watched the closed door warily. "I found somebody else who's seen somebody burn up. It ain't no coincidence. Got to be the wiseguys."

She considered for a second, gnawing on a broken nail, and said, "They're running scared. One of them beat the shit out of me to shut me up. I'll sell you names and facts for five hundred."

She hung up and watched the blue neon flare again.

Technically, she supposed, she was guilty of stabbing Robby in the back. Technically.

Five hundred bucks. She could get out of town on that, get someplace new. Robby would understand.

She stretched out on the bed and, after a minute, turned on her side and pulled her knees up to her chest to nurse an ache in her gut.

Incident Four:
CAMPBELL, LOUISIANA

Dwayne Elliot paced back and forth in the waiting area, fussing at the sleeves of the white robe he wore. They were too short, exposing thick hairy wrists. He was supposed to feel holy, he supposed. He just felt cold.

"Oh, you look fine, Brother Dwayne," said Missy Collier. She looked up from her mimeographed church program and gave him a smile. Missy, now, she was a pretty woman. A little old for his taste and married to old Vern Collier besides, but three children hadn't hurt her figure none, and he figured he wouldn't kick her out of bed if she fell in. It occurred to him (a little late to do any good) that a Sunday morning baptismal service wasn't the time to be thinking about that kind of thing, especially with her being married and all. Still, he had to wonder about what she was wearing under her white robe. Underwear, for sure. Front-hook bra? High-cut panties?

Through the closed waiting room door, Pastor Zeke's voice thundered like a jet engine, rising to a shout now to exhort the sinners to repent, glory glory glory. Dwayne imagined he'd be throwing up his arms and shaking his hands like tambourines. There'd be sweat stains under the arms of the suit by now. Pastor Zeke worked hard for his flock.

Dwayne paced over to look at a faded copy of Jesus raising Lazarus from the dead. Lazarus looked more like a man with a moonshine hangover than a three-day corpse. Dwayne knew what a three-day corpse looked like, because his Uncle Fisher Stevens had found one floating in the crick back of the house when he was fifteen. Three-days dead in Louisiana water, chewed by turtles and crawfish.

Awful hot in the church today. Dwayne mopped at the back of his neck with a wadded-up handkerchief; through the closed door he heard the organ break into a wheezing chorus of "Washed In The Blood." The only other baptismal candidate, little Alton Neames, bounced in his chair like he had to go pee.

The waiting room door swung open, and Pastor Zeke Clayburn stuck his head in and grinned with white square store-bought teeth, mostly at Missy Collier, who grinned right back.

"God bless, folks, we're ready. You ready, Alton? You ready to stand up for Jesus?"

Alton looked ready to raise his hand for the bathroom, but he hopped off his chair and took Pastor Zeke's hand. Dwayne stepped aside to let Missy go ahead, and took his place last in line. He followed her swinging white robe up three red-carpeted steps to the baptismal tank.

When he looked out into the church, Dwayne went weak. He'd never figured it would happen, but he was scared, scared to death to be standing up in front of all these folks. He knew 'em all— heck, he'd grown up with most of 'em— but suddenly they were a bunch of faces, and not very friendly faces, at that.

Pastor Zeke seemed to be about seven feet tall when he stripped off his powder blue suit coat and tie. He took a white handerkchief out of his pocket, kicked off his shoes, and stepped down in the baptismal tank, right down in the water up to his waist. His hair looked old-testament white, his eyes blue as swords. He gestured to little Alton to join him in the tank, and while the organ continued to play another chorus or two, Alton shook his head and hopped from one foot to another until Pastor Zeke managed to get him to take the first step, then one more.

"Glory Hallelujah!" Pastor Zeke boomed, and the congregation all shouted it back at him. Dwayne wished he had someplace to sit down where people wouldn't be staring at him. "Lord bless you, son, are you ready to accept the Lord Jesus Christ into your heart as your personal savior?"

Alton said something that not even Dwayne could hear, but it must have been the right answer, because Pastor Zeke crossed the boy's arms over his chest, put the handkerchief over his face and dunked him backward into the water, quick as you please, held him there for a second, then brought him up sputtering and blinking.

"Brothers and sisters, welcome Brother Alton into the body of Christ and this congregation!" Pastor Zeke said, and the folks in the auditorium sitting on velvet cushions on wooden pews all clapped and said "Praise Jesus!" Little Alton was allowed to escape wet and dripping off to the side, where Zeke's wife Sister Amalie was waiting with a towel.

No telling if Alton had peed in the water. No telling.

Missy Collier went right in like she was at the neighborhood swimming pool. Her robe ballooned up around her and made her look like the five-hundred-pound lady at the carnival, but she tugged it right down and said, "Yes Pastor," when he asked her about making Jesus her personal savior. And there she went, under the water, all that careful hair curling and makeup gone for nothing. She came up sputtering, too, mascara streaming down her cheeks, hair stringy over her face. Dwayne barely even noticed that he could see the outline of her lacy bra through the wet robe, because she was squishing off to the side where Amalie was waiting with a fresh towel, and now it was his turn. Everybody was watching him, and Pastor Zeke was waving his hand.

Zeke was working hard at it, all right. There was sweat dripping down his face, and his skin was blushing red at his collar and up over his face. *Working on a heart attack,* Dwayne thought. *Lord, maybe he'll have one before I have to do this.*

He'd been saved some sixteen times in the last twelve years, and every time he'd taken off the robe in the waiting room. Never gotten close enough to see the murky water in the baptismal tank, the dark shadows in the corners, Pastor Zeke's waiting open hands.

Dwayne froze on the first step down into the cold water. *I'll drown,* he thought. *I'll drown and float. I'll drown and float.*

No, no, this was holy. Nobody drowned at the baptism, that was plain stupid.

Everybody was staring. At the organ, Ginger Lee Olmstead was doing a key change into "Shall We Gather At The River," and Dwayne knew he had to either strip off his robe and run, or take those last two steps down into the water.

Pastor Zeke's smile looked like it was hurting him. "Come on, brother," he coaxed. He sounded like he was short of breath. Oh, Lord, Pastor Zeke was going to pop a vein if he didn't do it this time, he'd throw him right out of the church with his Momma and brother and Uncle Fisher all watching.

Dwayne took one step down into the water. The cold stroked his thighs.

"That's it," Pastor Zeke said. "One more."

He closed his eyes and took the step. The water gurgled up under his robe, closed over him like a clammy fist. He felt Pastor Zeke folding his arms over his chest and thought *I knew it, I'm going to die, I'm going to die right here, right now, and not even baptized.*

"Dwayne Elias Elliot, do you accept the Lord Jesus Christ into your heart as your personal savior?" Pastor Zeke shouted. His hands felt hot as fire on Dwayne's shoulders, ready to shove him down—

No! Dwayne thought. "Yes," he whispered. Something cold and wet settled over his mouth and nose. He sucked in a mouthful of cold cotton. The handkerchief.

Even though he was ready for it, the pull took him by surprise and he couldn't keep his balance; water swarmed over him, flooded up his nose and into his mouth. He opened his eyes and flailed against the hands that held him down. Roaring in his ears, shouting, screaming. He thrashed.

The hands let him go. He didn't go up. He went down, away from the light, the air. His thrashing sent the handkerchief floating away, and he banged off the side of the glass tank. Green mold in the corner. He needed to breathe, needed to, had to.

He closed his eyes and saw it again, that face, gray, bloated, the eyes gone, the skin ragged and chewed up, pale muscle poking out, a grin of white bone on the cheek—

His eyes flew open. There was a light up above him. A bright light. An orange light. If he could just get to that light he'd live, he'd live—

He found the bottom of the tank and pushed up.

More roaring in his ears. The congregation? Screaming like it was a hometown football game?

He burst up out of the water, choking, gagging, and for a second he couldn't see because of the water in his eyes. Reverend Zeke was bright, so bright—

Pastor Zeke was on fire. Lord have mercy, Dwayne thought in dumb amazement, tongues of fire, just like at the Pentecost. No wonder people were screaming, they were screaming in tongues—

The flames of the Holy Spirit weren't supposed to hurt, though. Weren't supposed to turn skin black and crispy. The pastor flailed desperately from side to side, slapping at his chest. His mouth was wide open and he was making a hiss like a snake, like a demon. His eyes were red and bloody.

Over the screams Dwayne heard the fat on the pastor's body sizzle and pop like bacon in a pan.

Dwayne finally grabbed Pastor Zeke by his Sansabelt slacks and dunked him backward into the water. Steam and bubbles stung his eyes, and a terrible smell, sulphur and hell and burning flesh and the swampy stink of drowned men and still water. He lunged out of the tank and laid full length on the red carpet, praying as fast as he could think of the words. Some of the deacons rushed over him, and he heard the wet thump of Pastor Zeke being laid down next to him.

He turned his head and saw Zeke gasp his last breath. The carpet was wet and sandpaper-rough against his cheek.

Dwayne had to wonder whether or not he'd really been baptized at all, or whether he'd have to go in there again.

Fifteen

Velvet

When Velvet rounded the corner, she saw Lenny Bradshaw huddled in the doorway of Fong's Deli, shifting miserably from one foot to the other while he blew on his white fingers. The cold had put little pink roses in his cheeks. He looked like an ad for L.L. Bean in his ski sweater and khaki coat and Docker pants. Hiking boots, too. Christ, he looked ready for the Vermont woods, not downtown Dallas.

"Forget your gloves?" she asked sweetly. He glanced at her, away, and then at her again as his eyes widened. She adjusted her brassy red wig— six bucks at the local Salvation Army store— and skated her dark wraparound shades down her nose to let him recognize her.

"My god, what happened to you?" he asked. She'd tried covering the bruises up with Robby's limited supply of makeup, but Cover Girl standard issue just wasn't cutting the mustard.

"Your mom punched me out."

"Very funny." He kept staring at her, fascinated. "Uh, the deli's not open yet. It's too early."

"No shit, Sherlock, they teach you that in reporter school? We're going down the block. Someplace quiet."

He didn't look especially happy about it, but he fell in next to her. His hiking boots made thick slapping sounds; they made Velvet's steps in Robby's too-large tennis shoes sound dainty. Don't dance with this guy, she reminded herself. And if you fuck him, make him take his shoes off.

A yellow DART bus chuffed by in a blast of warmth and diesel smoke; the driver had a glazed robotic gleam in his eyes. Overhead, the clouds clotted gray and ugly. The day had a metallic taste to it that clung to her tongue like fuzz. She swallowed and wished for breakfast. Coffee. Pastries that melted in her mouth. Sugar to jump-start the day.

Maybe a Baby Ruth.

"You said you had something?" Bradshaw prodded as he scuffled along. She turned the collar on her coat up to keep her ears warm against the wind.

"Yeah, well, don't worry, they have treatments for it." She glanced over at his choirboy face and saw him frowning as he tried to work it out. "Never mind. Yeah, I got something. Something hot. You'll love it."

"Well, *tell* me."

"Not so fast. Cash."

He tried to flash a roll but almost dropped it. She told him to keep it in his pants and took him around the corner. They went down a twisting flight of marble stairs in the shadow of a fifty-story high rise whose contractor must have had a brother-in-law in the marble business. At the bottom was a shopping mall, glass and aluminum with indoor-outdoor carpet with CLOSED signs in the windows, and some wrought-iron chairs and tables for fine outdoor dining. She parked herself in one of the chairs and gestured him to another one. He perched like a granny in a whorehouse.

"How'd you get the black eye?" Lenny asked. He sounded almost concerned.

"Do you want the stuff, or not?"

"I can't pay you more than three hundred. Orders." Lenny looked devastated. "My editor kicked my butt over the last time."

"My heart bleeds. Three hundred'll do it. This time."

She reached for the bills he passed over and slid them in under her blouse. Lenny took out his little Nancy Drew notebook and looked eager.

"Yeah, like I told you on the phone, my guy, Burt, he wasn't the first one."

"First one?" He was looking confused. "Well, I know you're a professional— "

"Asshole, I mean the first one to flame out, get it? There was some guy who was a fence or something, burned up in his apartment less than a year ago."

"Ah. Great. Name?"

She shrugged. Lenny bit his lip. He had small teeth that looked like he didn't use them much.

"You don't know his name?"

"Well, excuse the hell out of me, I didn't have time to do your job for you, newsboy. He died the same way as Burt, laying on the floor black as a Cajun steak. Another one of those darn 'smoking accidents.' "

Lenny looked a lot less than impressed. In fact, he tapped his pencil eraser on the table and stared at her, waiting. She scowled back.

"Like I said, the wiseguys did it," she finally said. He brightened.

"Wow! Really? The mob?"

"The *mob,*" she echoed mockingly. "You sound like a bad fifties movie. People are freaked on the street, Lenny, really. This friend of mine, she wouldn't even

tell me much about it, except she saw this guy bubbling on the linoleum. It's the wiseguys, all right.
People are scared shitless."

"Damn," Lenny breathed. He scribbled furiously,
tongue working in his cheek. "I'll get right over to
the *News* and see what they've got in the files. Maybe
make a couple of calls to some police friends. Great.
This is great. Mafia torches rivals. Great."

"Yeah, great." Velvet had already lost interest. The
three hundred was warming up in her shirt, getting
hot enough to spend. She needed some decent
makeup, a good thick breakfast steak, a really fine
piece of French Silk Chocolate Pie. Then she'd decide what to do next.

"Uh, I'll need your friend's name. For the records,
you know."

"Yeah," Velvet nodded absently. "Robby MacReady.
Hey, what is today?"

"Today?" Lenny sounded more mystified than
usual. He tapped his pencil on his lips. "Friday."

Friday. Something about Friday. Something—

"Friday," she said out loud, sitting up straight.
Lenny stopped writing and looked up at her warily,
like it was "Jeopardy" and he didn't know the question. "Jesus, isn't Burt Marshall's funeral today?"

"Yeah, that's right. Two o'clock." He continued to
look mystified as she dug in the pockets of her coat,
came up with three colored condoms, a stick of
Cinnaburst gum, two pennies, and a nickel.

"Quarter," she demanded. He dug in his pants
and found one. "Great. I'll owe you."

She left him still asking questions, and hobbled up
the steps as fast as her aching ribs would let her
move. Damn, they'd seemed a lot shorter going
down. Once she'd made it to the top, she stopped
and pressed a hand against her side before starting

across the big marble wasteland in front of the building. Some idiot had left the fountains turned on, and a spray of ice-cold water lashed across her bruised face. The pain would have made her sick if she'd had any food to be sick with and, always perverse, her stomach rumbled.

The rotunda in front of the building was thick expensive-looking glass. It looked kind of like a greenhouse, growing more marble. She pushed through two sets of revolving doors and entered a lobby with— surprise— more marble, and a big engraved metal sign that said SECURITY and pointed a discreet but urgent arrow left.

She went right.

She got about fifty feet before a guy in a blue polyester blazer and tan pants fell in beside her, looking pleasant except around the eyes. He had a cheap-looking gold badge pinned on his jacket. There was a bulge under his jacket that she hoped was a paperback book, but he didn't look like much of a reader.

"Help you, miss?" he asked. She shot him a quick cold look like she'd seen Ming do.

"Phone," she demanded. "Quickly, please."

"Are you visiting a tenant?" he asked. It didn't sound quite so pleasant. Damn.

"No, I'm just looking for a telephone, dear." She tried a smile. "Please."

He put out an arm to stop her. Just as well, she was heading for another dead-end marble wall; the place was decorated in Early Crypt.

"Ma'am, I'm sorry, there are no public telephones here. If you don't mind— "

At the end of the wall was a discreet little alcove that didn't have a saint's statue in it, or a vase full of dead flowers; the gold letters above it said TELE-

PHONE. Velvet smiled with all her teeth at the security guy, who didn't smile back.

"Oh, thank you so much for your kindness, I see it right there. Thanks. Won't be a minute." She darted around him and crossed to the alcove. When she looked back he was waiting, staring, ready to mow her down if she tried to pry a piece of marble off the wall or something. She stepped into the alcove and above her a spotlight came on, lighting up the phone. She fed it a quarter and dialed.

"Hello?" Robby sounded dead asleep. Velvet checked her watch. God, it was—almost seven o'clock. Didn't the woman ever get up?

"Hey, Robby, glad I caught you. Remember how you said to ask if I needed anything?"

Wet smacking sounds on the other end of the phone. Robby was tasting her morning breath, probably squinting at the clock and trying to figure out what century it was.

"Yeah," she said fuzzily. "Who is this?"

"Velvet. Listen. Want to go to a funeral?"

The church was as hot as hell's oven, and Velvet was sweating all over her borrowed clothes. She'd found Robby's only bright-colored blouse— mustard gold— and the most colorful of her skirts— rust— but the shoes were a disaster. They looked like penny loafers. Velvet stared down at them in resentment while the prayer droned on above her head.

"— And we thank you, O Lord, for your blessings and kindness in this, our hour of loss— "

God hadn't gone out of his way for Burt, that was for damn sure. She shot a sideways look at Robby, who had her head bowed, too. Robby looked dazed

with boredom. Well, how should she have looked?
She hadn't been there. She hadn't seen him.

"— commend the soul of our brother Burt into
your loving hands— "

"Are they always this long-winded?" Robby whispered. There was a stress fracture of Irish in her
voice.

"Nope. He's just clearing his throat. Wait'll he gets
to the actual praying." Velvet grinned, winced when
it dragged at a bruise. "You never been in a church
before?"

"Not a *Protestant* church."

It was a Catholic thing. Velvet rolled her eyes and
waited out the prayer, raised her head and twisted it
right and left to ease the muscle cramp. She tried
not to look at the centerpiece— shiny wood and gold
handles— and wound up looking at the carpet again.
Old nappy dark red carpet. Appropriate for churches
and movie theaters. She scuffed a penny loafer over
it and shifted from one cheek to the other on the
thin red-velvet pew cushion.

Burt had a lot of friends. The rows ahead of her
were full of suits and church ladies, buzz cuts and
big hair. In the second pew sat a fat woman wearing
black. Three young kids— the oldest a pimply teenaged boy, the youngest a restlessly squirmy girl— sat
close beside her. The only other person on the family
pew was a guy, small, neat-looking, weak-chinned. He
kept wiping his eyes, although the widow hadn't shed
a tear.

The organ crashed into a hurdy-gurdy version of
"Just A Closer Walk With Thee," and two guys who
had the professionally sympathetic look of undertak-
ers got up and collected the red, white, and blue
flowers from the casket and hinged open the top.

Velvet sat bolt upright, staring, though she couldn't

see anything but white satin. Jesus, they *couldn't* have
an open casket, they *couldn't*. All of a sudden she
couldn't breathe, because she knew she'd smell him.
The thought gagged her, but she couldn't get up to
head for the bathroom, she might accidentally see
into the—

The first two rows of people stood up. The fat
woman waddled past the casket; as far as Velvet could
tell, she didn't even look down. The gawky-looking
teenaged boy behind her didn't, either; he stared
right into his mother's back. The next girl in line
did look. She burst into tears, and the kid behind
her let out a big hiccuping sob and the two of them
ran off out of the sanctuary.

Velvet swallowed hard. The man who'd sat on the
end of the family pew stopped at the casket and
stared for what seemed like a long time. He sniffled
and blew his nose loudly. When he turned to walk
away, his eyes met Velvet's.

He stopped. His mouth dropped open.

She'd never seen him before in her life. She was
sure of that. So what? Did she look that much like a
hooker? Was everybody looking at her, pointing fingers, whispering?

Nope. Just him. He stared at her.

Velvet looked over at Robby and pointed to the guy,
making a question out of her eyebrows. Robby looked
and shrugged.

The guy was gone when Velvet glanced back.

The row in front of them stood up. Under cover
of their backs, Velvet grabbed up her coat and ducked
out, up the blood red aisle, heading for the door.
She heard Robby scramble to follow.

"Didn't you want to pay your respects?" Robby demanded in the vestibule as they shrugged on their

coats. Velvet shot her a dirty look. "Then why did you drag me down here?"

Velvet's hands paused in buttoning her coat. She frowned down at her penny loafers.

"Hell if I know," she said. "Seemed like a good idea at the time. I just didn't want to— you know— look at him again."

The side door to the vestibule opened. Burt's two daughters came out of the bathroom, still snuffling. They pushed past without an apology.

"I'm sorry about your dad," Velvet called after them. The younger looked back, surprised.

"Did you know him?" she asked; she sounded sad and miserable and lonely. Velvet stared at her, frozen. *Never should have said anything,* she kicked herself. *Stupid bitch.*

"She worked with him," Robby supplied, and grabbed Velvet's coat sleeve. "Come on, before you get yourself in bigger trouble."

The girl waved an awkward goodbye as the door wheezed shut behind them. Velvet shivered in the blast of cold wind.

"You didn't have to say that," she snapped. Robby sighed, her breath a white flag.

"I didn't have to come here at all, you know."

"Well, why did you?" Velvet demanded. Robby gave her a long level stare.

"Because you asked me to."

Robby's borrowed car matched her perfectly. Gray. Conservative. Not too new, not too old. Velvet slammed the door irritably and stared out the window at the church, where people were starting to straggle out. One of them was the guy who'd stared at her. He seemed to be looking for someone.

Robby hit the accelerator and Velvet closed her

eyes, resting her head against the cold glass of the window.

She still smelled burnt flesh. It had all been a waste of time, after all. Burt's ghost wasn't going to be put in the ground by anything so simple as a funeral.

"I have to work," Robby said. "I'm going by Jim's. Where do you want me to drop you?"

So that's how it was going to be. Dropped off at a corner, just like a street whore. Dumped with the clothes on her back and— luckily— the three hundred stuffed in her shirt. Well, that was no big deal. She'd call Ming. That was it, she'd call Ming, get set up with a couple of gigs—

The bruises. She'd have to explain the bruises.

"How come that guy knew me at the funeral?" she asked. "I'm sure I never saw him before."

"Maybe a former customer?" Robby asked; she couldn't quite keep the prissy tone out of his voice. "Somebody not very memorable?"

"Look, I don't remember everybody, but if he remembered me that good, I'd remember him. He looked like I was a ghost or something." Ghosts. Burt. Amy. Her mother's distant sobs on the telephone. Velvet pressed her aching forehead to cold glass. "Robby?"

"Yeah?"

"You ever killed anybody?"

The car slewed gently right, then sharply left. She knew without looking that Robby had taken the opportunity for a good long look at her.

"No," Robby answered cautiously. "No, I never have. Why?"

"I did." Velvet opened her eyes. The car window was cloudy with her breath. "You know what? That guy looked guilty. Guilty as hell."

Amy had looked so small in the coffin, skin pallid,

face bloated. They'd tried to talk Mom out of an open casket, but she'd been so sure it was all right, so sure Amy would look just like a sleeping angel. It had all been so hard, so hard to sit there with the family and know everybody was staring, whispering, pointing. *She's the one, you know. She was there when it happened. She should have done something. All her fault.*

Velvet gagged on the taste of Scotch and sperm in her mouth.

"Are you all right?" Robby asked. Velvet opened her eyes and swallowed hard.

"Sure," she lied. "Hey, I got an idea. Know where Elegance Dry Cleaners is?"

"Which one?"

"Uh, the main one. The one in Highland Park." That was a guess, but a good one. It was sure the priciest store in town, had the most blue-nosed customers. She'd probably find somebody to talk to there, somebody trustworthy. "Drop me there, okay?"

Whatever Robby thought about it, she said nothing, simply played taxi driver, turning down Mockingbird and onto Preston, winding into old money neighborhoods where every house had room for four cars and a Suburban for the maid. She slowed and parked in front of a discreet narrow storefront; gold script glittered in the windows, spelling out ELEGANCE DRY CLEANERS— LEATHERS AND SILKS A SPECIALTY. The sign on the frosted glass door read OPEN in small unencouraging script.

Velvet opened her door a couple of inches and looked over at Robby.

"Thanks," she said. Robby nodded. Her eyes looked preoccupied, like she'd already put all this behind her. *Well, fuck you,* Velvet thought. Even in her mind, it sounded sad instead of angry.

She got out and watched Robby drive away.

Velvet hugged her elbows and shivered as she turned to face the glass door. *I could find a bus stop,* she thought. Wouldn't be that long a wait.

No. She had to do this. Had to. She'd seen Burt's kids, after all. She kind of owed him something.

She pushed open the door. A silver bell tinkled somewhere in the back, past a marble counter and plush green carpet.

A young highly toned woman with mercilessly stylish hair looked up, and the smile froze on her face. "Can I—" Blue eyes swept up and down doubtfully. "— help you?"

"Uh, yeah. Was this— did Burt Marshall used to own this place?" Velvet shifted uncomfortably. Robby's penny loafers seemed Payless Shoe Store tacky, the clothes one step above homeless shelter giveaways.

"Marshall?" The woman gave her a brief contemptuous smile. *Her* outfit cost more than Velvet would have earned for a good round-the-world with a drunken stockbroker. "I'm sorry, miss, are you a customer?"

"No." Velvet shoved her hands in her coat pockets. *Not likely to be, either.* "No, I guess not. I was just looking for somebody who knew Burt Marshall. I got something for his family."

"I'm afraid—"

"What is it, Stacie?" a man asked. He swept in from the back, burdened with two handfuls of plastic-shrouded suits that he hung on gold hooks on the wall. "These are the special orders for Mr. Novacek. He'll be in at four-thirty."

He turned— a small man, thin, weak-chinned. Wide dark eyes that locked with Velvet's and got wider.

It was the guy from the funeral.

"Oh, Mr. Julian, this lady wants to talk to you

about Mr. Marshall." Stacie's tone was as dry as the Sahara, but it got odd at the end. She'd noticed, too.

Noticed Mr. Julian's shock.

"Uh, look, I don't want trouble or anything," Velvet blurted out. All of a sudden the idea of giving him two hundred bucks for Burt's family seemed pathetic, and even dangerous. There was something weasel-bright in Julian's eyes, a panic that looked rabid. "Never mind, okay? Just never mind. It was a mistake."

She backed up and stumbled on a Persian throw rug, caught herself with one sweaty palm on expensive wood paneling. Mr. Julian swung up the divider in the marble counter. God, she didn't like this, it looked wrong, all wrong.

When she reached for the door it swung open, blasting her with winter. An Arab guy stood in her way, big, staring over her shoulder at Mr. Julian. He had a face as sharp as a switchblade, and no expression at all. She'd seen enough enforcers to recognize the eyes of a killer when she saw them. The damn Persian carpet tripped her up again as she stepped back.

The model— what's her name, Stacie— behind the counter, said chirpily, "Sir, how may I help you?"

Mr. Julian said, from somewhere behind Velvet's left shoulder, "That'll be all, Stacie. Why don't you go in the back?"

I'm going to die, Velvet thought. *In a fucking dry cleaners. Oh my god, but I just made it up, I didn't know, I didn't—*

The Arab took a step inside. The door started to swing shut.

They're gonna lock the door. Turn the sign to CLOSED. I'm gonna—

Before she could finish thinking of *die*, she opened

her mouth and screamed at the top of her lungs, a
glass-shattering siren that made the Arab jerk backward. Across the street, two pink-cheeked junior
leaguers in fur turned to look with naked astonishment. Still screaming, Velvet dashed for the door.

Either he'd grab her, or he wouldn't.

His hand came up and brushed her shoulder. She
lunged past him for the cold thin air of the sidewalk.

She remembered to stop screaming once the door
had shut behind her, and turned to look at the two
men standing on the other side of the glass. Mr. Julian looked scared shitless.

The Arab was smiling a little. He tilted his head
to one side and watched her.

On the other side of the street, the junior leaguers
huddled together like pack animals and muttered.
They strode briskly off toward a corner drugstore
where, presumably, a mobile phone could be had.
God forbid they should call 911 from a pay phone.
Ooky.

"Sorry," Velvet mumbled, and started walking. At
the corner, a DART bus eased to a stop for the line
of minority housekeepers and butlers and nannies.
She lunged on before it could escape without her.
As she fed coins into the box, she looked back.

The street in front of the dry cleaners was empty.
Nobody was coming after her.

That was scarier.

Sixteen
Robby

Robby waited in the freezing shadows, rocking back and forth to keep blood moving to her feet. There wasn't any wind in the warehouse, but the temperature kept dropping and the humidity rising. Her bones felt as brittle and cold as ice.

If he doesn't come in five minutes, I'll leave, she told herself, and slapped her arms with gloved fingers. The ache burrowed deeper. *Three minutes. Three minutes more is enough.*

After only about thirty seconds, she stepped back up to the door and banged again, loudly, though he couldn't have failed to hear her the first four times. The echo rolled thickly through the dark warehouse. Things shifted and rattled in its wake . . . rats, maybe. She knocked again, harder.

Dumb. This is dumb, she told herself. *He's angry about Velvet. He's gone off with someone else. He's—*

Jim wouldn't let any personal disagreements affect professional relationships. They worked well together. It was profitable for everybody. Then where was he?

The street door opened with a rusty squeal, sending her heart thumping frantically. Robby stepped back into the shadows, glad she'd worn black to Velvet's idiotic funeral, and watched the man come closer.

"Jim?" she said softly. He spun awkwardly, almost losing the sacks he was holding. "Sorry. It's me."

"Kid, don't scare me like that." His voice was rough silk, a little sharp with alarm, but already welcoming. She came closer, and he handed her one of the sacks— heavy, filled with cans and bottles. "Sorry I'm late. The market was crazy."

He unlocked the door and stood aside to let her in first, a bit of unconscious courtesy or chauvinism all out of proportion to who they were, what they did.

"Hot cocoa?" He pulled a box out of the sack. She smiled and nodded. "You're here early. What, being roomies with the hooker wasn't quite the picnic you thought it might be?"

"She's just fine." Robby's ambivalence about Velvet melted instantly under the heat of Jim's disapproval. "It was nice to have a guest. I enjoyed it."

"Oh, really." He put blue cups of water in the microwave. "No accounting for taste. What'd you do with her, give her the keys and tell her not to steal anything over a thousand?"

"Just because you and I are thieves doesn't mean everyone is," she countered. The skin around his eyes crinkled as he smiled.

"She'd screw a priest for bus fare and you know it. Have a cookie."

Store-bought and not quite up to homemade standards, no matter what the advertising said. She licked crumbs from her lips.

"Heard from Mark?" She took another cookie from the box. "We need some more home cooking around here."

"He's taking his physics and literature finals this week. You know how he gets at the end of the semester. He swears he'll never steal again as long as he gets A's on the tests, then next thing you know he's pulling twenties out of somebody's backpack in lab class. The kid's incorrigible." Jim's smile faded like an old photograph. "He could have been good, you know. Really good."

"He doesn't have it," Robby said. "The touch. The patience. You know that."

The microwave binged for attention. Jim turned away and mixed cocoa, then handed her a cup breathing thick milky steam. She stripped off her gloves and wrapped her cold fingers around it gratefully.

"I know," he said. "You're the only one I know who *does* have it. The rest of them, they're good and lucky, but they'll get popped. Not you. Never you."

"You're jinxing me."

"Maybe." He leaned against a counter and watched her, smiling. He had on his professorial look today: a turtleneck sweater, a tweedy jacket with patches on the elbows, conservative slacks. All he needed was a thick book of literature, and the coeds would swarm. "Maybe the hooker's all the jinx you need."

"I'm sorry—"

"Don't." His smile disappeared. "Don't apologize if you don't mean it, and I don't think you do. You like her, and that's fine. So don't apologize for liking her. I won't apologize for thinking she's a worm."

"It wasn't about her, not really. You know that. I just couldn't take the idea of waiting while he beat her."

A cocoa-warm silence filled the cool fluorescent kitchen. Jim reached over and traced the line of her cheek with one finger.

"I know," he said. His finger found the bump at her jaw where the break hadn't healed cleanly. "Funny, even when you talk about him, you sound like you love him."

"He was my father," she said, as if that explained something. She leaned her cheek against his hand, closing her eyes. "Which mall today?"

"Oh, I don't know. We're going after the blue-collars at the hockey game tomorrow, want to go after the ladies who lunch? I like playing Robin Hood. Rob from the rich, give to us."

She felt her lips lift in a grin. His warm thumb traced them; she opened her mouth and nipped it lightly.

"Not fair," he said, and she opened her eyes to his smile. Warm, so warm.

With a surge of wickedness she had never known she had, she licked his thumb and took it in her mouth, sliding down to the base. His eyes widened. She flicked his thumb lightly with her tongue, let it slide out again, and said, "Is that better?"

"You've been hanging around the hooker way too much." She liked the unsteadiness in his voice. "Robby—"

She set her cup aside and came into his arms. His lips and tongue tasted of chocolate. He smelled of clean male skin with just a touch of sweat, and in the intimate body-to-body pressure she felt his erection nudge at her. His hands slid down under her coat and brushed over her sides, her breasts, her hips. Her breath sighed out into the hollow of his neck.

In one of those strange fits of chauvinism, he picked her up and carried her to the bedroom.

The afterglow left her lazy and jittery, more than an hour later. She had to concentrate to dip the wallet cleanly, concentrate harder to pass it to Jim's waiting hand as he passed. The deft brush of their fingers made her smile. She turned off into a store and examined a rack of women's suits— conservative, well-made, in solid businesslike colors. At the end of the rack a mustard-yellow jacket hung in forlorn exile. Robby's fingers brushed it lightly, gliding over the wool. She draped the sleeve over her skin and made a face.

No matter how bold she became with Jim, there were some things she just couldn't do. Bright tight clothes. Impractical shoes. The leather outfit still hung in the corner of her closet, as dejected as this mustard jacket. Perhaps she'd give it to Velvet. Someone ought to get some use out of it.

Perhaps— oh, naughty thought— she ought to wear it for Jim. Would he like it? She imagined herself in it, and felt embarrassment creep warm over her face. Robby the slut. No, it would never happen.

She chose a gray suit, held it up for the admiration of a mirror.

Velvet had seemed so surprised by the bright colors in her house. Was she that boring, truly? This morning the blues had seemed too bright, the reds too bloody, the whole house one long scream.

She put the gray suit back and went out into the mall, watching for Jim's loose-limbed, stoop-shouldered walk. There, coming toward her. She moved her head a little to the right, and he crossed on that side, their empty hands slapping together in a fleeting touch. He didn't seem to even notice her, but the afterimage of heat tingled in her fingers like money.

She went two shops down, paused to look blankly in the window, and turned to swim upstream through the crowd. Two scowling teenagers wearing belly bags; if they had any cash, it was pizza and beer money. A preoccupied mother dragged a squalling four-year-old toward her— a gaping purse, but the woman had enough trouble for one day. Behind her, a pinched-faced older woman in a designer dress and Gucci purse. Robby passed, fingers effortlessly drawn to the anorexically thin leather wallet.

The tingle was more like an electric jolt. She palmed the wallet into a sleeve pocket and walked steadily toward Jim.

Behind her, some kind of disturbance broke out. She didn't look back, just kept calmly walking and watching Jim's face. His eyes were riveted on what was unfolding behind her; if he changed direction, she'd run.

Something slammed into her back, sending her sprawling. She felt a sharp tug at her shoulder as she fell. Her knee banged painfully into cold concrete, her hand slammed down in an effort to save her head from the same impact.

The leather wallet slipped out of her sleeve and skidded two or three feet away.

The mugger who'd hit her ran on, head down, holding her purse like a football. He dodged around Jim— who tried to shove him off balance— and disappeared around a corner.

The wallet coasted to a stop next to a shiny pair of black shoes. The man who bent down to pick it up wore an ill-fitting black jacket with a silver badge pinned to the label.

Mall security.

Maybe he wouldn't look— maybe—

He unsnapped the wallet and looked at the pinched-faced picture, at Robby, back at the picture. His expression went blank, his blue eyes narrow. He leaned down and hooked an arm under her arm and hauled her up. She felt a twinge in her ankle and played it for an ace, going limp against him, screaming in pain. A crowd congealed around them, a forest of craning necks. She couldn't see Jim anywhere.

"Ma'am," the guard said. His fingers dug into the meat of her arm like pliers. "Ma'am, you'll have to come with me."

"Me?" She poured all the Irish she could find into the word. "Me! When your own thug knocked me down and took me purse? They all told me, they said America was worse than Dublin, but I didn't listen, no, I said it was a fine place, and look at you, draggin' me off like a common thief. I've been *hurt!*"

"Yes ma'am, I can see that. I'm taking you to get medical treatment." The guard was playing to the crowd, but she saw the cold glitter in his eyes. No use trying to slither free; his jacket bulged over his pumped biceps, and he'd lost his neck in muscle.

He pinched a nerve. She glared.

Over his shoulder she saw Jim standing on the other side of the mall, close to an exit, the smart bastard. At least she wasn't holding, thank god. She could talk her way out of it. Enough blarney and bluff. Musclehead would let her go before the police arrived.

Jim put his hands in his pockets and started walking.

Toward her.

No, she thought, frozen. *No, no, you stupid man, no!*

"Excuse me, young man, but that doesn't seem to be any way to treat her," piped up an older lady burdened under two huge shopping bags. She had kind eyes and a pug-dog face and an absurdly large diamond necklace that flashed fire as the woman leaned forward to pat Robby's cheek. "Poor dear thing, knocked down like that. I'd be *petrified.*"

"It was very sudden," Robby agreed pitifully. A few faces in the crowd— a thin artistic-looking man, another grandmother, a perfect-faced model— nodded in sympathy and glared at the guard. "I just want to sit down. Dear me, I've gone all shivers."

She wished she could burst into tears, but that level of acting wasn't in her. The best she could do was bat her eyes suggestively and gulp for breath. The guard looked disgusted; it was a pitiful display.

Jim shoved aside two sullen teenagers with hair in their eyes and reached over toward her. She looked up and met his eyes.

She could confuse the issue further, play him as an abusive husband, scream for protection— no, Jim was holding the wallets, he was vulnerable. She had to play his game.

She just wished she knew what it was.

"Sondra," he said, and grabbed her in a bearhug. "Jesus, Sondra, what happened? What's wrong?"

"Somebody knocked her down and took her purse," the diamond lady contributed helpfully. Jim's face folded into a map of distress.

"No! My god, are you okay? You look pale." Jim frowned at the guard, who'd loosened his grip but hadn't released it entirely. "What are you doing to catch this guy?"

"We have another problem," the guard said. "You know this woman?"

"Know her? She's my sister."

"From Ireland," Robby contributed helpfully.

"Just flew in today. God damn it, I knew something like this would happen. They can spot a tourist a mile off. Did you keep your hand on your purse like I told you?" Jim gave her another hug.

"No, I forgot, it's me own fault. I should have listened to you, dear man." She sighed and examined her shoes, the floor, the shiny black wingtips of the security guard. "All me own fault."

"She still has to explain the wallet," the guard said.

Out of the corner of her eye, she saw him display it. Jim stiffened.

"Sondra, damn it, you didn't— ah, hell, officer, I'm sorry. My sister is— you know— kleptomaniac. She's under a doctor's treatment. I guess all the stress, the strange surroundings, they must have got the better of her. Still, no harm done, right? You've got the wallet back. Sondra, you don't have anything else, do you?"

"No, not a blessed thing," she said, and thank god it was true. She looked up to meet the guard's eyes. "I suppose you'll be wanting to search me, then."

The diamond lady gasped in horror.

The guard's eyes went from blue to storm gray, and steroid-thick muscles jumped under his face. *He knows*, she thought. *But how far will he go?*

Jim put his hand on the guard's arm, drawing a glare; for all his thin build, Jim had the look of a dirty fighter, the eyes of a sniper. He smiled.

"Buddy," he said. "You don't want to do that."

The guard let her go. Jim's arm went around her shoulders and guided her limping away; the diamond lady patted her reassuringly on the hand as she passed. When Robby glanced back, the guard was following at a slow relentless pace.

The exit was about two hundred feet.

"How's the ankle?" Jim asked. She kept limping.

"Fine."

"Think you can run, if you have to?"

"Do I have any choice?"

His arm tightened, a friendly squeeze that was half warning.

"I've got to dump the wallets fast. You make a run for it, get outside, get under a car and hide. He'll be following you, not me."

"Rendezvous?"

"Home. Ready?"

She sucked in a deep breath and jabbed her elbow into his ribs. He crumpled back with a whoof of surprise. She leaped ahead, heard the slap of leather as the security guard chased her. Jim shouted something inarticulate, and she glanced back to see him urging on the guard while he faded back around the corner. He'd be okay.

Now all she had to do was run.

Truthfully, her ankle felt like burning sticks and baling wire, popping when she put her weight on it. The pain made her off-balance, and she stiff-armed the doors awkwardly; the massive pane of glass swung out and hummed like a bell when it hit a doorstop. She sprinted out into a wall of freezing wind.

The guard was close enough that she heard him grunt with effort. Her ankle popped again, a hot thick sound in the night air. Overhead, the moon glared, bloody with the edge of sunset.

A ghostly sea of cars and thick shadows. People walking to or from them stared as she ran, darting between rows of Cadillacs and BMWs and Infinitis; a few ticked like bombs as their engines cooled. She ducked behind a smoke-tinted gray Volvo and carefully peeked around for the guard.

He stood in the middle of the row, scanning cars. He had one hand in his jacket. Jesus, was he armed? He could have shot her. She felt a wave of weakness and ducked as his gaze swept her direction.

A police car, lights flashing cheery red and blue, turned in from the highway and cruised toward her. Robby swallowed hard and flattened out on the gritty asphalt, slid under the Volvo. The engine was still welcomely warm. She lay on her back in a sticky smear of oil, and breathed shallow gasps that tasted of exhaust.

The patrol car cruised by, tires crunching. She

folded her arms over her chest and waited, staring blankly at the blackened metal hovering a few inches above her nose.

Jim would have disposed of the wallets by now, changed clothes, exited at the other side of the mall. He'd be catching a bus.

Robby blew out her breath and grimaced as a drop of warm sticky oil fell on her forehead and oozed into her hair.

She remembered, for no particular reason, the lost look on Velvet's face as she'd left her there on the corner.

Seventeen
Sol

The hooker did a lot of bargain shopping. Sol Lipsky glared at the picture hanging crookedly on the wall by her front door— big-eyed fluffy cats in a flaking gold frame— and rummaged through the mail lying on the battered table. Sales circulars. Electric bill. An offer to apply for a secured credit card. A letter from somebody who used cheap white envelopes and blue ballpoints— Mom, he decided. Handwriting too good for anybody younger.

He ripped it open and read the first couple of paragraphs. Bullshit, bullshit, pig shit, farmer shit. It made a satisfying crisp crunch when he crumpled it and tossed it on the floor with the rest of the mess. She hadn't sent any money home, or Mom would have mentioned it in between the hog reports. That meant it was still here, someplace; he'd never met a hooker yet who'd believed in banks. She'd want it here, where she could touch it.

Little whore. He'd give her something to touch. If he had to kick her around to make his point, fine. He would, one way or another, get his money back, and make sure none of his people got any ideas about holding back again.

He'd already emptied Velvet's cheap dresser; the

cheap underwear lay in a red and black tangle on the ratty carpet, and now he yanked the drawers out and checked the backs, the sides, the bottoms. Nothing. Nothing inside the dresser frame, either. He kicked it apart, just to be sure.

"Honey?" That was Kelly, sitting on the bed where he'd told her to wait. He glanced over. She looked scared. That was good. He was doing half of this shit for her benefit. "Honey, let's go. This is stupid. She wouldn't keep anything here."

"It's here," he said flatly. "Whores don't keep Swiss bank accounts. You, sit there and shut up. Read a book or something. Let me do my job."

She looked down at her clenched hands, red lips trembling. He thought for a second about fucking her in the whore's bed, but he really didn't have the time and, anyway, Kelly was getting stale. Enthusiastic, but not too bright. Robby, now . . . Robby would fuck nice. He stared at Kelly's too-round breasts for a couple more seconds, thinking about Robby, and felt pressure build in his groin.

Shit. He reached over and ripped more pictures off the wall, big-eyed cats and big-eyed kids, something a teenager would hang in a locker. Nothing behind the prints but mildew-laced cardboard.

He yanked open the closet door and started pulling clothes. She liked Spandex and cheap plastic, everything tight. He held up a pair of thigh-high black patent fetish boots. Kelly brightened.

"What size?" she asked. He shrugged and tossed them to her, went back to ripping pockets and adding to the growing pile on the carpet. Behind him, he heard her grunt as she tried to squeeze fat legs into thin boots. That would keep her busy for a while.

"Ow!"

Sol picked a stiff black velvet jacket off a hanger

and probed the pockets. Second-hand from a dead old lady, it still smelled of mothballs and gardenias.

"Sol!"

"What?" he snarled, and glanced back to see her staring at something in her hand. A wad of green. Had to be at least a thousand.

"It was in the boot," she explained as he grabbed it off her palm. He snapped the rubber band and fanned the bills— old, limp, used. They smelled like mold and sweaty feet. "Is that all of it?"

"Shit, who cares? It's enough." He sat down on the bed next to her. Dead presidents stared up from his sweating fingers. "Good enough. Good enough."

"Sol?" She sounded tentative, scared. He looked over at her and flashed her a grin.

"Let's celebrate." He stared at her breasts and stroked a handful of money along her throat, down the shadow of her cleavage. "Right here. How about that?"

"Here?" She sounded doubtful.

"On the bed," he said, and met her eyes. "On the money. You'd like that, wouldn't you?"

Her lips parted, and her tongue crept out to trace her lips. He reached down and ran his fingers up the inside of her leg under her dress.

"On top of the money?" she repeated. He touched silky panties and wriggled his fingers around the elastic, stroking, sliding slowly in. She bit her lip. He added another finger.

"In the whore's bed," he said, and eased his fingers out, then in. Warm and wet and slick. He watched her face change, her body shudder. "Like a whore."

When she was whimpering and pushing hard against him, he stood up and unzipped his pants. He folded them neatly over a chair, draped his underwear on top, and when he turned around Kelly was naked on all fours, buttocks facing him like fat pink bubbles. Money sprayed green around her, crackled under his knees as he positioned himself behind her.

Robby. He thought of Robby, spreading herself for him. The surge of lust was almost painful. He guided himself into Kelly's hot slick hole and pumped hard, hearing money shift and crumple as she crouched back to meet him. She was saying something, but all he thought about was Robby.

It only took about a minute, beginning to end. He pulled out at the end. White drops spattered over the money, and Kelly moaned in frustrated disappointment and collapsed face down on the sheets. Sol sat back on his heels, sucking in deep breaths that tasted of sex and cheap perfume and baby powder.

"Get the money," he told her, and picked up his underwear. He checked the creases in his pants and frowned. "What'd you do with my gray suit, anyway? This piece of shit wrinkles like crazy."

"It's at the cleaners," she whispered. It sounded like she was crying, which pissed him off. He brushed lint from olive wool.

"Well, is it ready?"

"Yeah, I guess so. Sol—"

"Get your ass up," he interrupted. "We'll get some lunch."

He went in the bathroom to clean up. It smelled like the whore, more baby powder, more cheap perfume. As he pissed a big yellow puddle on the floor by the toilet, he said, "Something to remember me by."

Kelly had the money in her purse and was waiting, eyes down, as he came out. Afraid again.

He slapped her, lightly, to let her know he wasn't angry. In a final fit of humor, he locked the door back the way it had been when they'd come in.

"Surprise," he murmured, and patted the wood. "Don't fuck with me, sweetheart. Never again."

"No, Sol," Kelly murmured. His eyes cut to her face, the pouting lips, the trembling chin.

"Not you," he said, and smiled. "Sweetheart."

As they started down the stairs, a man turned the corner and started up, a weak-chinned, rabbity guy way too well dressed for this part of town. Sol took it slow and the guy kept his head down, his face turned away.

A john, definitely. She got the rich ones; Sol eyed the camel coat, the old-money suit. The guy looked scared to death.

Sol passed him whistling. At the last minute, he grabbed the guy's arm and swung him around; from the look on his face, the guy was about to piss his pants.

"Hey," Sol said in his friendliest tone. The guy looked too stunned to listen, so he slapped him. "Hey. Buddy. Tell Velvet that Sol Lipsky sends his regards."

When he let him go, the guy stumbled on up the stairs, chin down, shoulders hunched. Sol laughed and patted Kelly's hand as they strolled away.

He could hardly wait for the whore to come home.

Eighteen
Martin

He'd known by the sixth overhead that it wasn't going to work, and from that moment on it had been a hell of long, long silences, fumbling explanations, bored faces. Not only had he not convinced them, he'd unconvinced himself. Martin sat in the empty room with the lights blazing, picking up one overhead, dropping it, picking up another. They were spread out like playing cards. A losing hand.

Nobody had even bothered to take his handouts. They littered the table like the sad aftermath of a parade. He scraped four or five together, but they slipped out of his hands and spilled over the edge to the floor.

He put his head in his hands and rocked back and forth, back and forth. His chair squeaked in faint protest. Had he been right? Had he ever been right?

Watch me, Daddy. Watch me.

He sat straight up with a sharp gasp and saw Adrian Carling standing in the doorway. She walked in and picked up one of his handouts, flipped pages.

"How did it go?"

A laugh choked him.

"What did you tell them?" he asked. His voice sounded ragged, like his fingernails. "About me?"

She studied the handout as if she'd never seen it before. After a moment she looked up absently.

"I told them about Suzanne. About Sally." She raised a finger to her temple and made a small telling circle. "They drew their own conclusions about your competency."

The shocking thing was that he wasn't even surprised, not really. He couldn't remember what she'd felt like, last night; couldn't remember anything about it except a haunting feeling of loss. She'd arranged that. Not even tornadoes happened by accident around her.

"Aren't you going to call me a bitch?" she asked. He shook his head. "Why not? I am, you know."

He bent and scooped up his overheads from the floor and began painstakingly ordering them. He was missing number six, the point at which everything had gone so fatally wrong. Maybe it had burned up in the heat of his disappointment.

She handed it to him. He took it and ordered the corners of the stack, slipped the plastic pages into a white folder.

"Martin," she said. He was tempted to look up and conquered it by staring at a whorl of wood on the table. "I warned you."

He nodded. His reflection, faint as a ghost, nodded back.

"I had to do it. You were too close to right, and just too far wrong. I have new information." She shuffled papers and slid a photograph across the table to him. In it, a swarthy-looking man smiled genially. He was wearing a white sweater and white shorts, carrying a tennis racquet. "His name is Fathi el Haddiz. We think he's here in the United States to make a deal for something involving your dichlorhyradine."

"Why don't you ask him?" Martin asked quietly.

Carling's hand formed into a fist and slammed down on top of el Haddiz's picture.

"How stupid do you imagine I am? I'd love to, if we knew where the hell he was. We don't have a lot of time, and we need to focus. I needed to derail your little train, because I've got an express coming down the tracks, and I need you on board."

"Why me?"

She bent over. He sensed her warmth like a storm circling overhead. He met her teal green eyes, but couldn't hold the stare. His gaze fell to the table.

Watch me, Daddy! Watch me!

"Because you were at least half-right, and you *tried*. Martin, I have reason to think you're motivated to solve this problem. Am I wrong?"

"Go to hell," he mumbled. He opened his briefcase and stuffed in folders; one bent, pooched open, and spilled papers out in his lap. He gathered up crushed handfuls and threw them in. "You and your bugs and your damn politics, you go to hell. You go right to hell."

After a hesitation, her fingers picked up the photograph and he felt the weight of her shadow go away. He eased in a shaky breath.

From the doorway, Carling said, "I need you, Marty. I need people I can trust, and right now those people are few and far between. You call my office and let me know when you're ready."

She'd left a business card by his elbow. It had A. L. CARLING in raised black letters, and a phone number. Washington exchange.

He crumpled it up and threw it on the floor.

When he looked up, she was gone. He crossed his arms on the table and laid his head down, like a third-grader at quiet time.

Now, when he didn't want to remember, he felt her skin on the palms of his hands, tasted her lips.

After a long time, he bent and picked up her business card, smoothed it out, and put it in his jacket pocket.

As she'd known he would, of course.

She picked up the phone herself. He plugged his left ear with a finger and pressed his right closer to the receiver.

"Carling?" he shouted.

"Marty." He lost part of her reply in the blare of a loudspeaker. "—airport?"

"I'm at the airport," he agreed. "My flight's in fifteen minutes."

The line fluttered like a sheet in the wind. Silence went on so long, he thought they'd been disconnected.

"You're going back to Dallas."

"I think I have to." He twisted around to look at the flashing yellow message on the flight board.

"Then why are you wasting my time?" Offended. It was an act, he was certain.

"Because I wanted to tell you something," he replied. "Are you listening?"

"Yes."

"You're a bitch. I'm going home to get the data, all my files, everything. I'll be back tomorrow with it."

She said, "I'll meet you at the airport. Marty?"

"Yeah?"

The loudspeaker blared again, calling him to board. He thought she said, "Be careful."

Nineteen
Ming

Ming closed her eyes and let the braided leather of the whip glide through her fingers; smooth, flexible, warm as human flesh. She'd known a man in Singapore who'd had a whip made out of his favorite women. She often wondered what had happened to him.

"You want to know about Velvet," she said aloud. Her fingers found the cutting tip of the lash. "Why?"

When she opened her eyes, the client was staring at her with a strange expression. He had come to her door with no references, no history— but a convincing sum of money. Mundane tastes, so far. A little domination, mostly threat, but a little pain. He liked to keep his clothes on, a decision of which she approved. Naked men were so often disappointing.

"I heard she was good," he said hoarsely.

"From whom?" Ming touched the whip to her lips. His smile looked forced.

"A business friend. He said she sucked like a Hoover."

"How attractive." When he opened his mouth to reply, she snapped the whip in the air in front of him with practiced exacting grace. "I didn't ask you a question, little man."

"No ma'am," he said. He was sweating freely now, though the room was actually quite cool. Ming crossed one black-booted leg over the other and shook her hair back from her face in a black wave. It whispered like ghosts near her ears.

"Paolo," she called. The door slid open, and Paolo's large shadow loomed. "I can't quite decide about our friend here. What do you think?"

"Maybe you should whip him," Paolo suggested. His voice reminded her of glass grinding underfoot. "I'll chain him, if you want."

"No, not quite yet. Perhaps later." She stared at the client's eyes, watching the fear. She inclined her head to allow Paolo to leave. The door grated shut. "More than you expected, Ed? A little more . . . serious than you imagined?"

"I like it," he said raggedly. She shrugged.

"I don't care, as you know, whether you like it or not, as long as you pay." She snaked the whip out over the wood floor, watching it writhe like a live thing. "Would you like to fuck me, Ed?"

"I thought maybe you'd bring me the other one."

"Velvet?" Ming's smile felt tight on her lips. "Some other time, perhaps. Once I've broken you in properly."

He doesn't want to be here. The thought came to her suddenly, like a whisper, and she stiffened. *Something's wrong.*

But Paolo was in the next room; surely this little rabbit-chinned businessman couldn't be a danger, not to her. No strength in those eyes, only a blind panic. *Panic can kill.*

To still the doubts, Ming quick-snapped the whip, three, four times, each snap closer to the client's chest. He pressed back into his wooden chair, actually balancing it on two legs in his haste to get away.

When she stopped, the chair thumped back down
and he gulped in a deep breath.

"I think I've made a mistake," he said, and stood
up. Ming flicked her wrist, and the whip made a lazy
sinuous circle on the floor at his feet.

"Do you want to fuck me, Ed?"

His Adam's apple disappeared beneath the pressed
white collar, bobbed up again convulsively like a
drowning victim clawing for the surface. His face was
white, flushed with red around the ears.

"Yes," he said.

He was lying. Ming stood up and carefully coiled
the whip. She left it in the seat of her chair and
walked over to where he stood.

He didn't move as she unzipped the crisply pressed
trousers, teased his cock out, and persuaded it to stiff-
en in her hand.

"You know," she said, as she brushed her thumb
over the velvety head, "I taught Velvet everything she
knows. Is this what you want? My lips around you?"

She watched him nod convulsively and smiled.

"Ah, Ed, Ed." Her fingernails dug in just slightly,
enough to make him flinch and wither. "We don't
always get what we want, do we?"

She stood up and walked away, seated herself in her
chair with the whip on her lap like a favored pet. Ed
Julian stood miserably where she'd left him, cock
shrunken back into his underpants like a frightened
animal.

"See me next week," she told him.

When she heard the elevator rumble its way down,
she walked to the doorway and looked at Paolo, who
was reading a magazine by the light of a single small
lamp. She'd long ago instructed him that the magazines had to be pornographic, at least on the outside.

He put this one aside and revealed that *Leather Love* covered the latest copy of *Entertainment Weekly*.

"They're going to make a 'Gilligan's Island' reunion movie," he reported. She stared at him.

"He's asking about Velvet," she said. "I want to know why. Find out."

Paolo licked his lips. She read the hesitation.

"Don't make me ask you again," she said. He nodded and looked dejected. "Is there something you want to tell me?"

"I like her," he said. His dark eyes glittered from under thick eyebrows. "I don't want to hurt her."

It was as if he'd spoken to her in a Cantonese, the sounds familiar, but the meaning lost. She blinked.

"What does that matter?" she asked, honestly puzzled.

Twenty
Robby

As always, she'd slipped out of Jim's bed before the sun rose, like a vampire returning to her coffin. There was something about waking up with a man that seemed so final. The one time she'd violated that rule he'd woken surly and they'd fought over something stupid; now it was agreed that she went quietly, no goodbyes.

He mumbled in his sleep and turned over to put his hand in the hollow where she'd lain. He hadn't said anything about the fiasco at the mall except, *bad luck, kid*— but she was still smarting from it, angry at herself and the world, aware that luck had run out. The security guards would be looking for her. The police would have her description. Avenues of escape were narrowing.

Jim didn't seem worried, but he had lived on the edge for so long that he'd gotten addicted to the view. She was still a tourist, and liked it that way.

As she rode the deserted bus to her building, she thought about alternatives. Leaving town seemed logical— after all, any good-sized city could support a decent pickpocket— but she'd built up so much here. A change in hairstyle? Clothing? Jim was the chameleon, changing to meet the world; she had a set unchanging camouflage, and that was the way she preferred it.

The bus driver, in no particular hurry at this hour, idled at the curb until she opened the building's front door, a bit of kindness that made her wave thanks. He didn't seem to see it as he rumbled away, an island of yellow glow in the thick night.

No lurkers in the dim foyer tonight— no muggers, rapists, serial killers. Television to the contrary, she had never seen one except for the kid who'd bowled her over in the mall. She watched the elevator panel over her head count down floors and thought longingly of a hot shower, a cool bed that she could stretch out in, covers she could wrap tight in.

Something moved in the shadows. Robby flinched and backed away as feet scraped, and a body lurched upright.

Velvet, puffy with sleep, technicolor with bruises. She held a thick lumpy suitcase that spilled balloons of garish cloth out of the broken zipper.

"They were in my house," she said, and burst into weary tears.

"Who was it?" Robby asked, and held out a plate of cookies— store-bought again, to her regret. Velvet ate three in quick succession.

"Paolo, maybe— he's Ming's bodyguard. Maybe she's pissed at me, Jesus, I don't know."

"Maybe it was a robbery."

"No," Velvet said, and picked up another cookie. She nervously nibbled bits from the edge. "Okay, maybe, they took some stuff, but it was, like, personal, you know? They tore my pictures off the wall, piled all my clothes in the floor, pissed all over the

bathroom. Kicked in the TV set. They didn't have
to do that, they could have pawned it.''

Robby nodded slowly and settled back in the cool
embrace of her mint green chair. She'd loaded a CD
into the stereo, and the cool soothing music of
Enya— as Irish as she could stand, lately— floated like
mist around the room. Behind Velvet's bowed head,
the Ringling Brothers clown laughed.

"What did they take?"

"Huh?"

"Velvet, what did they take? Drugs?"

Velvet straightened indignantly and brushed her
hair back from her face.

"I'm not a junkie," she snapped.

Robby tipped her head back and sighed toward the
ceiling. "Did they take any drugs?"

A pause, and Velvet said resentfully, "No. I don't
use."

"Then what did they take?"

Velvet stood up and walked nervously around the
room, clicking her ragged fingernails on the back of
a chair, the wall, a small black table. At the window,
she stared out at the sullen orange of sunrise.

"Money," she said. "There. Happy?"

"How much?"

"Couple thousand. Enough to get me out of town,
keep me alive until things settled down." She blinked
back tears again and wiped at her swollen face. "Bastards. I worked for that money."

Robby reached for the cookies. Oatmeal, sugar, va-
nilla; she inhaled the warm perfume and crunched
a bite to ease the cramp in her stomach.

"We all work for our money," she said. Velvet snuffled wetly.

"Yeah, well, some of us work a little harder, if you
know what I mean. Hell, all you do is steal."

"Stealing is worse than prostitution?" Robby asked. She reached for a half-full glass of milk on the table and took a thick cold mouthful. Velvet covered her face with her hands and leaned her forehead against the window. "You really know how to make friends, Velvet."

"I'm sorry," she mumbled. "You gonna throw me out?"

Robby stood up and carried the cookies and empty milk glass back into the kitchen. From there, with warm water running soothingly over her hands, she said, "You know where the guest bedroom is. Sheets are in the closet. If you want anything else, look for it."

She felt rather than heard Velvet behind her. She looked over her shoulder and saw her slumped against the wall, tears glittering in her tired wounded eyes.

Velvet reached out and touched Robby's shoulder, a quick brush of fingertips. The tears spilled over.

Robby turned back to the dishes, scrubbing furiously. When she looked again, the room was empty except for the morning light.

"Two fingers," she instructed, and moved Velvet's hand slightly. "Relax. Relax. There."

Velvet jerked the wallet triumphantly out of her pocket, whooped, and tossed it in the air. Robby caught it deftly and slipped it back in her jacket.

"That was terrible. Remember what I told you. Two fingers, move with your mark, let his momentum take the wallet. If you jerk it like that, he'll know the second you have it. Try again."

Velvet, face tight with concentration, slipped two fingers into the pocket and snagged the wallet. When she had it halfway out, Robby took a step forward, and Velvet lost her grip. The wallet flopped on the carpet, spilling credit cards.

"Shit!" Velvet kicked the wallet into a skid across the hardwood floor, sent credit cards skittering. "You moved! No fair!"

"That should make an impressive defense in court." Robby bent and scooped up a Gold American Express, a Visa, a Discover. None of them had her names. She retrieved the wallet and slotted them back in place. "Do you want to stop now?"

"No. I just want to do it right, just once."

"In a day?" Robby shrugged and handed her the wallet. "Here. Put it somewhere."

"Where?"

"Anywhere."

Velvet grinned and stuffed it in the inside pocket of the blazer she wore— Robby's, of course, a muted green that was the brightest of her wardrobe. Robby considered for a second, examining the fit of the coat, and reached out to straighten the lapels. She pursed her lips, cocked her head, smiled, and walked away.

"Hey! Aren't you even gonna try?"

For an answer, Robby held up the wallet. She looked over her shoulder to see Velvet slap at the pocket, lips parted.

"You are totally great," Velvet said, and grinned. "Can you teach me to do that?"

"In a day? No." Robby pocketed the wallet, outside pocket, and came back to face her. "Try again."

"So how long have you been practicing?" Velvet bit her lip as she reached in the pocket, eased the leather out. Not bad, considering. Robby let it pass.

"I began when I was six. At fifteen I apprenticed to a magician named Alex the Magnificent; he taught me true sleight of hand. The rest of it came from my father. Try again. This time, do it faster."

Velvet had clever fingers— not God-given instinct,
perhaps, but she was trainable. Robby stood patiently
while she practiced. She'd learned on a threadbare
sewing dummy, bought from a second-hand shop,
draped with ragged coats and unraveling suits. Da
hadn't tolerated clumsiness, not from someone who
so clearly had the gift. Funny, how she could remember
the smell of that room, the close musty scent of old
clothes, dried sweat, old whisky. Tweed had felt so
rough on her young fingers, leather so smooth. He'd
watched her while he drank, nodding approval, slamming her against the wall with a casual slap when she
faltered.

For all that, what she most remembered about him
was how warm he'd felt when she'd clung to him that
last day. Fever-warm, in the chill of the trainyard. As
if, somehow, he'd known it was the last time.

"How's that?" Velvet crowed, and held up the wallet. Robby blinked.

"Good. Very good. Now do it left-handed."

"Left-handed?" Velvet's grin collapsed. "What do
you mean, left-handed?"

She was spared by the jingle of the doorbell. Robby
checked the peephole.

Sol, dressed in unseasonable off-white. As she
watched, he smoothed his hair back and checked the
shine on his fingertips, frowned, and punched the
doorbell again.

"So who is it?" Velvet asked. She clutched the wallet like a life preserver, and her eyes were wide and
tragic and ready for betrayal. "That guy? It's the suit,
isn't it, the one from the warehouse?"

And for a second, Robby thought about opening
the door and pointing to her and saying to Sol, *there
she is, go on, leave me out of it.* Jim would have, without
a second thought.

She could see from Velvet's eyes that she expected it.

"It's Sol. Go in the bedroom, lock the door, stay there. Don't make a sound." Velvet fled without argument. Robby waited until she heard the click of the bedroom door, then began unlocking deadbolts.

Sol's smile looked worn razor-thin by the time she swung the door open for him. When she stepped aside, he sauntered in and looked around like a landlord.

"Nice," he said, and shrugged off his coat to hand it to her. "Hang it up. I don't like wrinkles."

She resisted the urge to throw the damned thing in a heap on the floor, found a hanger and put it in the hall closet. When she returned, he was sitting at ease on the sofa, feet up, flipping channels on her TV. The sound was too loud.

"Cable," he said approvingly. "Great. I like those pirate shows on— what's it?— the Discovery channel. And those mysteries. Good mysteries. And that 'American Justice' show."

He settled on ESPN, the roar of a hockey match. Robby sat on the edge of the magenta chair, waiting, ready to move if he came at her. Would he be that crude? Was she giving him too much credit for subtlety?

"Robby," he sighed, and shook his head. "Here I am, a guest in your house, and you don't offer me anything to drink? Where'd you grow up, a barn? Some wine, if you have some. Red. And some crackers, pretzels, something like that."

She went to the kitchen and opened a bottle, poured two bubble-fragile glasses full. The hockey game continued to rage in the living room. She paused to stare at the wall phone next to the counter. Jim's number was on speed dial, as if it would do any good, as if he'd ever cross Sol.

Sol took the glass with evident relish, sniffed the woody scent of the beaujolais, swirled the wine, and sipped. Robby put hers aside untasted.

"Young," Sol said with a prissy twist of his thick lips. "A little nosy. Peppery."

She had no idea what he was talking about, and suspected he didn't, either. She waited until he'd drained the glass.

"Anything I can do for you, Sol?" she asked. He tilted his empty glass suggestively; she fetched the bottle and poured him a second. No shilly-shallying about tasting, this time. He guzzled it. She put the bottle on the coffee table in front of him. "Is something wrong?"

"Something's got to be wrong for me to visit you? What if I just like your company, sweetheart?" His eyes looked like black glass, full of pupil. The suspicion came to her too late that he was on something, that she'd lost her chance to call Jim and might never get another. There was a phone in the hall bathroom; she might be able to plead indisposition . . . "Robby, Robby, I like you. Why do you have to double-cross me?"

"D-Double-cross?" The stammer betrayed more than she wanted him to know. She saw lazy killing pleasure in his eyes. "I don't know what you mean."

"I'm talking about the hooker," he said, and leaned over confidentially. "You fucking her?"

She jerked as if he'd stabbed her. He sat slowly back upright, watching her face.

"Good," he said. "I wouldn't like to think you were that kind of pervert, know what I mean? So, she's, what, blackmailing you? Giving you the soft-soap? What?"

She spread her hands, helpless. He smiled and

nursed a mouthful of wine. A drop spilled on the lapel of his off-white suit like a bloody flower.

"Not that it matters," he continued. "Couple of object lessons, we don't have this problem anymore. The hooker, she got hers. Time for yours, Robby."

She didn't have time to move at all before his hand was under his jacket, before the gun was out. The muzzle was a huge black eye, staring. Her brain continued a helpless litany, *stupid, this is stupid, how can he do this, it's all a mistake—*

Sol put the muzzle to her forehead, the circle a cold tattoo. She pressed herself back against the chair and just had time to cry out before she felt the pistol press harder against her head.

Click.

She opened her eyes and watched Sol holster the gun through a sudden blurring curtain of tears.

"No bullets," he said. "Not this time. Next time we come up short, *cara mia,* you get one in the knee. If it happens twice, you get one in the brain. Got it?"

She nodded convulsively, unable to speak past the rage. He finished his glass of wine and stood up.

"Get my coat."

She didn't mean to obey, but then her hands were full of heavy wool, and he was taking it from her and shrugging it on.

On his way out, he kissed her hand.

She locked the door behind him, all the locks, all the alarms, picked up the wine bottle and glasses, and carried them to the kitchen.

"Robby?" Velvet, behind her, voice trembling. "Are you okay?"

Robby opened the bottom drawer and took out a hammer, and without any feeling at all, smashed the wine bottle and glasses into tiny glittering fragments.

"We have to kill him," she said.

Twenty-one
Martin

Martin Grady deplaned with the rest of the cattle, shuffling down a long narrow hall with strange angles and sloping floors. At the end of the hall the crowd dispersed like aerosol spray, all on their separate urgent missions, their strange little lives. He shifted his suitcase from his right to his left hand and looked around, wishing he could have slept on the plane, wishing he'd been able to sleep the night before. Exhaustion had made him odd.

A uniformed limousine driver was holding up a hand-lettered sign that said MR. GRADY. He headed in that direction and was almost there when a hand slid under his elbow and turned him quickly away. He looked down and saw a plain matronly-looking woman with a pleasant smile clinging to his arm.

"Don't cause trouble, Mr. Grady," she said without breaking her smile. Something pressed into his side under the cover of their linked arms. "Feel that?"

"Yes— "

"It's a gun. Keep walking. Do not make eye contact with the limo driver."

He walked with her, sweating. Kidnapped by a grandmother at JFK. He was going to end up a movie of the week, just as he'd feared.

"Do you have any other bags?" Grandma asked, and patted his arm.

"No." He resisted the urge to add, *ma'am*.

"Why, very good, that'll save us quite a lot of time. Might even save your life. Right through here, young man, through that door."

The door in question was blank wood except for the knob. Should he try to hit her with the door and run? He'd never expected to be a secret agent, no one had bothered to inform him about the proper procedures for being abducted. Behind the door could be anything— interrogation, a quick bullet, a body bag. He had to do something.

But it just didn't seem possible.

He opened the door and went through, Grandma still clinging tightly to his arm. The lights were much lower inside the room; he blinked as she let go of him with one last fond pat and stepped away.

"Where are we?" he asked. The room was furnished with comfortable couches and chairs, reading lamps, shelves of books and magazines. A TV played quietly in the corner. Only the muffled rattle of aircraft and the lack of windows made it clear it wasn't a normal living room.

"VIP lounge," Grandma said, and opened her purse to slip a round gold tube of lipstick inside. He stared at it.

"Where's your gun?"

"Oh, sonny, we're in an airport. I don't have a gun." She gave him a wink and ducked back out into the airport again. He stood helpless, bag dragging at his hand, and flinched when another hand fell on his shoulder.

Adrian Carling. He looked down into her deep blue green eyes and had a sudden longing to kiss her, but her expression was all business.

"You almost went with the limo, didn't you?" she accused. He shrugged. "Damn it, Marty, we'd be picking your body parts out of the Potomac if you'd made that mistake. Be a little more careful, would you?"

"You said you'd meet me."

"I *am* meeting you." She shook her head in disgust. "Martin Grady, meet Special Agents Jennings and Mendoza. You just met Mrs. Womack, who's on loan to us from another agency."

"CIA?"

"AARP," Carling said. Nobody else laughed. His chuckle trailed off into strained silence.

The two men who got up to shake hands might have been twins, except that Jennings was big and black-skinned, and Mendoza big and bronze-skinned. They both had football builds and chilly eyes, and wore earpieces like Secret Service men.

On the whole, he liked Mrs. Womack better.

"Martin is our data specialist," Carling explained. "Mendoza, take his bag. I assume the disks and files are in there? Good. All precautions, Mendoza. If you're ready, gentlemen?"

Carling, like a good defense attorney, always knew the answers before she asked the questions. They exited another door. This one led to a hallway that looked administrative. At the end of a long T-square hall loomed a guard station with metal detectors; Carling reached in her pocket and showed her FBI badge, beeped through without a pause. Jennings and Mendoza followed like the Crimson Tide in plainclothes. Martin was content to hold up the rear; alone in the parade, he didn't set off the detector.

"Where are we going?" he asked, darting around the linebackers to get to Carling as they went out on the sidewalk. Carling had no time for him. Like the other two agents, she scanned the streets, eyes alert and paranoid, as a dark gray sedan slid to the curb in front of them. She jerked open the door, gave the driver a glance, and jerked her head at Jennings and Mendoza, who crammed into the backseat. She slid in the front and beckoned for Martin to follow.

The driver was Mrs. Womack, she of the deadly lipstick. She swung the sedan out into the traffic circle, watching the rearview mirror.

"Limo?" Carling asked.

Mrs. Womack smiled. "Mechanical problems. I don't think there's anybody on our trail, ma'am." Mrs. Womack's eyes wandered over toward Martin. "He seems like a very nice young man. Interesting. You know, I think he actually considered whacking me over the head and running for it."

"My god," Carling said, and laughed. "Bowling over a granny. Marty, you surprise me."

"Where are we going?" he asked again, plaintively. Mrs. Womack made a right turn and drove at a sensible law-abiding speed.

"We're going to take the suitcase to the office, where it'll be secure. Jennings and Mrs. Womack will spend the evening digging up information about the cleaner with the limousine."

"Cleaner?" he repeated.

Her smile faded. "Assassin, Marty. They were going to kill you."

He'd been right about her office; thick burgundy carpet, Persian throw rugs, mahogany desks. The air smelled faintly of oranges and fresh roses. Martin sank into a red leather chair and closed his sand-coated eyelids. Carling gave whispered instructions to Jennings and Mendoza. When he woke up again,

Mrs. Womack was in front of him, holding out a thin china cup full of coffee. He took a burning sip and swallowed. It tasted like burnt motor oil, but that must have been his exhaustion, because Carling would have had Jamaican Blue Mountain in her private stock, brewed with pure spring water. Brand name filters.

"How do you feel?"

While he'd been staring at the translucent white cup, Womack had vanished and Carling now perched on the edge of a desk, legs crossed. She had a penchant for above-the-knee skirts that cast interesting shadows. Good thighs. He was too tired to wonder how calculated the display was.

"Okay," he lied. "You didn't tell me people were trying to kill me."

"I told you to be careful." She stretched her legs lazily, smooth as velvet. "I was worried about you. Who'd you talk to?"

"Nobody." She stared at him until he gave up. "Dr. Westfield. I had to explain why I wanted the raw data. She caught me copying the files."

Carling nodded without breaking the stare.

"Dr. Westfield," she repeated. "Jill Westfield. She's been on your staff for—five years. Right?"

He nodded, mesmerized by the slow circles of her foot, the sensuous rasp in her voice.

"Well, I think we'll have to assume that Dr. Westfield is a bad risk. Anybody else you talked to? The cleaning lady? The nurses at the hospital?"

It was no use wondering how she'd known. He was already convinced that she'd bugged his underwear.

"I told the head nurse that I'd be going to Washington for an extended period of time, and told her I'd call with the number. Look, they had to know. Sally's condition . . ."

She let him run out of words, pulled a pad of paper across the desk and wrote, handed it to him. He looked at the number uncomprehendingly.

"That's a secured beeper. You have them call if there's an emergency." Carling held his gaze, and even though her expression hadn't changed, he felt some connection again, sparking back to life. "How is she?"

"The same," he said, cleared his throat and corrected himself. "Worse, really. They're worried about renal failure."

"How's her brain function?"

Her eyes were so calm, so remorseless.

"She doesn't have any. She hasn't for nearly a year."

Mrs. Womack rounded the corner and cheerfully held out a silver platter of sandwiches with the edges trimmed away. He chose something that looked like tuna and ate it quickly without much noticing how it tasted. Carling ate, too. Neatly.

"Mrs. Womack," she said as she swallowed her last bite of sandwich, "take Mr. Grady to the phone room and get him a clear line. He has to make a phone call."

She hadn't asked him why he'd kept his daughter alive for so long on the machines; he was grateful for that. Other people asked. People who thought they understood what it was like. She'd been so tanned when it had happened— a long hot Texas summer, hours in the pool. He hardly recognized her now, white and thin, with eyes that sometimes opened but never focused. Her skin felt clammy and cool.

Carling hadn't asked, *How can you force her to live that way?* Maybe Carling understood. Maybe.

He had a brief conversation with Nurse Varnas—

no, her condition hadn't changed— yes, they'd beep him immediately if it did. Nurse Varnas had a cool judgemental voice. When he was finished, he sat staring blankly at the squat black phone until Mrs. Womack put a warm hand on his shoulder and reminded him that his presence was needed in the office.

Carling had moved to sit behind her desk. She had on a pair of reading glasses that magnified her eyes. She looked at him over the top of the frames and tossed a red folder across to him. Papers skated over mahogany wood.

"Got another one," she said. "Pastor at a church in Louisiana. No connection to the other cases, except that the majority of them seemed to be centered in the south and southwest. I'm sending Mrs. Womack and Mendoza down to do data collection."

Grady pulled the papers closer and skimmed through the report, settled on the pictures. The upper half of the face was almost normal, except for the boiled-egg eyes. Whoever had tried to save him had gotten to him quickly. Even so, the tissue damage was incredible. It was impossible to tell what in the red and black mess was clothing, what was skin, what was muscle.

"I want to go," he said. When she didn't answer, he looked up at her. "I *need* to go."

"My people can handle things."

"I'm not disputing that, but— "

"Mrs. Womack?" Carling interrupted. He'd forgotten all about the older woman, who still sat in the back of the room, hands neatly folded on her lap. Mrs. Womack fussed with her floral skirt, picking invisible lint from it. "Your opinion?"

"Ma'am, I'm just an employee." Mrs. Womack shot him a look that was nakedly ungrandmotherly. "However, if this nice young man insists on acting like a Junior G-man, I'll cheerfully shoot him in the back. I don't need your help, son. Just do your job, and I'll do mine."

After a long chilly silence, Grady managed to clear his throat and nod.

"Lovely. Now, dear, Mendoza and I will need a few things from storage. I trust that's all right?"

"Perfectly," Carling agreed, and opened a desk drawer. She passed over a card key. "Try to get the body transferred to Quantico, or, failing that, get the forensic reports and get me some tissue and blood samples. Anything else, Martin?"

"Uh—yes, his clothes. I'll need to see test results on those. Also, local water samples."

"He was in a baptismal tank," Mrs. Womack reminded him. "I think they've drained it, but I'll see what I can find."

She bustled out, shutting the door behind her. Grady looked at the photos again, flipped through the narrative reports.

"What are we missing?" he asked. On the other side of the desk, Carling shrugged and played with a Mont Blanc pen. "It's not random," he added. "If it were random, we'd have female victims."

"Unless women simply are immune to it somehow."

"That doesn't fit with the standard pattern of spontaneous human combustion. The typical SHC victims are usually women, usually over forty, and the cases occur during the late evening and early morning. These have almost exclusively been daytime occurrences. Public."

"Strikes a little more terror that way, doesn't it?" Carling asked. He gave her a disgusted look. "Oh, come on, Marty. You said yourself, it isn't random. And it doesn't follow established patterns, if you believe in that sort of thing. So what do we have left? *Human agency*. Deliberate murder."

He continued to study the picture of Pastor Zeke Clayburn, mouth open in a rictus of horror. Nearly normal down to his nose, charred meat from mouth to waist.

His white Sansabelt slacks looked sooty but intact. No burning of the legs and pelvic region.

"Files," he said, and snapped his fingers. "The El Paso file. Where is it?"

Carling dug in a desk drawer and passed him another red folder. He pulled the picture and stared at the mashed charred corpse. The feet looked intact in battered running shoes. Other than that, he was a mess.

"Clayburn was in a baptismal tank," he said. Carling came around the desk to examine the photos side by side. "No combustion below his waist. I'll bet he was sopping wet."

"So?"

"So if the water's making them burn, why would it keep him from burning below the waist?"

Carling met his eyes.

Grady sat back, photos still held at eye level, and shook his head.

"The water's safe. My god, the water's safe! It *is* murder. God, that's great!"

Carling leaned over and kissed him, a chaste gentle peaceful kiss. "I like to think so."

Twenty-two
Velvet

Two pimply teenaged boys in oversized pro football jackets were staring at her. Velvet pointed her shoulder at them and curled closer around the pay phone, wishing the wind would let up, wishing she had her day-glo blue jacket with the fake fur lining. Damn, that thing was warm.

Instead, she had to settle for Robby's hiking shit— L.L. Bean or something, made for one-hour hikes in the fall, not for winter windstorms. Besides, she looked like shit in flannel.

And the goddamned penny loafers were killing her feet.

A thin recorded voice in the phone receiver said *The number you have reached is not a working number. Please check your number and—*

"Fuck you," Velvet grumbled, and slammed the receiver down. She chewed her lip and fingered a quarter in her pocket. She'd lost Lenny Bradshaw's number, of course; never had been able to hang onto things like that, not even when her life depended on it. And here she had things to tell him, too. Big things.

She needed to replace the money she'd lost, fast. What the hell was that rag he worked for? *Weekly*

World— no— *Dallas Met*— no— *Big D Gazette*. That was it. *Big D Gazette*.

She dialed 1411 and demanded the number. A computer that sounded like the one she'd just told to fuck itself gave her a number that didn't sound at all familiar. She scribbled it on the back of her hand with a ballpoint pen, and fed her last quarter into the phone.

The two teenagers were still staring, nudging each other. She gave them a shark smile and dialed the number, listened to the grinding blurry rings. Five. Ten. Jesus, didn't they ever—

"BigDGazette. Holdonaminute." Before she could tell him to fuck off, he'd jammed her on hold— silent hold, not Muzak hold— and she spent another minute rubbing her chilled hands together, smearing the phone number. Great. She'd have to get it again, if she needed to call back. "Yeah. Whatdoyouwant?"

"Lenny Bradshaw." She had to say it slow, because her teeth were chattering. The plastic of the phone felt like a block of ice on her ear. "Hey, buddy, hurry it up, I'm dying out here."

The guy grunted and put her back on hold. Silent hold. She danced uncomfortably from one foot to the other, thinking about central heating and peeing. She was on her left foot when a voice picked up and said, "Yeah, go ahead."

Not right. Didn't sound right.

"Hey, you got two seconds to start talking or I'm gone." He breathed heavily into the phone, a wheeze at the end like a three-pack-a-day addict. This wasn't Mr. College Boy Dimple-Chin. No way.

"Lenny Bradshaw?" she asked, like an idiot. He wheezed some more.

"Yeah, yeah, you got him. What?"

"Lenny Bradshaw, like, the reporter, with the *Big D Gazette*?"

"No, baby, Lenny Bradshaw with the fucking Peace Corps. What are you, crazy? You called me, right? So?"

So. She leaned heavily against the pay phone, almost rested her forehead on the cold metal, but realized it was covered with some mysterious white stuff that could have been snot.

"So— let's say, just for grins, I been talking to a guy who says he's Lenny Bradshaw. Only he isn't you. He's been giving me money for information."

"Money?" Bradshaw's laugh sounded more like springs squeaking. "Baby, you got a guy paying you to talk, I'd hang on to that bad boy, 'cause it damn sure ain't me, and anyways, I don't pay for information. I'm a journalist. People give it to me."

"Yeah, sure. Listen, this guy, he's been pretending to be you. Isn't that like, against the law or something? 'Cause, you know, I told him a lot of stuff." She hesitated. "Personal stuff."

"Like what?"

Here she was, scared to go home, stranded at a snot-laced pay phone in the freezing wind wearing L.L. Bean shit, for god's sake, shacked up in a house that Ringling Brothers decorated. Why worry about one more asshole?

"Like, I'm the one who was in the hotel room with Burt Marshall when he burned up."

The silence seemed to go on forever. Papers shuffled, or static hissed, she wasn't sure which. Finally, he said, "Burt who?"

"Come on, you did a big story about it, I read it. Guy burned up in a hotel. You were offering a reward. I was there. I saw it." She sucked in a deep breath. "That isn't all, not by a long shot. I saw plenty. I think it was murder, and I think I know who did it."

"Yeah, I remember this guy. That was *last week*, fer

crissake. But, uh, yeah, there's a reward. If you've got good info. What's your name, honey?"

"Velvet. Velvet— uh— look, don't print my name, okay? Just call me an unnamed source or something. Look, I need the money. I need to get out of town, like, fast. Get it?"

"Got it. Okay, Velvet, you want to come down here?"

"Here where?"

He gave her an address out in the 'burbs, a long cold bus ride. She wrote it on the back of her hand next to the smudged telephone number and chewed her lip some more, winced when a cut opened and she tasted blood.

"Yeah, okay, it'll take a while. Like, a couple hours. Okay?"

"I ain't going anywhere. Come on down." Bradshaw sounded friendlier now, like a tamed bear. "Got a pot of coffee with your name on it."

"Long as you got a check with my name on it."

"We'll discuss it." He hung up without any goodbyes, which was fine; she felt warm and fuzzy enough. Whoever Mr. Dimple was, fuck him. If he came back, she'd get some more cash out of him, even if she had to do him a favor or two.

Things were starting to look up for her, she decided, and gave the two teenaged boys another smile. The taller one wandered over, deliberately casual.

"You waiting for somebody?" he asked. She lifted an eyebrow. Under the glasses, her eyes were still puffy and red, but what the hell, the only thing he was going to care about was her mouth.

"Why honey," she purred, and linked her arm in his. "I was waiting for you. How about your friend? Might as well make it a party."

Might as well. She didn't intend to make her

money back one blow job at a time, but, hell, she had to start someplace.

And the bus would be late. It always was.

The offices of the *Big D Gazette* had an office-supply-warehouse feel— assemble-them-yourself desks, cheap bookcases that leaned forward like vultures, computers that looked put together from garage sales and public auctions. None of the chairs matched. Most of the desks were empty— and too clean.

"What happened?" Velvet sidestepped a dented trash can and waved a hand at the empty bullpen. Lenny Bradshaw— who turned out to be tuberculosis-victim thin, pencil-necked, and a big fan of garlic and Old Spice— shrugged slumped shoulders. He had on paisley suspenders, a blue-striped shirt, and a polka-dot bow tie, a man in terminal pattern indecision.

"You know. The usual."

Cutbacks? Mass cult suicide? Ptomaine? She hadn't seen any funeral wreaths on the door, but there hadn't been a receptionist, either.

"Okay, Miss— what's your name again?"

"Velvet."

"Velvet." His voice turned nasal and snide. She knew the tone, knew without looking that he'd be staring down her cleavage, except that Robby's L.L. Bean wardrobe didn't give that kind of view, not without a lot of work. "Yeah. So, you want to tell me what happened at the hotel?"

"Gee, Lenny— may I call you Lenny?— I'd love to, only I got this problem." She seated herself in the chair he waved at, leaned over, and rested her elbows on his desk. It was clean, too— not ex-employee clean, but not-much-to-do clean. "See, I need money. That's why I just took a long boring bus ride to get here."

He coughed in her direction, a wet rattle that smelled like a six-day-full Dumpster. She'd bought a trial-sized bottle of Listerine and gargled at the bus stop— just to get the taste of the condoms out of her mouth. She thought about offering the bottle to Brad-shaw.

"Ah." He tapped a sharp-pointed pencil on a clean pad of paper. The eraser had never been used. "Well, why don't you just let me be the judge of that."

"Hey. Buddy." Velvet pressed her hands flat against the desktop and stood up to lean over him. He either had a dandruff problem, or it had started snowing outside while she wasn't looking. "Let's get something straight. I'll deliver. I . . . always . . . deliver."

She used the patented Ming low-octave purr in the last of it, saw it register in his eyes. The pencil stopped tapping.

"Yeah." He cleared his throat, "Yeah, I can see that. Tell you what, I got five hundred bucks that says— "

"Let me see it."

He opened his desk drawer and pulled out a ragged cigar box. He flashed it open, showing an equally ragged stack of bills.

"Count it."

Bradshaw's eyes were a washed-out brown, squinty and tired.

"Count it," she said again, very quietly. "Or I walk right out the door."

"Cocky bitch," he muttered, and slammed the lid back on the box. He laid out twenties, old and used, in stacks of five. At five stacks, he'd emptied the box. "Satisfied?"

"I believe in total quality management. I'm never satisfied." She grinned when his eyes started to narrow more. "Forget it. We're cool."

When she reached out for the money, his hand came down over hers, hot as summer sweat.

"Uh-uh. Not until I've heard what I want to hear."

Before she was done, he'd let her take the five hundred, fold it into neat halves, and stick it in her socks. After that, he took out a half-full bottle of Chivas Regal and poured two paper cups.

When that was empty, he found a full bottle.

" 'Slate," Bradshaw mumbled. He tried to pick up his paper cup, but turned it over. Whisky peed off the edge of his desk onto his pants. "Shit. Shit. See that? Shit."

For some reason, it was ungodly funny. Velvet laughed until the room started spinning, then put her head down on the desk until it stopped. From time to time, giggles bubbled up and dribbled out of her mouth, gooey with Chivas.

"Not the first time," she said. "Not the firsht time shomebody died with me. Y'know?"

"Yeah?" He snorted wetly and searched for a handkerchief. "Damn. Damn."

"My sister."

He started laughing, a high thin laugh like a jackass. She wished she was close enough to slap him; it seemed like way too much effort to go around the desk to do it. She settled for throwing the rest of her drink on him, then reached for the bottle and poured. Most of it missed the cup.

"Don't fuckin' laugh, you asshole. Ash-hole. Good kid. She was . . . you know . . . young."

"Lemme guess." Bradshaw's laugh sawed at her again. "Drunk driving."

"No." She tried to sit up straight, but the room took a funny lurch. "Drunk, not driving. Blow jobs."

"Huh?"

"I was blowing this guy— y'know— in the backsheat. Seat. I dinnit know she wanned to go home. She started walking an— an— thish other guy he— " All of a sudden she was crying, bawling, shaking all over. "Amy— "

She didn't remember any of it too well— just crawling out of the car, half-dead from the booze, seeing the other boy throwing up in the bushes. Seeing Amy lying in the mud, her face in the mud.

"Suffocated," she said, clearly. "Dinnit mean to do it."

That's what he'd said on the witness stand, *I didn't mean it, I didn't know she couldn't breathe, I didn't mean it—*

And she'd sat up there looking out at the courtroom, at her friends, her mom, and said, *I didn't know, I didn't hear it, I was drunk, I was in the backseat giving his friend a blow job while he raped my sister and she choked to death.*

God, oh God.

"Life sucks," Bradshaw said solemnly, and heehawed like a jackass. Velvet stood up with all the dignity she had left and pointed her ink-smeared left hand at him.

"Fuck you," she said, and staggered away.

The freezing night air cleaned her up a little. She sat down shivering on the curb and waited for the bus. Her mouth tasted like Scotch and semen.

She opened the trial bottle of Listerine and gulped it down in two quick shots.

She had the distinct feeling that when she sobered up, she was going to regret this whole thing.

Twenty-three
Ming

Ming liked the quiet, late at night. Sometimes, in the distance, she heard a siren wail, but all in all it was silent, and cold. She never turned the heat on unless it was cold enough to kill, and even then only enough to keep her alive.

Cold focused. Cold crystallized purpose.

She sat naked on her rough cotton mattress, hands clenched into fists, and stared at a blank brick wall. There was nothing in this room. No clothes were allowed here. This was the place of utter nakedness.

The room of punishment.

There were no light switches; the bulbs were unshaded, too bright, harsh. They burned constantly. The light slid gold over her skin, black over her hair. She opened one fist and watched blood flush pink back into her palm.

Paolo had been to Velvet's apartment. Someone had been there first. She was gone— either fled or dead. Dead, she was a great loss.

Fled, she was a great liability.

Ming turned her hand palm-down and laid it on her thigh, never quite relaxing.

Velvet did not know very much about this room. About the drain in the center of the floor, the water taps placed low to the ground to flush the floor clean. Velvet had never watched the red whirlpool disappear.

"No one leaves," Ming said softly. The air in the room was dead, no echoes. Voices fell into immediate silence, lost. "No one leaves here. It is the rule."

She had managed to conquer her need for this place— now she indulged it only once a year, rarely more than that. She had planned to bring Velvet here, to let her understand the silence.

It might still be possible. It might still be *necessary*.

A knock on the door. She smiled slightly, though she felt no joy.

"Come in," she said. The door creaked. "Come inside."

Paolo hesitated in the doorway, looking nervously at the empty walls, the plain concrete floor, the drain like a dark eye in the center.

"Uh, no, ma'am, I just— uh— "

"Did you find her?"

Paolo's silence gave her an answer. She closed her hand into a fist again.

"Unfortunate." She considered the uneven bricks in the wall, the red brown that concealed so many stains. "Perhaps it's time to have another session with Mr. Julian. He seemed so— eager."

"He didn't call."

"Then call him. Tell him Velvet's ready for him."

"Uh— " Paolo straightened when she looked at him. His eyes went blank and businesslike. "Ma'am. Uh-huh."

She turned her head back to contemplation of the wall.

"Close the door when you leave."

Such a small sound, the closing of the door. She shut her eyes and listened to the metal snick of the

lock closing, played and replayed it in her head like a
favorite song.

She liked the quiet, late at night.

Twenty-four
Sol

"The note says she's sorry," Kelly said as she laid the jacket over the back of the couch. Sol threw her a look that slid off her face and landed on the jacket, stuck like Superglue. He hit the mute button on the TV, derailing the movie in mid-scream, and reached over to touch the fabric.

"Who says?" Eggplant wool, soft as a baby's butt, rich as butter. He pulled it over to look at the label—small, discreet. His eyebrows went up like balloons.

"Velvet," Kelly said. She sounded suspicious and pouty. "The hooker. Why's a hooker sending you presents?"

"Think, sweetheart, think. She learned her lesson." The lining was pure silk, dark blue. It felt like warm skin. "She learned it perfectly."

"Well, try it on," she sniffed, and flounced down in the leather armchair, crossed her legs, and swung her left foot impatiently. "Go on. See if I care."

"Did she call?"

"Huh?" She looked up from examining the TV schedule. "Oh. No. Came with a note. In the pocket."

There were, of course, no outside pockets in such a beautiful piece of work; he reached inside and found a plain white piece of paper, plain sloppy writing. *Dear Sol,* it said. *Sorry for the misunderstanding. Consider this an apology. Sincerely, Velvet.*

"Yes indeed," he murmured, then crumpled the note and tossed it toward the kitchen wastebasket. "My god, yes. I had no idea she had such taste."

Kelly mumbled something mutinous. He stood up and shed his wrinkled off-white jacket, slid his arms into the buttery embrace of the eggplant coat.

Perfect. Utterly perfect. He checked the cuffs, tugged at the lapels, sauntered down the hall to check the fit in the mirror. His color, his size, every line in place.

It made the rest of his clothes look like shit. He frowned and sucked in his gut, turned sideways, tried again. A new shirt, that was what he needed. Something in dark blue silk. One of those raw silk ties, light yellow. The trousers had to go, too. Time for a housecleaning.

"What do you think?" he asked, and did a runway spin for Kelly. She glanced up from her crossword puzzle and shrugged. "Come on, what do you think? It's nice, eh?"

"I don't like purple."

If he'd had time to think about it, he might not have hit her quite so hard. He flexed his fist and stepped back, careful not to get any blood on the jacket.

"Time for a housecleaning," he said aloud. "Get your things."

"But Sol—" Stunned, she started to bawl. He resisted the urge to punch her again—hell, there wasn't any point—and walked back to the bathroom to rinse his knuckles off. When he came back, she was stuffing things in a suitcase—one of his suitcases, the Gucci. He dumped the shit out on the floor, went to the kitchen, and grabbed a garbage bag from under the sink. She sat on the floor, legs splayed, sniffing back blood, and stuffing her clothes into the garbage bag; he felt sick at the sight of her.

New jacket, new wardrobe, new day, he thought. *Today, I change everything.* God bless that little whore, she'd made him wake up. He'd go over to Robby's, sweet-talk her, take her out for some Italian. She'd like the jacket.

Kelly tried to sneak some of the jewelry into the bag. He convinced her to leave it. When she was packed up, he made her go wash her face and comb her hair, even carried her garbage bag down to the car and threw it in the trunk. When he slammed it shut, he found her staring at him with wide fixed eyes.

"What? What now?"

"You— aren't going to— kill me, are you?"

He stared at her, stunned. "I don't kill people, sweetheart," he told her kindly. "Mama mia, why would I? I'm in the business end. Look, it's over, that's all. I take you home, you don't come back, you don't make any trouble for me. End of story. Okay?"

Tears spilled out of her eyes, down her pale cheeks. She wiped them away with trembling fingers.

"Okay," she whispered. He opened the door of the Mercedes like a gentleman, closed it for her, walked around to the driver's side. When he opened his door, she said, "Sol?"

"What?" He fastened his seatbelt, slammed the door, started the car. The heater smelled like burning socks.

"I love you." She continued to cry. He backed the car out into weak sunshine, felt the crunch of the tires as they hit the street. "I really do, Sol. Nobody else loves you like I do."

The saddest thing about it was she really believed it. He handed her a Kleenex, winced when she blew her nose. He was tired of her, sick and tired, but it was important to be a man about these things. Let her down gently.

"I know you do, sweetheart. You're one in a million." He searched for a new cliche. "I don't deserve you."

"Yes. Yes, you do." The tears died off to wet snuffles. He gave her another Kleenex. "Oh, Sol, you're great, you're really great. I never thought I'd find anybody like you."

"That's great, but— "

"Please don't leave me. Please." She batted tear-clumped eyelashes at him. He sighed and kept driving, turning left on the Tollway, out to the 'burbs where she still kept a cheap one-room apartment. She hadn't planned on keeping it much longer, he knew. Good thing he'd made up his mind.

At the tollbooth he blew through at fifty miles an hour without paying; red lights flashed, bells rang, no cops.

"Fasten your seatbelt," he said. Sniffing, she did, then folded her hands in her lap and sat like a schoolgirl, head down. "Look, it's time for you to move on, find somebody else. It's better that way. Better for both of us."

She started crying again. He took the Mercedes up to seventy and let her cry.

Fifteen minutes later, he eased to a stop in the parking lot next to her building, switched off the engine, sat for a second with his eyes closed. He didn't feel so good— he'd turned the heater up too high, maybe he was catching something. Cold. Flu. Something. He needed bed rest, some hot soup.

"Sol?" Kelly hadn't moved. She sat twisting a loop of red hair in her fingers, watching him with big hopeful eyes. He unhooked his seatbelt and reached across her to pop the trunk. "Oh, Sol, please— "

The freezing air felt good on his skin. God, he was sweating. As he hauled her garbage bag out of the trunk, a knife of pain went under his ribs. He winced and fell heavily against the car.

"Sol?" The car shifted up as Kelly got out and came around the back. He couldn't get his breath. Heart attack. That was what it was. No big deal, an ambulance'd fix him right—

He was sweating all over the jacket. The wool was blotching dark in places, all ruined. He brushed his fingers over the damage.

Hot. Hot. Hot.

Kelly said, "Oh, honey, it's okay, I won't leave if you don't want me to go, it's okay—"

She hugged him. When she felt the heat she tried to yank free but he held on, not because he wanted to hurt her but he wanted *help*, wanted her to make it *stop*, this terrible thing, this awful pain. Knives. Knives everywhere. Skin coming off in strips. Heat burrowing in everywhere, burning, everything burning.

Kelly's fingernails clawed at him, sank deep into his skin and pulled it out by handfuls. He couldn't hold her anymore but when his legs gave way and he fell she was still with him, screaming, beating at him, clawing.

Stuck to him. Before the skin went black on her face, he had time to think, *You got what you wanted, baby.*

Twenty-five
Velvet

It was dark when she woke up, morning or middle of the night or some damn thing. Velvet groaned and put a pillow over her head, but that only made the pain echo more, like a pinball trapped inside her skull. She blinked dry eyes until the digital alarm clock swam into view.

It said 7-something. She couldn't tell if it was A.M. or P.M., didn't really matter, anyway except there was better shit on TV if it was P.M. She was in no mood for "Good Morning America."

Christ, how the hell had she gotten home? Speaking of that— where the hell was she? She fumbled for a light and found one on the bedstand. When she flicked it on, she moaned and turned it off just as fast. Neon blue. God, she'd made it to Robby's, maybe the bus driver had walked her upstairs. Lucky she hadn't gotten busted.

With the pillow held firmly over her head, she turned the light on again. She let the glare in in stages— through closed eyes, then just a peek, finally eyes open at half-staff. No way were they coming open any more, not yet, not in this technicolor hell. She kicked the suffocating covers off and stumbled naked out of bed, found a T-shirt and slipped it on, a pair of discarded panties that felt suspiciously stiff. What the hell. She'd change later.

She was sitting on the end of the bed, head in her hands, waiting for the pounding to die down, when Robby knocked on the door.

"Are you all right?"

"God damn nosy Irish bitch," Velvet whispered into her trembling hands. "Yeah. Yeah, I'm okay."

"Can I come in?"

"No."

She hadn't figured Robby would pay any attention, and she was right. The door opened and light— a lot brighter than the little nightstand glare— hit her like a white wall. She wailed and shut her eyes.

"Poor thing." Robby sounded unsympathetic. "Time to get up. I've got to go."

"Where?"

"Work. Come on, get up, you'll feel better if you move around. Do you remember getting here?"

Velvet tried to shake her head. It was a bad idea.

"You opened the door at three in the morning and hit the floor like a sack of bricks. On top of that, the intrusion alarm went off. I didn't know whether to kill you or call the paramedics." Robby was doing something behind her, straightening up, pawing through clothes in the closet. The rattle of hangers was enough to make Velvet's eyes bleed. "I put you in a cold shower just in time for you to start throwing up. All in all, it was a glorious morning, and don't you *ever* do that to me again, *ever,* or you're out on your ass, understand me?"

Velvet pried her fingers away from her eyes and blinked until Robby's face came into focus. Hard. Cold brown eyes. A mouth like a straight razor.

"Sure," she agreed, and gulped back a hot mouthful of something she didn't want to identify. "Sorry. Won't happen again."

"It had better not." Robby glared at her another minute, then went back to rattling hangers. "Have you seen my brown pants?"

Actually, from where she sat, Velvet could see them real well. They were crumpled in a ball under the dresser, probably covered with vomit and Chivas and Listerine. She covered up her eyes again.

"No. Got any aspirin?"

"Bathroom."

She tried to get up. She managed to get about two inches off the bed. The resulting fall back to the mattress made her think her brain might actually explode, but it only throbbed until her teeth rattled. Scotch. She knew better than to get drunk on Scotch.

"Uh, could you . . ." The question died under the weight of Robby's stare. "No. Didn't think so."

Somehow, once she'd got her feet under her, the room stopped swaying like a rope bridge and just felt like a tilt-a-whirl instead. Not so bad. She kept both hands pressed against the hallway on the way to the bathroom, averted her eyes from lemon yellow and cheery day-glo orange, and dug aspirin out of a cabinet. She swallowed four of them dry, found vitamin C capsules, and swallowed them, too.

As she stood slumped and miserable, staring at her bruised swollen face in the mirror, Robby appeared in the doorway and handed her a frosty glass of orange juice.

"There's coffee on the counter," she said. "Turn the pot off when you've had enough. Unplug it, too. And wash out the pot, just water, no soap."

Nodding seemed to still be a risky proposition, so Velvet waggled her hand in agreement. Funny, it had ink stains on it. She blinked and finally remembered jotting the address on it.

The paper. Oh, God, she hadn't meant to tell him *all* of it, surely she hadn't— God. Oh, God.

No telling what she'd done. Told the story on nationwide TV. Screwed her way across Dallas. Who knew?

She tossed back a mouthful of orange juice and gagged, but Robby was still watching, so she kept drinking, and drinking, until all she got was a frothy mouthful of pale bubbles. Robby took the glass back.

"Thanks." The word came out rough around the edges, not quite the way she'd meant it, but Robby nodded and went away. "Where're you working?"

"Hockey game," Robby called. "Good business, especially around the beer lines. Lots of flush people at hockey games for some reason. Sports events are always good."

"Good in my line of work, too," Velvet managed to say, and sat down on the toilet. Mercifully, the lid was down. "Guys are always horny after a good game."

Robby came back from the kitchen. This time, she was holding a steaming cup of coffee. Velvet wrapped chilled hands around it and sighed in gratitude; the steam cushioned the ache a little, made her feel a little more normal.

"Does it ever bother you?" Robby asked. Velvet met her eyes. After a long uncomfortable silence, Robby turned away. "Sorry. Not a very polite question, I suppose."

"No," Velvet agreed, and sipped coffee. It was bitter and hot and tasted like the bottom of a grease pit, and she didn't care at all. "It's not a very polite question."

She waited in the bathroom until she heard the door shut, wandered out to check the locks, eased herself carefully down on the sofa. The leather was as cold as ice, but warmed up quickly.

She went to sleep, curled up under a clown-red afghan with bright yellow fringe, with the TV on ESPN as she waited for the hockey game to start. She didn't know how long she'd been asleep— long enough that there were guys fighting on the ice on TV— when a volley of knocks on the door woke her up. She came bolt upright, and met the wall of her hangover with bruising force.

It's that guy. The suit. Jesus, what do I do?

She hit the mute button on the TV and huddled under the afghan. The knocking continued. After it got quiet again, she ventured over to the door and looked through the peephole.

"Well, well, well," she murmured, and flipped the deadbolts, tossed her hair back over her shoulders, and opened the door. She clung to it in what she hoped looked like a sexy way, instead of a way to stay upright.

Mr. College-Prep-School-Dimple-In-The-Chin-Not-Lenny-Fucking-Bradshaw stared at her with those big soft eyes. She batted her eyelashes at him— it still hurt— and said, "Hi, Lenny. Come on inside."

He hesitated only a couple of seconds, giving her exposed legs a wide glance. She locked all three deadbolts behind him, making sure he got a good view of her butt.

"Uh, Velvet, I didn't know you'd be— "

"No, of course you didn't. I told you about Robby, didn't I? You must have come by to see her, not me." She kept smiling. "Have a seat."

He did, perching uneasily in the magenta chair. She offered coffee. He refused. She sucked on what was left in her cup— cool, getting cold— and watched him watch her. Little prick. Lying little sonofabitch.

"When's my story coming out?" she asked. He shrugged.

"Editors. You know."

"Uh-huh. So, what'd you want to talk to Robby about?"

"What you told me. The man she saw." He took his eyes off her thighs long enough to give the apartment a quick glance. "So, is she here? Can I talk to her?"

"Gosh, Lenny, I'm real sorry but she's out. Working. So, how's the newspaper business?" She crossed her legs, slowly. He swallowed hard.

"Good. Since I'm here, do you, um, have anything you want to tell me? Anything new?"

"Cash," she said. He dug in a pocket and laid a hundred on the coffee table. "Keep coming."

He stopped at two hundred, and not even uncrossing her legs could make him go to three. She sat up, grabbed the money, and stuffed it in her panties.

"Sorry you had to skip the table dance, but I'll make it worth your time." She gave him a wicked toothy grin and made sure she could make it to the kitchen and Robby's knife rack before she said, "You want more information, read about it in the papers."

Lenny's college-boy face smoothed out. The dimple looked like a special effect.

Funny how fast those eyes could cool off.

"Pardon?" he said softly. She put both feet flat on the floor and leaned forward, ready to run. "I'm sorry, I don't understand."

"No? How about this one— I lost your number, Lenny or whatever-your-name-is. So I called the *Big D Gazette*. You don't look anything like Lenny Bradshaw."

She expected some babble of lies and apology, but he just sat there, watching her, quiet. She didn't like the calculating look on his face. There wasn't any more of the college boy; this guy looked old now, older than she did, fine lines of wrinkles around his eyes that she guessed didn't come from smiling.

"But, hey, whatever, no skin off my nose—" she continued.

"What did you tell him?"

"Who?"

"Bradshaw. At the *Big D Gazette*."

Funny, how her hangover vanished under stress; she could feel it jittering madly down in her guts, vibrating up around the top of her head, but right now her brain was working hard.

"Nothing," she shrugged. It seemed the safest thing to say. Lenny— or whoever— leaned back in the magenta chair and smiled.

"Oh, come on, Velvet. I know you better than that. You couldn't keep your mouth shut if somebody put a gun to your head, could you? And you're always looking for a buck. So you went looking for bucks at the paper. How much did he pay you? Three hundred? Five?" He laughed softly, a street laugh, not college-boy at all. "Did you have to blow him on top of that?"

"Fuck you," she said; it was half-automatic, and it was half-fright. God, who was this guy? Had he already been to the paper, talked to Bradshaw?

"How much?"

She blinked and said, "Pardon?" His smile was as thin and red as a paper cut.

"How much? Fifty? Twenty-five? Ten? Are you a ten-buck-a-fuck whore yet, Velvet, or is that coming in the next couple of years? Is that your career path?"

She stood up, opened her mouth, and sprinted for the kitchen while he was still waiting for her retort. She grabbed Robby's big black-handled Ginsu knife and gasped in deep scared breaths, as she waited for him to come around the corner.

From the other room he said, "Come on, Velvet, I'm not going to hurt you. Come on out."

She firmed up her grip on the knife and jammed herself in the corner between the coffee machine and the sink.

"You get the fuck out, right now!" she yelled.

"I'm afraid I can't do that." He sounded relaxed as hell. Something made a metallic click in the other room. She froze and thought, *It's the heating, the central heating, that's all. Goddamn old buildings, they creak all the time, maybe he knocked something off the table, maybe his knee popped, maybe my knee popped, oh god, maybe it was a—*

He came around the corner in one long, graceful step. Over the top of the gun, his eyes were cool and calm.

"Drop the knife, Velvet," he said quietly. "I don't want to hurt you."

She had never in her life had a gun pointed at her, never. Funny how it made things happen deep in her guts, funny how her eyes kept coming back to the sleek silver gun and the big black hole pointing at her. *I need to remember what kind of gun it is, in case they ask me later,* she thought. *It's big. It's a big fucking gun.*

Her hand was trying to drop the knife. She wrapped her left hand around it, too. Lenny's eyes stopped looking quite so calm.

"I mean it. No joking around, Velvet, put the fucking knife down or I'm going to blow a hole right through you. Don't be stupid."

The knife wriggled out of her hands and clanged noisily on the tile floor, spun away out of her reach underneath a cabinet. The silver tip of it winked up at her. She didn't know what to do with her hands, and settled for holding them up.

"Come on out here," he told her, and flicked the

gun just a fraction of an inch. "Come on, I'm not going to hurt you. Let's go."

She didn't remember walking from the kitchen to the couch, but the shock of leather on her legs was like a wet towel. Lenny settled in the magenta chair again, gun resting comfortably on his knee, still pointed right at her.

"You like hockey?" he asked conversationally. She shook her head and swallowed hard. "Me neither. Too much violence."

He wanted her to laugh, but she couldn't. Her arms ached from holding them over her head.

"Simon says put your arms down, Velvet. Relax. Nothing's going to happen here. Why don't you tell me what you told the paper?" He grinned that college-boy-innocent grin again. "I already paid for it, didn't I?"

She swallowed and said, "Just what I already told you, I swear."

"I don't think I believe that."

The headache was coming back, stomping iron boots along the inside of her skull; orange juice and coffee boiled in her stomach. She wondered if he'd believe her if she said she had to go to the bathroom.

"Would you please just tell me who you are?" she asked wearily. God, she was tired, her whole body ached, her throat throbbed. "Please?"

He dug in his jacket and took out a black leather wallet, flipped it open and slid it across. The plastic identification card in the top said FBI in big blue letters. Under it, he flashed his college-boy smile. His name was Garrick James.

"Now you know. Have you ever seen this man?" he asked, and dug in the pocket of his preppy jacket for a black-and-white photograph. He slid it over the table toward her. She took a quick glance at it.

"No," she said, and then took another look. Her hesitation was too long.

"Yes." He said it for her. "Okay, where? Where'd you see him? Who was he with? Burt Marshall?"

The photo glared at her. She swallowed hard.

"I never saw him."

He sighed and took the picture back. She kept staring at the coffee table where it had been, as if it had left a scorch mark.

"Velvet, please, I'm not the enemy here, I promise. I'm trying to help you, but you're making it pretty damn hard. You do understand that if you've seen this man, if you have any knowledge of what he's doing, he'll stop at nothing to kill you? I can protect you, if you'll just level with me."

"It wasn't an accident, was it?" she asked. "Burt, I mean. Somebody really did kill him."

Leather squeaked as he shifted. When she looked up, he'd put the gun in a shoulder holster under the preppy jacket.

"Yes. Somebody really did. You're lucky they didn't kill you, too. Maybe they just didn't get to you in time."

Even though the hockey game was muted, a dim whisper came from the TV set, a roar as somebody scored or somebody bled. She stared blankly at the screen.

"Robby thinks it's the wiseguys," she said.

"Robby's probably right. Where'd you see this guy, Velvet?"

The roar on the TV was loud enough that it was audible even through the muting. She looked up at the screen. The cameraman was confused, the picture shaking unsteadily. She couldn't figure out why he was panning the crowd.

"At the dry cleaners. Elegance. Highland Park."

After a stunned silence, Lenny repeated, "Elegance
Dry Cleaners. Burt Marshall owned part of it."

"Yeah. The Arab guy from the picture, he was there,
and this creepy little asshole named Mr. Julian—"

She forgot to finish. The cameraman had managed
to get his shot stable, a crowd shot; the picture jerked
unevenly as he pulled the focus, shocked confused
faces, a blur of motion— he pulled back again

Velvet screamed.

A burning man plunged down the steps of the
arena, arms waving, bright enough to fuzz out the
TV picture. People piled out of his way, mouths
open, eyes wild.

Velvet fumbled for the remote, but Agent James
got there first, found the mute button. Screams exploded into the cool air of the apartment, ringing,
echoing. Over them, the announcers.

Not sure what we're seeing here

*My god, Jim, it looks like that man is on fire. Yes, he's
definitely on fire. As you can see, Security is right behind
him*

*Anybody see how it happened? When did it start? He's
fully in flames now, folks, pushing a hot dog vendor out
of his way*

Agent James looked over at Velvet, his face tight
and pale, and said, "I guess it's a little late for damage control now."

Twenty-six
Robby

It was a good thing that Mark had arrived to act as bank, because Kelly hadn't bothered to show. Robby brushed past him on her way to the beer stand, passed him three thick wallets, and made sure he had them before she continued on her way. Of all of them, he was the only one with an actual pick-pocketing conviction.

He had a tendency to cockiness that made her nervous. This time, he caught her eye and winked, an absolute violation of common sense and every rule. She swept her eyes blankly on and decided to tell Jim, once and for all, that she didn't want Mark to bank for her. No matter what.

Two drunks were arguing ferociously near the beer stand, drinks sloshing as they gestured. One of them demonstrated high sticking with his forearm. Robby ducked the struggle and continued on. Ahead, a weaving couple of teenaged girls giggled and gossiped in line. The brunette had an open purse and a vacant look, but Robby decided against it; the blonde looked too intelligent and only a little drunk. She passed them up for a party of business people still dressed in wrinkled, beer-spotted suits and lightened two pockets and two purses, a heavy enough haul to make her immediately turn and scan for Mark.

He caught the signal and started in her direction, a loose easy walk. He'd lost most of his stiffness over the last year, but there was something about him, something that made cops' eyes turn in his direction even when he was innocent. He was a bad choice for bank, she felt it in her bones. Something would happen.

He brushed past her, and she passed two of the wallets over— Jim could have taken three without breaking a sweat, but two was the limit of Mark's agility— and watched helplessly as Mark fumbled the second one. It fell to the concrete floor with a meaty smack that sounded like a bomb explosion to her. As Mark bent down for it, she kicked it with the side of her foot and sent it sailing away into the crowd. When he straightened up, she fixed him with a glare.

He knew better than to try to pick it up. He'd *always* known better than that.

He mouthed, *Sorry*, and moved on. She blew out a shaking breath and decided to take a break. The hockey game sounded as if it had reached a fever pitch of excitement. She ambled through a short dark tunnel and paused on the crowded landing, thinking about lifting the wallet that stuck half-out of the blue jeans in front of her.

A hand grabbed her arm. She looked up into Jim's chalk-pale face.

"What's wrong?" She had to shout to be heard over the screaming of the crowd. He pointed. Directly down the stairs, toward the ice.

A man wrapped in white fire staggered down concrete steps, arms waving helplessly. People bobbed backward from him in waves. He missed a step and fell face forward, sliding down several risers and leaving a trail of burning flesh behind.

He was still moving. Oh, God, he was still moving. She watched as he clawed his way upright and smashed into the plastic screen around the ice, smearing it with oozes of blood and flaky black skin— and then the plastic slumped with him, as if it were tired of holding him back.

He slithered over the barrier and crawled onto the ice. Hockey players veered off to one side of the rink, like birds wheeling. The man crawled, or slid, another foot or two.

The ice bubbled. He was still burning.

She realized that her hands had gone to her mouth, turned to bury her face in Jim's chest. His arm went around her. She could feel him shaking.

Somebody on the P.A. yelled, "Be calm, everybody please stay calm, there's no cause for alarm, stay in your seats." Nobody listened. Jim tugged her back down the tunnel, forced her into a run. She heard the rumble of feet behind her.

They attained the safety of the bathroom alcove as a wave of people erupted from the tunnel, shoving, screaming, blind with panic. A young black man fell only a few feet away, curled into a ball. Robby couldn't see the kicks that hit him, only the blood. He crawled toward them, far enough that she could grab his hand and pull him into the relative peace of the alcove.

"Jesus Christ," Jim kept saying, over and over, like a prayer. "Jesus Christ."

The black man, sitting at Robby's feet with blood streaming down his face, said, "Man, I hope somebody got that on tape."

Twenty-seven
Martin

Martin was having a dream about chickens when suddenly, without any warning at all, one of them blew up with a BANG that sounded as big as the world. He jerked upright in his leather chair, blinked, and saw the massive shadow of Agent Jennings standing in the doorway. The door was just swinging back from its impact with the wall.

"Agent Carling," Jennings said urgently. "Ma'am, you'd better come see this, now."

Carling had been napping as well, but her eyes were clear and her movements precise when she got up to follow him. There were fabric wrinkles on her cheek where it had pressed against her suit sleeve. As he stood up, Martin realized he had one hell of a crick in his neck.

Jennings had a hockey game on TV—at least, it looked like a hockey game, a big ring of ice, plastic walls to protect the crowd from flying pucks and sticks, a huge crowd of people. Only the people were emptying out in a stampeding frenzy. The hockey players circled at the far end of the rink, swooping in confused Brownian motion near the goal. A knot of uniformed security stood on the ice to one side, near the wall, around—

"What the hell is that?" Carling put her finger on a bright spot of white in the screen.

"Watch," Jennings said, and turned the sound up.

Jim, I'm not sure what we're seeing now— the crowd is panicking, running for the exits— I think that's— yes, that's the paramedics coming down the aisle now— Jim, can you— camera two, can you focus on— yes, thanks. There you see the paramedics approaching, and there's the man who's down. You can still see the fire on his back, my God, he's still burning, it's unbelievable—

"They didn't catch the beginning of it," Jennings said. "Just started showing him when he came down the stairs burning."

"Where is it?" Carling demanded.

"Dallas. Dallas, Texas. Stars versus the Mighty Ducks."

On the screen, the picture froze and blacked out, replaced almost immediately by a slow-motion image of a man wrapped in flaring white flames, staggering like a movie monster. A vendor in a blue and white apron fell backward, mouth open in a silent O of astonishment, spilled popcorn a white halo around his head.

Okay, folks, here's the original picture we had of this terrible tragedy— looks to me like he's already fully on fire here— could this be some kind of publicity stunt gone wrong, do you think?

Greg, I certainly hope that's not the case. As you can see from the slow motion, he continues to go down the stairs— sorry about the picture quality— and people are beginning to realize something's wrong— some of them must think it's a special effect because they aren't moving— Greg, what is that, do you think? There, hanging off of him?

Uh, Jim, I don't think we should go into that right now. That looks like the remains of a sports jacket he's wearing, wouldn't you say? Maybe a business suit?

The slow-motion footage cut back to real-time and the jittery motion of a hand-held camera, as it panned the faces of hockey players pressed against plastic, staring. The camera panned down to a team of paramedics working feverishly on a lump of red and black, no more fire, just meat.

Carling said quietly, "The cat's out of the bag, gentlemen. We're out of time."

On the screen, announcers continued a feverish play-by-play.

Uh, Jim, perhaps we'd better update our late-tuning viewers. Folks, we're at Reunion Arena in Dallas, Texas, where the Stars-Mighty Ducks game has just been tragically interrupted by a man who appeared to burst into flames—

That's right, Greg, he appeared to burst into flames at the top of the stairs and run down toward the ice, collapsing near the bottom and sparking a panicked rush for the exits— we have people wounded in the crush— we don't know the condition of the man who caught on fire— Greg, what exactly do we know right now?

Uh, Jim, the score of the game stands at 2 to 1 in favor of the Stars—

Carling said tightly, "Jennings, get us on a plane."

Twenty-eight
Paolo

"Coors Light," Paolo whispered in the direction of the waitress's apron. She leaned over to hear better.

"Sorry?" She cupped one shell-pink ear toward him. He stared down the expanse of her cleavage. Pale skin, thin blue veins showing through. He liked that.

"Coors Light," he repeated louder. She nodded and stalked away toward a yelling table of drunks half-out of their business suits. The floor was crisp with peanut shells and sticky with spilled beer, like bad peanut brittle. He'd always liked peanut brittle, he thought, and munched contemplatively on a dry unsalted pretzel stick. Pralines, too. The kind that turned to raw sugar on his tongue.

There were plenty of hookers working the bar, but Velvet wasn't one of them. He'd been to her place, but it was a wreck, trashed. No sign of her in any of the usual hangouts, no word on the street about her. None of the other girls had heard from her or about her.

He nibbled his pretzel and felt the pressure of anxiety in his stomach. He didn't have any other leads; there were no other hangouts. If she didn't show here, she didn't show.

And he'd have to explain to Ming where Velvet had gone. That wouldn't be pretty at all.

A beer thumped down on the table in front of him, sweating with cold. He slid the money across the table so he could watch the waitress bend over again, then forgot her as soon as she walked away. Velvet had skin like that, pale and pretty, and everything else, too.

Nobody in the room competed.

He sucked down beer and stared blankly at the big-screen TV; the table of drunks had started screaming and throwing peanuts at it. One of them stood up on his chair, leaned slowly left, and toppled over on the guy next to him.

He couldn't see what they were so upset about, except that the hockey game had stopped. The players were skating around in tight circles at the far end of the ice, hands on their hips, shaking their heads. There were a bunch of people who didn't look like players on the ice, too, near the edge; one of them was lying down. Great. A fan jumped the wall and had a heart attack, or got slammed, or something. Who cared?

The picture fuzzed out and was replaced with blurry footage of a guy on fire staggering down the steps, while hockey fans scrambled back from him in human waves. Paolo sat riveted, beer half-raised to his lips, staring.

One of the drunks threw a beer bottle at the TV, but it missed by a mile and pegged a big burly-looking guy in the back of the head. He had a table full of friends who looked like linebackers. They all had Marine haircuts.

"Turn it up!" somebody screamed, and the crowd in the bar took it up like a chant. The bartender messed with a remote control, and the sound buzzed and whispered until it finally competed with the shouting in the room.

Appears that security reacted very quickly to deal with

*this potential threat to the fans and players— as you can
see, three of them arrive very quickly after the man is down
and begin trying to beat out the flames with their coats—
also, as we clearly see in the tape, helpful fans tried to
help the victim by pouring drinks on him as he passed—*

*Well, Jim, if you ask me, what we're seeing is exactly
what's wrong with professional sports today. The fans just
get way too involved in things. I'm sure this guy was flicking his lighter up in the rafters and—*

*Thanks for that insight, Greg. Excuse me for interrupt-
ing, but I have definite word now that the victim is dead,
I repeat, the victim has just been pronounced dead from
severe burns. What a tragedy for the sport, the players,
and the fans.*

*I'm telling you, Jim, this is the kind of thing that gives
hockey a bad name.*

"What's the fucking score?" one of the drunks
yelled.

The five jarheads at the table near the TV were
up and walking. Paolo sipped beer and munched
pretzels and thought about Velvet's story of the client
bursting into flames.

Could happen, he decided. Definitely could happen.

The fight was okay, but the businessmen didn't have
much of a chance against the jarheads, not even with
a couple of bouncers joining in to break it up. Not
much of a substitute for the hockey game. Paolo
watched until he'd finished his beer, dropped a dollar
on the table for tip, and took one last walk around the
bar.

Not there. Ming was going to be very unhappy.

By the door, a delivery guy was loading papers into
a machine marked FREE. The logo on the side said
BIG D GAZETTE. Paolo grabbed one off the top
and flipped to the back for the personal ads. He sat

down at an empty table nearby and started circling the ones that caught his eye.

Young, shy SWF seeks M for friendship and companionship. Favorite colors: black and blue

Friendly curvaceous SWF seeks WM for cuddles and communication

Bored? See me. I'm a MF with vast experience in what's most important to you— marital status no obstacle

Not bad, he decided, and folded the paper up.

Velvet's face stared at him from the inside bottom right. It was an old mug shot, not very flattering. She had that defiant crazy look in her eyes. He laid the paper out carefully and found the article that went with the picture.

He read it silently, lips moving, one thick finger marking his place. While he was still working on it, two or three cops showed up to haul the businessmen and jarheads out; he hardly noticed.

When he was done, he sat back and closed his eyes.

"Jeez, Velvet," he whispered aloud. "Oh, Jeez."

He knew he'd have to kill her.

Twenty-nine
Velvet

Agent Garrick James bought Velvet a hamburger and fries and a shake, which was a good thing, because even though she wanted to throw up she needed the stuff in her stomach to do it with. She took tiny dogged bites of the hamburger until she got it all down, licked the ketchup off her fingers, and munched nervously on french fries while he drove down Industrial to Oak Lawn. The shake was chocolate and too watery, and every time she sucked on the straw the taste of plastic made her want to gag.

"Where're you from?" she asked, to take her mind off the throb in her head. Agent James looked over, surprised, and almost ran over a man in a red flannel shirt shuffling across the street.

"Kansas."

Farmer country. She wrinkled her nose and took another gulp of shake. Shakes for the shakes, that was what Cousin Floyd had always said, and if anybody should know, it was Floyd. He'd emptied out every liquor store in Verbina County.

"Where in Kansas?"

Another look. She wondered if he was lying to her, or only wondering what the hell she was doing.

"K.C. How about you? Where're you from?"

She looked out the passenger window of the car at a bunch of ragged-looking men sitting in an empty lot, passing a bottle back and forth. None of them seemed to be enjoying it much.

"Hell."

"That's melodramatic," he said. She shrugged. "Look, I promise, you won't be in any danger. You just sit in the car while I go into the dry cleaners and ask a few questions, then I'll take you to my office. We'll find a safe place for you, until we're ready to arrest these men."

She perked up a little at the thought of that. Witness Protection. Didn't that mean, like, expensive hotels and nice food? Of course, the bad part was the testifying, but she'd done that before. At least this time she'd get something more in return than the dead shattered look in her mother's eyes. *Hey, Mom, I'm a fucking hero, how about that?*

She could almost see Mom's absentminded smile and hear her say, *That's nice, Amy. Happy birthday.*

Agent James made the turn on to Oak Lawn. They cruised past the gray buildings in the Design District— squat concrete buildings that were almost aggressively ugly— passed under the freeway, and headed toward Highland Park.

"Hey, Agent James?"

"Yes?"

She twisted around in her seat to face him. He still looked like a college boy, but the eyes were different— cool, calm, distant. A guy with a purpose. She wasn't sure if she liked him that way.

"Remember when you tried to shake me down for a blow job?"

He braked for a red light and kept staring straight ahead as he said, "Yes, I remember."

"Did you mean that, or was that just, like, part of the investigation?"

He blushed pretty well, a Valentine-red flush that worked its way up from his collar and along his cheeks. His ears turned shell pink.

"I was wearing a wire, Velvet. I was just doing my job."

"I'm good at it," she said. "Blow jobs, I mean. I'm okay at the other stuff, but man, I'm a fucking artist at blow jobs. Want one?"

The ears turned the color of maraschino cherries.

"You're not in my price range."

"I'll do it for free."

"Why?"

She started to answer, stopped, and turned back to face the road.

Truth was, she didn't know.

After the third traffic light, the stores took on a glossy look, like they'd been Tefloned. The houses had a heavy dignified self-satisfied look, like overweight bankers. The street narrowed to discourage casual visitors.

"It's up ahead," she told him. "On the right."

It was just the way she'd remembered it— standoffish, stuck-up, dark. Agent James eased the car into a narrow parking space and shut the engine off. She couldn't tell if the place was closed or open, but he didn't seem to have any doubts.

"You stay here, keep the doors locked, wait for me," he said. She nodded. His eyes locked with hers, but she couldn't tell what he was thinking. "Thanks for the offer."

"No charge." She flinched when he slammed the door, dug her nails in her palms, and sat stiffly. The door opened for him, but, of course, it would, wouldn't it? Through the dark-tinted window, she saw him go to the counter and talk to a model-perfect blonde that might or might not have been the same one from last time. The model went in the back. Agent James followed her.

The rest of the chocolate shake disappeared in one hissing slurp. She looked for someplace to put her trash and tossed it in the back floorboard. As she did, something sticking out from under the floormat caught her eye.

It was an ID card. In this one, Agent James was squinting at the camera, looking older than he was, and his name was David Van Housen. It said he was Miami police.

She fumbled open the glove compartment. Two more IDs, one Dallas PD for Brian Groves, one Texas Rangers— -the cops, not the baseball players— for Henry Samms. They all had his picture on them.

She clutched the three IDs like a bad poker hand and swallowed hard.

The FBI one was fake, too, had to be. Real feds didn't carry around an assortment like this.

There was no witness protection. There was no protection at all.

She was sitting right where they wanted her.

Thirty
Ming

Ming opened her eyes to the awareness of someone with her in the darkness of her bedroom, someone unknown. The fear felt like a wave of heat over her skin, muscles tensing and twitching under the strain.

She lay still and waited. After a few seconds, someone struck a match. The bloom of yellow illuminated an evil mask— no, it was only a man's face. He touched the match to the end of his cigarette.

"What do you want?" Her throat felt as dry as concrete, her tongue as thick as lead.

He didn't answer. The glowing tip of the cigarette bobbed in the dark as it moved.

Something struck her across the legs. She caught a scream in her throat and bowed her head to swallow the pain she knew would follow— but there was no pain. She reached down and found that he'd dropped a newspaper on her bed.

"Read it," he said. She cleared her throat, but it didn't help.

"May I turn on a light?"

"Sure."

She flicked on the bedside lamp. He leaned against a bare brick wall, smoking, staring at her— an average-looking man, brown hair, casual clothes. He'd just showered; the ends of his hair were damp and stuck in sharp points to his neck. Beside him was a larger man in blue jeans and a plain black cotton T-shirt. He had a gun in a shoulder holster.

She scanned the first half of the page, lingering over items about police department reorganizations, a salmonella scare, the latest HIV statistics. The man took the cigarette out of his mouth and said, "Bottom of the first page."

She unfolded the paper with a snap, and Velvet's face stared at her, caught defiant by a police camera six years ago. She began to read, forcing herself to do it slowly, each and every word.

When she was done, she looked up at her visitors. The one with the cigarette dropped it on the floor and ground it out with a twist of his foot.

"Phone call," he said, and pulled a cellular phone from his jacket. He pressed a button and held it out to her. She took it and held it to her ear as the number dialed.

It was answered on the second ring, by a man who said, "Ming?"

Surely her throat was full of concrete now; every swallow seemed a monumental effort, every breath a victory. She closed her eyes.

"Yes."

"I have to explain to you how disappointed I am about all this. I am pretty fucking disappointed."

"Yes, I understand."

"Somebody took off one of my people yesterday. Burned him alive. You understand me?"

"Yes."

"Today I get this paper on my desk, Ming, and I am seriously unhappy about the way this girl shot off her mouth."

He waited for her to say something, but she couldn't. Breathing was enough of an effort.

"She even mentioned your name," he said.

"Yes, I know."

"I'm going to ask you one question, Ming. Have you found her?"

"No," she whispered. There was a long silence.

"You call me back in eight hours, Ming. When you do, the only word I want you to say is yes, understand?"

"I understand." The line went dead. She offered the phone back; the brown-haired man put it in an inside jacket pocket.

His companion went around to the other door and opened it, looked through. He nodded. The smaller man said, "We'll wait in there. When you have her or you know where she is, you tell us. If you don't have her in eight hours, we take you in."

She understood that as clearly as she'd understood the cold voice on the telephone. It had now become a matter of survival, hers or Velvet's.

There would be no question of the winner.

Two hours later, she listened to Paolo's wind-ruffled voice on the telephone say, "But she's not there, Ming, I already looked. I went to all the places, and wherever she is, it ain't around here. Nobody around here's seen her for two, three days."

"Who was she with two or three days ago?" Ming had to fight to keep her voice calm, for the benefit of the two men next door waiting to kill her.

"Nobody, I guess. Nobody regular."

"You guess? I have no time for guessing, Paolo, find out. Find out *now*. Go everywhere and ask everyone, hire people if you must, but find her. She's not gone. I know she's not gone."

The wind fuzzed his reply, but she knew he'd do what she said. Paolo was a dog, loyal and mildly intelligent and willing to love the one who kicked him.

Yet he could be a rabid dog, when necessary. That was the most valuable thing of all. At the end of the evening, when the blood was cool, she wanted to look down at the broken body of Velvet Daniels and be unable to recognize her from any other pile of meat. Paolo would do that for her.

At the end. But there would be a long slow red crawl to the end.

Thirty-one
Martin

The airlines wouldn't let Carling use her cell phone on the flight. Seething like a volcano, she used the credit-card driven model the tight-lipped flight attendant indicated. The strain was starting to show a little; her hair looked a little ruffled, her suit a little wrinkled. Martin was almost sure he saw a glint of weariness in her eyes.

"Mrs. Womack?" Carling said into the phone, and breathed a long sigh. "I'm not on a secure line, so we'll have to make this brief, not to mention that it's going on my VISA. What did you get?"

Martin had the window seat, which coincidentally was the emergency exit seat. He'd been reluctant to take it, because he'd once seen a special about getting out of airplanes in emergencies. He'd had nightmares after that show of being in this very seat, people screaming, flames all around, and the instructions kept getting smaller and smaller and longer and longer. He decided to read the special card in the seat pocket again, just in case.

"Not much," Carling was saying. He looked over at her and raised his eyebrows in a silent *what?* "Okay, that's something, anyway. You take the next flight into Dallas— yes, that's right. Perfect."

She cut the connection and gave him a small quiet smile. He hadn't seen that one before, and he liked the way her lip curled.

"AARP to the rescue?" he guessed.

"Mrs. Womack has some very interesting chemical analysis of the preacher's clothes. I think you'll be satisfied." She reclaimed her VISA card from the slot and studied it suspiciously before putting it in her purse.

"We'll get there just about midnight. Any thoughts about procedure?"

"Would I be out of line, if I asked about a hotel?"

She gave him a long serious look, smile fading.

"You're right. We need the sleep. Womack and Mendoza will arrive about three o'clock, we might as well wait for them to arrive before we do any serious thinking." She looked around for the flight attendant and lowered her voice. "Don't eat the food here."

"Words to live by."

The plane hit turbulence, bounced, dropped. He felt his stomach hit the ground hard.

"I'm not just talking about the normal hazards of mystery meat. I think we may have picked up a couple of traveling companions who aren't exactly tourists."

"What?" He craned his neck in an attempt to see over the blue headrest. "Who?"

"Quiet!" She squeezed his knee for emphasis and let it stay, a light distracting pressure. "They're behind us. Two men, traveling light. The flight attendant had a long conversation with them, and I didn't like the look of it, so don't eat anything, don't drink anything, don't even get up to go to the john, if you can help it."

Her hand felt warm as sunlight on his knee. He stared at it and said, "What do we do when the plane lands?"

"You leave that up to me and Mr. Mendoza, I'm sure we'll think of something." The words sounded confident, but she looked tired, almost vulnerable. Her hand moved a couple of inches. Up his thigh.

"Are— " Martin cleared his throat and glanced around for the flight attendant, small lurking children, nosy grandmothers. "Do you think we could— stay together? Tonight?"

She cocked her head to one side, eyes luminous and controlled. He felt something bend in his fingers, and realized he was still holding the emergency exit procedures card. He missed the pocket twice trying to put it back.

"Is that a proposition?" She sounded amused. He didn't dare look at her directly.

"Uh— " He cleared his throat again. "Yes. I think so."

Hard to believe she was the same woman he remembered from the Washington basement— smooth warm skin, a hot hungry mouth, she'd been so completely real, so amazingly *present*. He wanted to cross the distance again, hear her say his name in a whisper like raw silk.

She leaned over, and the smell of her overwhelmed him— perfume, skin, hair, even the slightly stale smell of her clothes. Her lips brushed his, warm and moist. Her hand traveled further up his thigh.

"I think," she whispered, and lightly kissed the skin just under his ear, "I think we'd better get some sleep, Marty. We'll need it."

She had just effectively zeroed his chance for sleep, and she knew it. He saw it in the flash of her eyes, the crooked half-smile.

He kissed her, felt her lips part under his. It only lasted a second, before she put her hand flat on his chest and pushed him a safe distance away. The air felt thick and hot between them.

As he gulped in deep breaths, he saw the flight attendant watching them like a nun. She hustled off down the aisle when he caught her eye.

"Let's not do that," Carling said, smoothing her skirt. "I need to keep a clear head."

He nodded and turned face forward, staring at the headrest in front of him. The plane dipped down, descending, and a constellation of lights wheeled outside the windows.

"Won't happen again," he said to the headrest, and thought he heard her laugh just as the captain turned on the NO SMOKING and FASTEN SEATBELTS signs and announced the weather in Dallas. Cold, windy, expected freezing rain and sleet in the next few days.

"No smoking," Carling said, and snapped her seatbelt shut. "Words to live by, Marty. Words to live by. Have you thought about what would happen if somebody flamed out in an airplane?"

He closed his eyes, opened them, and reached for the emergency exit procedures again.

"Who are they?" Martin turned to look over his shoulder at the headlights of the cab behind them. Carling nudged him none too gently.

"Quit staring. Want to know about Fathi el Haddiz?"

"Well, I assumed he was political. You know, an extremist."

Their cab driver, obviously not a native Dallasite, was taking advantage of a long red light to consult a Mapsco. He muttered something under his breath, tossed the street map on the floor, and drummed his fingers on the steering wheel.

"He probably started out that way, but he went commercial. He's a businessman. If what we suspect is true, he's going to take this technology— or this process— whatever it is, and sell it to the true believers for whatever he can get. He's just as likely to sell to the IRA or the Neo-Nazis as he is to any Arab group." Carling smiled grimly. "He's very good. Also, he's very well staffed, which is something of a problem right now. He knows we're on his trail, and he's going to be assigning people to cover us, if he hasn't already."

Martin resisted the urge to glance over his shoulder again. It didn't save him from another nudge in his ribs, a harder one. He looked down and saw the handle of a gun.

"Are you going to shoot me?"

She gave him a disgusted look. "Just take it. If I wanted to shoot you, I'd point the *barrel* at you. Keep it with you. I assume you know how to shoot?"

She said it like it was something everyone learned in grade school, like multiplication tables. Her face went blank as he shook his head.

"I thought everybody in Texas knew how to shoot. Never mind, here's the safety, I've already loaded a round in the chamber. Just take it off of safety, point and shoot. And try not to shoot me, if you can help it."

It was a minor miracle that the cab driver had missed the whole exchange; he was busy squinting at street signs and muttering again. Martin gently pushed the gun away with two fingers and shook his head.

"I'd just blow my foot off." She was going to protest, he could see it; to stop her he leaned forward and tapped on the glass separating them from the driver. "Hey! Buddy! Take a left up here."

"What're you doing?"

"Giving him directions to my office. We can pick up my car there. It'll save us a few hours of driving around while this guy figures out street signs."

She didn't seem to approve, but didn't protest, either; she sat silently, eyes narrowed, while the cab darted down one street after another. From time to time she took a hand mirror out of her purse and checked the cab behind them, which seemed a little too much cloak-and-dagger for his taste. Six blocks before he told the driver the last turn, the other cab turned off and disappeared.

"Free and clear," he sighed, and slumped back against the worn leatherette upholstery. The cab driver lit up a cigarette and rolled down the window to let in a blast of chilling air. "Up ahead on the right. Turn in to the parking garage, I'll use my card to let you in."

Carling did not seem to have relaxed much. As they descended into the dark tunnel, she looked back over her shoulder, the first overt sign of nervousness he'd seen from her.

"What's wrong?" he asked. She shook her head.

The fluorescent-striped swing-arm of the gate swung up like an ax, and let the cab clatter through. Martin leaned forward and told the driver to go down three levels.

Nobody else was moving. What cars were left in the structure sat mute and dark, like modern sculpture. The patches of lights looked weak and watery, the dark as thick as oil.

The cab eased to a stop at the third level, crept forward toward the plain white Lincoln Martin indicated. He passed over too much money in cab fare, since Carling didn't jump to volunteer. The cabbie grinned and demonstrated perfect dentures, then left them standing in a cloud of stinking exhaust.

As his tires squealed into the turn, Carling did a slow circle to survey the garage. Fluorescent tube lights buzzed like colonies of flies, and somewhere metal squeaked in the wind.

"Let's go," Martin suggested, and fumbled his keys out of his coat pocket. She grabbed his wrist and held up one finger; she bent and looked in his car window, shifted right, then left. After a long shivering silence, she shrugged.

"Go ahead." She waited until he'd put the key in the lock and opened the door before going around to the passenger side. He reached over and flipped up the lock.

As she slid in, he said, "Did you think they'd put a bomb in it?"

She shut her door and clicked her seatbelt shut, and smiled.

Tires squealed somewhere up above, moving fast. They both froze, staring at each other, and Martin swallowed hard and started the car. It took two coughing tries and shuddered when he threw it into reverse, a plowhorse forced to race.

Carling's hand came out of her coat pocket with the gun she'd tried to hand him. She laid it in her lap, casually; he was relieved that the barrel was pointing away.

As he shifted into drive, lights exploded out of the darkness behind them. He floored the Lincoln, felt it hesitate and then lunge forward. Slow. Too slow.

At first he thought the tire had blown out, but the wheel stayed steady in his hands, and the booms continued, and he realized somebody was shooting. Not Carling; she had turned to face backward, but was only starting to raise her gun.

Jesus, she'd been right, she'd been right all the time. He wondered if he'd ever have a chance to apologize.

He took the uphill turn too fast, skidded, felt the back end of the car slide and bounce off a concrete stanchion. Carling steadied her right hand with her left, sighted, and fired straight through his back window. It exploded in a network of stars. The noise was like a slap, a physical sting on his skin and a punch to his ears; he gagged on gunpowder. She fired again, two shots he thought, or three. His ears rang too much to be certain.

They picked up speed in the straightaway and he touched the brake for the curve, not too much, just enough; the tires screamed and shimmied, but held. He couldn't see the car behind them through the cracks in the rear window, but he heard them hit something with a thick metal crunch.

"Did they stop?" he yelled. The wind cut through the shattered window and blew Carling's hair back like a wind sock, revealing the stark pallor of her face, the fixed wide eyes.

"Drive!" she shouted back. He hit the gas hard and saw the EXIT light ahead, a beacon in the dark. The fluorescent gate was down.

He fumbled for his card, dropped it, fished frantically. *What are you doing?* he thought. In the middle of a car chase, he was trying to pay his toll.

He put his foot all the way to the floor. The Lincoln growled and hissed forward over the concrete.

The barrier had a core of metal; he heard the squeal as it bent and slashed a screaming cut down the side of his car. More booms. He pulled his head in toward his shoulders like a turtle, and the Lincoln slammed down the short ramp. The front end hit the street in a shower of sparks, but then the tires grabbed and the building fell away behind them, the dark mouth of the parking garage closing in the distance.

Martin became aware that his chest hurt. He let

his breath out and gasped in a fresh sweet lungful of air, and looked over at Carling.

She was still facing backward, one hand clutching the headrest, the one with the gun hanging at her side. She still looked chalk-white, hair wild around her face.

"Are you okay?" he asked. She didn't seem to hear him. "Carling, are you—"

She fell back slowly, like a rag doll, hitting the back of her head on the dashboard. Martin screamed her name and slammed on the brakes. The car fishtailed to a stop, the rear window fell out of the frame and spread square pieces on the backseat like parade confetti.

The whole front of her shirt was soaked red. The bullet hole looked very small, the size of a button, only in the wrong place, just below her right breast. He gathered her up in his arms and got her in the seat, tilted the back down so she was lying nearly flat.

Her eyes fluttered open and found his.

"Marty?" she said, her voice was shockingly soft, a little girl's voice. "Don't put me on the machines. Please don't do that."

He remembered the other car and looked back. Nothing. Nothing he could see.

As he ran red lights and broke speed limits, he dialed her cell phone one-handed and told Parkland Hospital that he was bringing her in.

They were waiting by the ER doors, two tired residents, three nurses. Martin held Carling's hand as they wheeled her in. She opened her eyes again, but didn't seem to see him at all, like the day he'd found Sally and she'd opened her eyes, but they'd just rolled like marbles, hadn't seen him, had never seen him again.

They left him at the double doors with Carling's blood on his hands. He wasn't even aware that he was crying until a passing nurse handed him a tissue.

Thirty-two
Robby

Mark had a broken nose and two broken fingers, courtesy of the rush for the exits. Robby waited with him while the paramedics fixed him up. Jim was nowhere to be seen. She had no way of asking Mark with all the inquiring ears around, but she thought Jim had probably collected the take and taken advantage of the confusion to get home safely.

Mark tilted his head back and snuffled loudly. The cotton plugs in his nostrils were thick with blood. He gave her a puppy-dog look as the paramedic taped his fingers.

"My dose," he said. "How's it look?"

"Swollen," she told him, and patted him lightly on the knee. "It'll give you that sinister look."

"Wodderful. I gad't breathe." He stared morosely down at his fingers, as the medic finished with them. "This sugs."

"At least you're alive, pal," the paramedic said. He had the war-weary look of a career man. "Got at least one guy ain't so lucky."

"The man who burned?" Robby asked. The paramedic met her eyes, but his face was as blank and impersonal as looking in a mirror. "Was it murder?"

"Tell you what, I worked a lot of burn cases, and

I never seen nobody just burst into flames, I don't care what they tell you at the wacko conventions. Always something chemical involved, if you ask me. Murder, accident . . ." He made a seesaw motion with his hand. "Who the hell knows? Whatever it was, he was one messed-up guy, I can say that."

"Did he smell of anything? Gasoline? Anything like that?"

This time he really looked at her, but it wasn't much of an improvement; now it was suspicion, not weariness.

"Playing detective?" he asked, and gave her a cool smile. "No, nothing like that. Smelled like any other burned body. Okay, pal, you're fixed up. Make sure you get those breaks X-rayed."

"Danks," Mark mumbled, and stood up. He had a large waffled shoeprint on the front of his shirt, and a smear of blood along his collar. "Gan I go home dow?"

The paramedic had already closed up shop, snapping his red box together like a fisherman who'd caught his limit. He nodded toward a harassed-looking black patrolman a few feet away.

"See that guy."

Mark actually started walking toward the policeman. Robby caught his elbow and pulled him gently aside to stand next to an overweight woman wearing a Rolling Stones T-shirt. The woman was arguing loudly with her son, a pale young man with brittle eyes.

"I wadt to go home," Mark said again. "Robby—"

"You don't go through him. I've had about enough trouble for one day. Go to the bathroom and go out the other exit. It's around the corner, he won't be able to see you leave. I'll talk to him and meet you outside."

He walked toward the bathroom like a condemned man going to the chair. She waited until she was sure he'd got it right before approaching the patrolman.

As she'd suspected, the cops were too busy, too confused, and too harried to do much more than take
a name and an address. She provided both— completely fictitious— and stood with a crowd of gawkers
as a white-sheeted lump was carted out of one of the
tunnels. She couldn't tell if the crowd's silence was
respectful or avid, and decided it didn't really matter,
not to the man on the cart.

What did he have in common with Arnold, burned
to death in his kitchen? Velvet's Burt, dead in a hotel
room?

The thought occurred to her that it might be random. She shivered, pulled her coat closer, and
walked, head down, to the exit.

A blue-white glare hit her in the face like lightning;
she put up one hand to shield her eyes and heard
shouting. The glare zipped away, leaving green after-
images like hostile ghosts.

The news crews were chasing the cops, paramedics,
and the white-sheeted gurney, a stampede of expensive on-camera suits and ragged-jeans cameramen, of
boom men swinging mikes like medieval lances. The
circus rushed by her, elbowing and shoving, and she
stood looking after them.

After a few seconds, she smiled and fingered a calf-
skin wallet that she'd tugged out of the pocket of
one of the newsmen. A prominent one, she thought;
she remembered his face from billboards.

She'd never liked reporters.

Mark was waiting by the car, shivering and miserable. She tuned out his mumbled complaints and
drove to the exit, which was jammed with incoming
news vans and rubberneckers and cars waiting to
leave. She watched the sullen glow of taillights and
thought about how strange it had been, how very
strange, watching a man die like that. No one seemed

to have felt much about it, really. No one seemed to care who he was, or how he'd caught on fire.

She wasn't sure she cared, either. Velvet had cared about the one in the hotel room— cared enough to try to help him, at least.

She'd looked down at Freddy Arnold and felt nothing except horror and revulsion, really. No sorrow for a man she'd known at least casually. No fear.

The stealing had been a shock reaction. She'd blanked out for a few minutes, and then his wallet was in her hand, and she was looking down at him from a great height, as if she'd floated to the ceiling. The smell—

It had been like Dublin. Like reaching for her father's blood-smeared wallet, that last piece of him still whole.

"Robby?" Mark touched her on the shoulder; she jerked as if he'd slapped her. "Uh, are we goidg?"

The line had moved forward two car lengths. Behind her, a Mercedes blared its horn. She took her foot off the brake and let the car creep on.

"Weird dight, huh?" said Mark. She nodded. "Did you see id?"

"I saw him running." It had all been so *strange*.

"What was id like?"

She looked over at him. His nose had swollen to twice its size, and bruises were forming around both eyes. He looked half-dead.

"Like a movie," she said. "Just like a movie."

By the time she had dropped Mark off and got back to the warehouse, it was nearly midnight, and all she could think about was a cup of Jim's hot cocoa, his arms around her, and the weightless oblivion of sleep. Through some trick of memory she kept smelling burnt flesh in the air, on her skin, on her clothes, or maybe it was just the smells of woodsmoke, barbecue pits, exhaust.

She was grateful for the dark stillness of the warehouse, though it made the hair on the back of her neck prickle to cross that empty, empty room toward Jim's door.

It wasn't dark enough. She slowed as she realized that the door was not completely closed, and a thin slice of yellow light glowed around the jamb. Jim was careful about things like that— kept his door locked, all the time. She stopped where she was, debating, heart racing, and heard a whisper.

No, a moan.

Jim.

She crossed the rest of the distance in a sprint, slammed the door back, and stared in stunned disbelief at the wreck of his room. The couch was slashed and thrown against one wall, the chair shoved on its side. The shelves had spilled out their books on the floor. Jim's prized big-screen television had a gaping hole in the center.

Jim lay against the couch. She threw herself to her knees next to him, unable to get her breath, saying his name over and over, but knowing he couldn't hear her. His face was swollen and bloodied, his legs clearly broken, the left badly enough that a knife of bone had sliced through his pants and blood soaked the carpet around him.

Worst of all were his fingers, his long clever magician's fingers. She bent her head and cried helplessly, desperately, at the sight of them broken like matchsticks.

As she dialed 911, still trying to force air into her aching lungs, he whispered, "They were looking for Velvet."

Thirty-three
Velvet

Velvet had gotten across the street by the time Agent Dimples came out to get her from the car. She ducked in an entryway, but knew he'd seen her, knew he was coming after her. She darted from one storefront to the other, but they were locked, closed up tight.

The response time of the Highland Park Police was legendary. She picked up a brick from a flower-bed and pitched it through a plate-glass window; as she'd hoped, alarms went off, whooping to the skies.

Not enough. He was coming at a loping run, as if he ran a lot. She took off down the sidewalk, regretting all those hours at the bar, those candy bars between tricks. Her legs felt like mud. She heard the slap of his shoes behind her.

She gained the next corner, a cluster of imposing houses with high rock walls and ornate gates. The second one down had a plain-looking gate of six-foot-tall wooden boards— operated with a motor, of course. She got her fingers under the gate and shoved it open enough to wiggle in, leaving two fingernails in the wood as it slammed back against her. She surveyed the back yard— Christ, what a yard!— and circled the pool to a tall stand of something that looked like corn but probably was more expensive.

She dropped gratefully down on the cold ground and hugged herself, shivering, waiting. The wind carried an echo of laughter. She pulled the corn plants aside and saw a family inside eating dinner in a kitchen from *Better Homes;* they were having something that looked like lasagna. Her stomach pitched.

From where she sat, Velvet had a perfect view of the garage— three cars, one heavy-looking Mercedes, one boxy-looking Volvo station wagon, and one white Jeep Cherokee, since everybody in Highland Park seemed to think they couldn't live without four-wheel drive. She wondered what the chances were that the rich left keys in their cars, and decided they weren't too good; the rich had invented paranoia, what with their alarm systems and electric gates and big dogs. She glanced around nervously for dogs, but found only evidence of kids— bright yellow and red plastic tricycles, ragged-looking dolls, dismembered pieces of toys she couldn't identify. If they had a dog, they kept it in at night.

An outside light snapped on, bathing the corn row in harsh white. She dropped flat and pressed her cheek to the cold dirt as the back door opened. Someone clumped down three steps and across the flagstones to the garage. She lifted her head and clawed hair out of her eyes to watch a tall guy in a blue shirt gather up an armload of firewood. He was whistling something that sounded like a commercial, or opera.

Velvet heard wood creak and turned her head the other way, her other cheek now in the dirt. A dark shape dropped over the top of the gate and landed lightly, knees bent, in the shadows.

"Oh, Christ," she whispered, and bit her lip. The guy in the garage dropped a stick of firewood and bent over to pick it up; his whistling broke off and started again as he straightened up.

Agent Dimples came a step closer into the light;

he was smiling slightly, not even out of breath. He'd put on gloves, and in one hand he had the gun he'd pulled on her at Robby's apartment. He was watching the garage, but he was also looking around the back yard for potential hiding places. Any second now, he'd look at the corn row.

No time for subtlety. Velvet opened her mouth to scream.

The back door opened, and a little girl said, "Daddy?"

Velvet's scream hitched in her throat like a gag. She swallowed hard and stayed very still, cheek pressed to the ground, wind pressing like cold fingers on her exposed face.

"Coming, sweetheart. Go on back inside, it's cold out here."

Think, Velvet screamed at herself. *Do something. Anything. For god's sake, don't just lay there!*

She realized she was looking at a playhouse hidden behind the corn, a little princess house with miniature glass windows and heart-shaped shutters. She started to crawl for it, moving slowly, and eased her head and shoulders inside, curling her legs and feet in behind. The kid had furnished the place with some good blankets and pillows— Mom would probably have a cow when she found out— and Velvet wrapped herself up and sat next to the window, looking out at the guy in the garage.

He'd put down his firewood, and was looking toward the wall where Agent James waited. She watched him pop the door on the Mercedes and get something out of the glove compartment.

He picked up his firewood, walked to the back door, and slammed it shut behind him. Through the glass door, Velvet saw him say something to the dark-haired woman at the table, whose face went blank and then tight with fear. She got up and left the room.

She hadn't seen him move, but all of a sudden Agent Dimples was standing there in the corn rows, scuffing a shoe in the outline where Velvet had pressed her face in the dirt. She wiped at the grit on her cheeks and pulled the blanket over her head as he looked at the playhouse. Dark. Her sweat smelled like Scotch, she couldn't get her breath, was he coming? Was he right there, *looking* at her, aiming the gun—

She screamed when she heard the shots, two quick loud explosions, and waited for the pain.

When she stripped the blanket off her head and pushed her hair back, she saw Agent Dimples face down in the dirt, blood spreading black under him. The rich guy stood in the doorway, holding onto it with one hand, like his knees weren't quite ready to do the job. Behind him, the kids were screaming, Mom was running and grabbing and hugging.

The rich guy had a gun in his hand. Velvet watched it fall from his hand and bounce on the steps. It spun to a stop a couple of feet away, shiny as a roach.

The guy sat down and started to cry, big gulping gasps of air she felt all the way across the yard. While his head was down, while the kids were screaming, she clambered out of the blankets and snaked out of the playhouse, ran to the gate, and pushed it open enough to wiggle through.

Sirens wailed in the distance. She ran.

Incident Five:
DALLAS, TEXAS
Spontaneous Human
Combustion (SHC)

Minnie Abramson woke up crying.

In itself, that didn't scare her; she often woke up crying. Sometimes she felt so lost, so strange . . . nothing seemed right anymore, not the way it had been when she was a child. In her dreams she was eight, skipping down the sidewalk in a blue dress, proud of her new black patent leather shoes. She skipped rope with Verna Henderson. The sun had been hot and tasted like lemons.

It had all been so different then, the neighborhood full of good Christian people, full of kids who weren't afraid to play in the street or in the yard. The ice cream truck had come around every couple of days, and sold blue ices and chocolate Fudgsicles. The driver had worn a crisp white suit and his truck played popular songs like a giant music box.

Minnie looked across the room— not her room, just an apartment, she'd moved out of her room and her house five years before— and made sure the chain was still on the door. She'd done her best with the room, scrubbed and cleaned and kept everything neat

as a pin, but it just never seemed to help. It wasn't
her house, wasn't her room.

She laid in bed and sobbed into her pillow for all
the lost things, for the ice cream truck, for the jump
rope, for the heavy whack of her braided hair on her
back as she skipped. From down on the street she
heard jungle sounds booming, all drums, no music,
and remembered how her mother had always been so
careful to keep the radio turned low, because the
neighbors might be sleeping. Now everybody just
turned their own radio up louder and louder to cover
up the noise.

She felt sick, but not sick to her stomach— hot,
maybe feverish. She climbed out of bed and put on
a fluffy pink zip-up robe, put on her faded fraying
houseshoes, walked slowly across to the kitchen. Hot
tea. She'd have some hot tea and lemon and honey,
and that would make her feel so much better, she
just knew it would.

She put the kettle on to boil and sat down at the
table, rubbing her forehead. Her skin felt like crepe
paper, old and frail. She looked at her gnarled aching hands, and felt tears welling up again, useless
tears, hot as the water in the kettle.

"Oh, Minnie," she sighed, and patted her white
hair back into place. She usually wore a satin cap
over it at night, since she couldn't afford to go to the
beauty shop more than once a week, but she'd forgotten and now it was a wreck, curling every which
way. "Don't be such a silly billy."

When the kettle whistled she filled up a cup and
put a tea bag in it, found a plastic bottle of lemon juice
and added two drops, then a thick stream of honey.
Doctor said she wasn't supposed to have honey, but on
nights like this, she decided doctors weren't always
right, and anyway she didn't have it very often.

The tea tasted just right, tart and sweet. She sat back in the rickety wood chair and looked out the window at the bright glare of downtown; they were playing with the blinking lights on that silly old ball at Reunion Tower again, she could never figure out what it was supposed to be. It looked like the world now, then it didn't look like anything at all. She watched it for a few more minutes until her eyes started hurting, then she blinked and sipped her tea and thought about Verna Henderson, dead these eight years.

It started like indigestion, a bright burn in her stomach that got hotter and hotter and made her pant through the pain. The pain didn't last long. She fell forward, pushing the teacup away, and was dead in less than a minute.

Her body smoldered for an hour, turning gray and black and then falling into ash. Her hands stayed untouched on the table, burnt off at mid-wrist. Her feet, still in the faded houseshoes, fell over to the right and left.

There was nothing left of the rest of her but ashes and a yellowish film of fat over the ceiling of the room.

There was a scorch mark on the table where her head had lain, and one in the seat of the wooden chair, but nothing else burned.

Nothing but Minnie.

Thirty-four
Martin

Mrs. Womack had stopped looking grandmotherly some time ago. As she looked at him from the other side of Agent Carling's bed, she seemed like some evil old witch dug up from a fairy story, blue eyes gone cold, smile gone mean.

"This is your fault," she said. Martin looked down at Carling's too pale face, at the tubes going into her arm and mouth and nose. "Don't bother to deny it, Mr. Grady. You wanted to play secret agent, and here we are."

"I'm sorry," he said. He felt the lash of her scorn without looking up.

"How nice. I'm sure she'll feel much better once she knows that. As far as I'm concerned, young man, the only reason I haven't taken you out and put a bullet in your back is because that nice young doctor says she's going to live through the night."

When he finally had the courage to look up, he saw her dabbing her eyes with a tissue, hands trembling.

"She's like my own. I don't suppose you can understand that."

Martin reached down and moved a strand of auburn hair away from Carling's face, touched the curve of her cheek with one finger.

"I think I do," he said. She huffed indignantly and crumpled the tissue in her fingers, over and over, until it was a wad the size of a walnut.

Agent Jennings looked in the door, gave Martin a cold stare, and addressed his remarks to Mrs. Womack.

"Ma'am, Agent Mendoza has those results you wanted. Want to look them over?"

"Have him bring them in, Bryce, thank you. Oh, and get yourself a cup of coffee. I'm sure we'll be fine." Mrs. Womack gave Martin a sharp-toothed smile. "Mr. Grady here will protect us."

Jennings said, "Yes, ma'am," and held the door open for Agent Mendoza. Mendoza gave Carling an expressionless glance and didn't bother giving any notice to Martin at all.

"You have the report?" Mrs. Womack asked. He crossed the room to hand it to her and then stood in the corner like a Coldstream guard, hands at his sides, eyes on the still form of Agent Carling. Mrs. Womack flipped pages and raised her eyebrows. "My. How very interesting."

She let Martin stew in silence while she read, pulling her half-glasses down her nose and holding the folder almost at arm's length. The benevolent grandmotherly mask was back in place. She smiled at Agent Mendoza.

"Oh, Antonio, do sit down, dear, please."

Mendoza sank into a chair, stiff as a corpse. A nurse came in and bustled around adjusting tubes, checking monitors. Mendoza's lethally intense concentration shifted to observe her. Martin pulled up a chair to Carling's bedside and sat, holding her hand. She had neat clever hands. He turned one palm up and winced at the long needles in her forearm, the outlines of forming bruises. He traced her lifeline with one fingertip.

"I expected you to ask," Mrs. Womack said, sounding peeved. He stared at the thin blue line of Carling's vein.

"I figured you'd tell me when you were ready."

"Hmm." She fixed him with a sharp-eyed stare and passed him the folder over Carling's unconscious body. "Page three. It's a chemical analysis of the preacher's clothing."

"Give me the short form," he said, an automatic bureaucratic reflex.

"Executive, aren't we?" She paused long enough to let him know who was in charge. "The principal thing is that there is no dichlorhyradine present, although it's definitely in his tissue samples."

"So it starts from the body and works its way out."

"I'm afraid you're jumping to a conclusion, Mr. Grady. You're assuming that dichlorhyradine is the agent of chemical ignition."

"It's present in every one of the victims. It's highly exothermic under laboratory conditions— "

"It's a byproduct," she said. "Page three."

He waded through about four paragraphs and looked up at her, eyebrows arching a question. She smiled and opened her purse, a large black leather thing. He half-expected her to take out a gun, but she took out a ball of blue yarn and two knitting needles and a pebbly length of scarf-in-progress.

"Pretend you're in Catholic school, Mr. Grady. What is present in the clothing?"

"Um . . . traces of salt, an alcohol-based mixture that the lab identified as Old Spice cologne, tobacco residue— the preacher liked his cigarettes and— what the hell is this?"

"Benzine and toluene. Dry cleaning compounds."

"Oh." Martin continued down the list. "Benzoic acid— "

"A distillate of benzine. Not a very good dry cleaners; all those chemicals are present in far greater concentrations than they should be." Mrs. Womack counted a row of stitches and started clacking, a dry quiet sound that reminded him of dice. "Go on."

"Sulphur dioxide—"

"Commonly used as a disinfectant and preservative."

"Sulfonmethane."

"A hypnotic agent."

"Hydrochloric and hydrocyanic acids."

"Also used as clarifying agents in dry cleaning."

Grady watched as Mrs. Womack calmly knitted an entire row.

"Are you trying to tell me," he said slowly, "that somebody killed him with *dry cleaning fluids*? That these chemicals combined will burn?"

"Not at all." She started a second row. "But it might interest you to know that Burt Marshall— who died right here in Dallas, Texas— was half-owner of a dry cleaners. And that earlier last year he applied for a patent for a new dry cleaning solution, but withdrew the request within three weeks. Isn't that interesting?"

"But if these chemicals don't burn—"

"By themselves." She inspected the row and adjusted it with nudges of her fingers. "Do you think you love Adrian?"

"Pardon me?" He blinked and sat upright. He had to look down to be sure Carling wasn't awake. "What?"

"Do you think you're in love with her?"

He opened his mouth to say no, shut it, and tried again. "I don't know."

"Well, I do. Let me give you a piece of advice, son. I love Adrian like she's my own, but I'd never let a boy of mine marry her." She smiled wolfishly. "She's too much for you."

"What makes them burn?"

Mrs. Womack looked over at Agent Mendoza, who sat impassive and still in his chair. Without any visible signal, he stood up and left the room.

"Body heat," she said, and went back to her knitting. "Most of the early chemicals used for dry cleaning were unstable and flammable, you know— boiling points of as low as ninety degrees. Up to the turn of the century, they were still using kerosene and gasoline to fume clothes. I think our Mr. Marshall stumbled onto what he thought was a new dry cleaning process— but it turned out to have a low boiling threshhold. And once it's combined with salt from sweat— "

She shrugged. One of her knitting needles slipped and fell with a clatter to the floor.

"Whoosh," Martin said.

"Naturally, not a market for that kind of thing in commercial applications. As a weapon, though— "

"Good god. Do we know what dry cleaners— "

Mrs. Womack went back to her knitting, serene as Whistler's mother.

"Elegance Dry Cleaners, Mr. Grady, right here in Dallas. Isn't that funny? It was right under your nose the whole time. Did you ever get your clothes cleaned there?"

His mind went blank, and for a second he couldn't honestly remember whether he had or not. His suit coat itched over his shoulders.

"Agent Mendoza believes that the surviving partner, Edward Julian, is the one responsible for the burnings. Whether he's targeting people he doesn't like, or people who might have caused trouble, or just likes the thrill of it, we don't know."

"What about this terrorist— el Haddiz?"

"Ah." Mrs. Womack found this serious enough to put her knitting in her lap, fold her hands, and give him her full attention. "Mr. el Haddiz is quite probably making a deal to buy the formula, or at least some garments treated with the product. You can imagine how effective those might be in some of the warmer climates notorious for political unrest."

He couldn't think of anything to say. Carling's monitors beeped a steady gentle rhythm. He saw her eyes twitch under the fragile lids and hoped she was dreaming.

"Did she know any of that?"

"Some. Not all." Mrs. Womack picked up her knitting again and adjusted the angle of her glasses on her nose. "I imagine Mr. Marshall's establishment does a lot of business in uniform cleaning. Police uniforms, for instance. Girl scout uniforms. Marching band uniforms."

The scope of it made him dizzy. He shrugged his jacket off and piled it in a heap on the floor, loosened his tie, and put his head down on the cool sheets of Carling's bed, next to her loose empty hand.

"My god," he whispered. Mrs. Womack made a dry sound of agreement. Her knitting needles clacked.

Thirty-five
Velvet

Velvet was three-quarters of the way through a fifth of Scotch by the time she heard the front door rattle. All those damn locks. Fire hazard, that's what it was. *Fire hazard.* That was so funny it was sick. The Scotch went down warm on her tongue, scorched her throat, added fuel to the bonfire in her stomach. Nice and warm now. In a minute or two she'd forget all about it, all about the dead man in the garden with his dimples all shot off. She'd forget the look on that rich man's face as he cried.

Robby got the door open and slammed it, jammed the locks shut as fast as she could. Velvet watched her with unfocused eyes and smiled.

"Hey. Saw the hockey game. Hell of a game, 'cept for that guy melting the ice." She was trying to be snide, but it all came out sad instead. She drained the last sip of whisky from her glass and poured out another splash from the bottle on the coffee table.

Robby slapped the glass out of her hand. Velvet watched it spin off through the air, pinwheeling Scotch. She licked the drops off her fingers.

"Hey," she said. "Hey, I was drinkin' that."

Robby pulled her to her feet, or tried to; Velvet couldn't seem to stand up. Robby finally let her drop back to the couch. Velvet tried to focus both eyes on her, but it was way too much effort; she closed her right eye and focused her left. Something wrong with Robby's face. Tears. Tears in her eyes, on her cheeks.

Velvet got the bottle and tried to hand it to her. "Have a drink."

"No more, Velvet." *Na morrh.* Robby's Irish brogue had taken over, and so had her temper. She reached for Velvet's shoulder and grabbed a handful of hair, too. Velvet batted feebly at her, making *oww* sounds. "You've got to stop lying to me, Velvet, you've got to, understand? We're in trouble, both of us! Why did you do it? Why?"

Every time Robby got to the end of a question, Velvet got shaken. In between the shakes, the room spun around, a neon technicolor whirl like a kaleidoscope, only Velvet was one of the little glass beads tumbling around.

"Stop it!" she shouted, and slapped wildly, connected with skin. Robby pulled back. "Goddamn it, stop that!"

Robby slapped her back hard enough to bring tears to her eyes and numb the whole side of her face. Unfortunately, it didn't last. In the next few seconds her bruises woke up yelling, and she put her hands over her face and doubled over, moaning.

Something smacked the floor next to her feet. She looked over the tips of her fingers and saw a newspaper. Her face looked ghostly and wasted, a beat-up hooker with dreamy-dead eyes. Her first thought was, *God, he could've used a better mug shot than that.*

Robby said, "They put Jim in the hospital looking for you. It's just a matter of time before they find both of us, and God help us then."

"J-Jim?" Velvet wiped her eyes on her sleeve and looked up at Robby's face. Robby had stopped crying, but the look in her eyes was just as bad. "Jim? Wh-what happened?"

"They broke his hands," Robby whispered. "His hands."

I'm sorry sounded so lame when she tried it that she covered up her mouth with Scotch-damp hands. Sorry. Sorry. Always so fucking sorry, sorry about Amy, sorry about life, sorry for poor little Velvet. She was sick of being sorry.

Then don't keep fucking up, some part of her whispered. She gulped back tears and reached for the Scotch.

Robby moved it out of the way. Their eyes met.

"You have to get out of town," Robby said, very clearly. "Tomorrow at the latest. Do you have any money?"

"At— " Velvet bit her lip, did it too hard because of the Scotch, and tasted blood. "Shit. Had a stash at my apartment, but it's gone."

"Anything?"

"Not much." That was the truth. She'd had money at some hazy, earlier point, but there'd been cab fares and meals and a couple bottles of booze and things she didn't remember that had seemed real important at the time. "Not enough."

Robby looked around at her living room as if seeing it for the first time— the stereo, the CDs, the leather furniture.

"I can sell some things, but not tonight. How much do you need?"

"You— you'd sell your stuff for *me?*" Velvet pulled back, stunned and suspicious and strangely angry. "How come?"

Robby stood up and walked over to the stereo cabinet, opened it and touched the black components inside, little sad touches of her fingers.

"How come?" Velvet demanded again, leaning forward. "What the fuck makes you my social worker?"

Robby steadied herself with one hand on the cabinet and turned to look at her. Her eyes were blind with tears.

"Nothing," she said. "Nothing at all."

It was gymnastics to stand up, ballet to keep from falling over. Velvet pulled herself as upright as the alcohol would let her and pushed her tangled hair back from her face.

"Don't worry about it. I'm getting the hell out of here, and I won't be coming back." She took two steps and her foot went limp as a noodle under her. She pushed herself straight off the back of a chair and tried for an exit again.

"Take anything you want," Robby said when she'd reached the hallway. Her voice sounded so strange, so faraway. "I'll have to leave it all behind anyway."

By the time she got to the bedroom door, Velvet was so angry she was sick. She limped to the closet and threw back the doors, yanked clothes off the hangers and tossed them on the floor, on the neon blue bed, anywhere they'd fall. Tans. Off-whites. Browns. Muted this and pastel that, little fucking girl clothes, Jesus, didn't she have—

At the end of the closet, shoved behind a pair of threadbare blue jeans with bleach stains, hung a butter-soft leather jacket with long threadlike fringe. Velvet slid it off the hanger, and it collapsed like a pet in her hands, purring. There was a skirt, too, short, slit up the side. She laid them reverently on the bed, staring.

She touched the fringe the way Robby had touched the stereo components, gently, like someone petting a friend's show dog. God, it was beautiful. She'd never seen anything so beautiful.

From the doorway, Robby said, "Take it. I don't need it."

When Velvet turned around, jacket clutched tight in her arms, Robby wasn't there. She listened, but she didn't hear any footsteps.

Another fingernail split as she fought the buttons of her flannel shirt, the tight zipper on the pants. She kicked the dirty clothes off to mix with the clean ones she'd thrown out of the closet, and slowly, so slowly, slid the skirt up over her hips.

The zipper sounded like a whisper. The fit was perfect. Velvet kept her black front-close bra and slid the jacket over it, silk lining cool on her skin and warming up, leather a thick soft cushion around her.

In the corner she found her black patent leather fuck-me pumps, only a little scuffed at the heels. She stood in front of the mirror on the closet door and turned slowly, unsteadily, watching the leather gleam.

"God," she said reverently. It was as close as she'd gotten to a prayer in years.

The doorbell rang; she lost her balance on the high heels and sat down on the bed hard enough to make the springs squeak. The room lurched into spin dry.

God, it was Sol, come to beat her up again— or worse, it was those assholes from the dry cleaners— or—

Robby ran by the door, backtracked and traded a look with her.

"Stay here," she said, and swung the door shut. Velvet clutched handfuls of neon blue comforter and waited, eyes shut, while the room dipped and danced.

She didn't hear anything from the hall, not even the locks clicking back. She'd hear something, wouldn't she, if somebody broke in? If they started kicking the shit out of—

Wouldn't she? Oh, God. If they did, what would she

do? No back way out, no place to hide, nothing to fight with. Oh, God. She was suddenly convinced that she would throw up, and looked frantically around for a trash can, a plastic bag, anything. There was a trash can across the room, but that was ten steps, at least.

She covered her mouth with her hands and bent over to put her head between her legs.

Two, maybe three breaths later, she heard the bedroom door open, and a man's voice said, "Are you okay?"

She looked up with both hands still wrapped around her mouth.

It was Paolo. He had a gun.

She passed out.

When she came around, he had put the gun away and was holding her in his arms, wiping her face with a warm damp cloth. She choked on the taste in her mouth and dry-heaved; he grabbed a trash can he'd brought over and held it under her mouth, but she didn't do much more than drool in it. He wiped her chin.

"Better?" he rumbled. She'd never noticed it before, but his eyes were green with brown rings. "You shouldn't drink so much, Velvet."

"Thank you, Betty Ford. Hey, sorry about the mess, I— I got the flu. My friend's been taking care of me."

Paolo took a folded newspaper out of his pocket and handed it to her. She didn't have to look to know which article he was pointing to.

"Yeah, I know, it looks bad— but honest, Paolo, swear to God, I didn't— this guy, he fucked me over, I told him not to use my name, honest."

"Doesn't matter." Paolo looked sad, as much as his

blocky massive face could. "Ming's unhappy. Very un-happy."

"I know." She swallowed hard and looked at the bedroom door; it was open. "Um, where's my friend? Robby?"

"In the living room."

"Uh-huh. Um, sorry, but is she, like, okay? You didn't— "

Paolo stared at her with his eyebrows bunched to-gether like hairy spiders, green eyes the color of old grass. He shook his head.

"Oh. Good. So, she's, she's okay. Right?"

He didn't nod. Oh, God.

"Do I have to go back? Is that why you're here?" More blank stares. She felt a shiver in her back pull her shoulders tighter. "I have to go back, right? Take my medicine?"

"Medicine," he repeated. "No. Don't go back."

He took the gun out of his jacket pocket and looked at it through slitted eyes. She held very still while he thought about it.

After a minute or so, he looked up and said, "Don't go back, Velvet. She wants to kill you."

She opened her mouth but couldn't think of a damned thing to say, just watched him fiddle nervously with his gun. He finally jammed it back in his pocket, threaded his fingers together, and stared down at them.

"You look nice," he said at last. "Real nice. Except for the bruises."

"Story of my life," she whispered. "Thank you, Paolo. Really. Thanks."

He nodded, little delicate bobs of his head that looked crazy on a guy his size. She fingered the fringe of her leather jacket and watched him from the corner of her eye.

"You want something?" she asked. He stopped nodding. "For, you know, old times' sake? If you want, I'll do it."

His head moved slowly, like it didn't want to, until he was looking her in the eye.

"I love you," he said. "I do. You don't have to do anything. Just don't go to Ming."

Kissing him seemed like the right thing to do, so she gave him one quick moist one; he didn't try to hang on to her when she pulled away. Instead, he reached in his pocket again.

Oh, Christ, I knew it. He's going to kill me because he loves me.

He pulled out a piece of paper and a short stack of twenties.

"You should leave town," he said. "I know you don't got any money, but here's some, about two hundred. And this guy, he wanted to hire you for a night. He said he'd pay real good. Ming told him no, because she was mad at you, but if you call I bet he'd still pay good."

The name was Henry Parriott. It was a local phone number.

"Are you going to be okay with this?" Velvet asked. He shrugged toward his shoe tops.

"Ming wanted me to find you. I didn't find you. It'll be okay." He cleared his throat, a sound like rocks grinding. "Be careful."

"Yo, you bet. You too." He deserved one more peck on the cheek for his money. "Hey, Paolo? I always liked it with you. Really."

"Really?" He smiled. It shocked the hell out of her, because he had a nice smile, when he wanted to use it. "Thanks."

He stood up and walked out. She wobbled after

him on her high heels and slowed when she caught sight of Robby lying on the couch.

"It's okay, she's sleeping," he said, and opened the front door. "I had to hit her, but I didn't hit her too hard. Bye, Velvet."

"Bye."

As she locked the door behind him, she heard him humming something. It sounded like the theme to the "Love Boat."

Robby was going to have a hell of a bruise on her chin.

After four rings, a man's voice said, "Hello?" He had a high thin voice that reminded her of telephone wires humming in the wind.

"Mr. Parriott?" she asked, and took a short sip from a glass of Scotch. Her buzz had passed with her fright, and she was doing her best to spin it back up.

"Yes-s-s." He sounded doubtful. "May I ask who's calling?"

"Maybe." She swirled the liquor and watched the overhead lights through the thick amber filter. "Maybe it's somebody you want to hear from."

"I'm afraid I don't— "

"Velvet," she said, and took another drink during his silence. "Interested?"

He cleared his throat and said, "Yes, of course. But I understood you were not available."

"Yeah, well, plans change. What exactly do you want?"

"Well, I— I don't know— the night. I'd like to book you for the evening."

"All evening?" She finished the Scotch and set the glass down with a tinny clink on the kitchen counter. "My, my. You're ambitious."

"How much?"

"One thousand."

She'd intended it as a starting point, the rock bottom price being five hundred, but he only said, "Fine," which made her feel a little nervous, but not enough to pass up a thousand bucks. One last fling in Dallas. Might as well make it a big one.

"Where do I go?" she asked. He fumbled the telephone and dropped it. She sighed and tapped her pencil on a pad of paper. "Yo, buddy, you there? Where?"

"Meet me in the street behind the Spaghetti Warehouse downtown. You know where it is? Across from the Alley?"

"I know where it is. Look, the weather's pretty—"

"I'll pay extra," he cut in. She wrote down *alley spaghetti $*. "I'll send you something special to wear."

"I have my own stuff."

"But these clothes are very special." His voice cranked a step or two higher on the tension scale. "Where can I send them?"

"Whatever. Send them to 2212 Ross. Leave them hanging in the lobby." That was the building across the street. She'd watch until the delivery guy was gone before going over. "When do you want me there?"

"At three."

"Three?" Velvet checked the clock over Robby's blood red sink. "Jesus, it's already one-thirty."

"The clothes will be there in thirty minutes, I promise." Mr. Parriott giggled like a breathless teen-aged girl. "I'm looking forward to it."

"Me too," she breathed, and poured herself another slug of Scotch. "I can't wait to see you." She hung up while he was still giggling, stared at the phone, and said, "Jesus, what a prick."

"You don't have to do this."

She whirled around, forgetting the fuck-me pumps

and her general lack of balance, and almost pitched
face forward to Robby's Purina tile floor. Robby— pale
and narrow-eyed and sporting a bruise like a rose tattoo on her chin— grabbed her arm and got her steady
before reaching past her for the Scotch bottle.

"Do what?" Velvet asked innocently. "Hey, I was
using that!"

"Too bad." Robby took a glass from a cabinet and
poured herself a tall drink. She tossed it back in two
gulps, hardly pausing to make a face. "Mary Mother,
that stuff's awful, where'd you get it? Somebody's
bathtub?"

"All that Irish crap rotted your taste buds."

Robby held the bottle out to her and said, "You
don't have to meet him. I told you, I'll give you the
money as soon as I can sell a few things."

There were about seven drops of liquor left; Velvet
tipped the bottle and got rid of them. Before she could
practice her three-pointer skill, Robby grabbed the
bottle and dumped it carefully in the trash can. She
rinsed out the two glasses and put them in the dish-
washer.

"If I'd wanted your money, I would have taken
your shit while you were gone," Velvet said, and
straightened the hang of her black leather jacket.
"Snazzy. So, you get this as a gift or what?"

"A friend talked me into it. God knows I would
never wear it, so you might as well. You're going to
meet this man at three? No matter what I say?"
Robby looked sick in the white fluorescent light,
green around the eyes.

"Yep. You might find this hard to believe, but I
don't want to fuck you up any more than I already
have. Look, I know all this is my fault— if I'd kept
my mouth shut the way everybody wanted, none of
this would have happened, Jim wouldn't have got

beaten up, people would still be—anyway, the best thing I can do is get the hell out of here, now, tonight. I spend the night with Mr. Prick and pick up enough cash to travel, and tomorrow I see a new skyline. It's no big deal. I did it before."

More than once, new towns and new Mings and bruises that never quite healed. But with a little money in her pocket—

Who was she kidding? A little money in her pocket would be gone in a week, and she'd be moaning in the backseat of a car, only the cars would get cheaper and the guys would get meaner, and pretty soon—

What was it the fake Agent James had said? *Ten buck a fuck whore?*

Robby was mopping up little smears on the countertop with a neatly folded rag. She looked ready to drop.

"It's the only way they won't come after you," Velvet finished, and walked over to watch out the window for somebody bringing clothes to the building across the street.

Thirty-six
Martin

Martin had never worn a bulletproof vest before, and he didn't like it much. It felt like wearing one of his Aunt Martha's hand-knitted sweaters, lumpy and suffocating and ugly as hell. He picked at the Velcro fasteners until Mrs. Womack slapped his hand.

"I don't like bringing you into this at all," she said, and stepped back to admire the fit. "Still, I suppose we have to make do. Agent Mendoza simply must stay with Carling in case anyone tries to get to her, which leaves me without a driver. I assume you can drive."

"I did okay earlier." He knew he sounded defensive, but couldn't tell if he sounded scared, which was how he felt. Mrs. Womack looked at him over the top of her glasses. She was wearing a bulky black sweater, a loose black skirt, and sensible black orthopedic shoes. Her support hose were black, too. She blended in to the dark shadows of the parking lot where they stood, except for the silver blue gleam of her hair and the glitter of her eyeglasses. He shivered in a new blast of arctic-cold wind and reached for his coat and gloves.

"You got the car shot half to hell, lost the back window, and managed to let Agent Carling collect two bullets along the way," she corrected. "I believe you'll have to do better this time."

She dug in her big purse and came up with her ball of yarn and knitting needles, frowned, and dug again. She came up with a handful of ammunition clips that she slipped in the pockets of her big black slouch coat.

"Do I get a gun?" he asked. Agent Jennings, who was silently donning his bulletproof vest a few feet away, looked up. He had two expressions, the second one was disgust. It vanished as quickly as it appeared. A car drove through the parking lot, speakers booming bass. Agent Jennings turned to track its progress and only relaxed when it disappeared back to the road and sped away.

"No, dear," she said, speaking carefully as if Martin had a hearing impairment. "You drive the *car.*"

"Shouldn't you be calling in the local FBI agents?" he guessed. "The police? The boy scouts? Somebody?"

Mrs. Womack left him to join Agent Jennings at the trunk of the car. She reached in and clicked open a case, took out a shotgun, and racked the shells with terrifying precision.

"Bryce dear, I think you might want to take something with more range, perhaps the Mac-10. We should have some extra clips in here somewhere." Without looking away from whatever assortment of death-dealing weapons she had in the trunk, she said, "Mr. Grady, I don't think you fully understand our position. We are not, per se, here in an official capacity."

"What?" He watched the two of them load guns and felt weak at the knees. "What? Excuse me?"

"Oh, it'll be quite all right, you'll see. All you need to worry about is driving." She paused a second and sighed. "I do wish Adrian were here. I wish that very much. She'll be so disappointed to have missed it."

Agent Jennings slammed the trunk shut and walked around to open the passenger-side door for Mrs. Womack. Martin stood flat-footed and open-mouthed, breathing in air cold enough to sear his lungs, until she clucked her tongue and came back to him, rooting in her oversized purse.

"I almost forgot," she said, and came up with the blue scarf she'd been knitting in Carling's room. "Here, dear. Keep your neck warm. It's going to be very cold tonight."

The car was a nondescript-looking blue, American-made, new but not flashy. He wasn't even sure what model it was, but it was automatic and had a lot of power under the hood. He pulled out of the hospital parking lot and followed her directions east. Apart from the directions, she had nothing to say to him. He felt like he was sixteen again, taking his driver's exam. *If she asks me to parallel park, I'm dead.*

"Where are we going?" he asked after ten minutes. She gave him a beatific smile.

"Don't ask silly questions." Her tone was steel. "Agent Jennings?"

He was doing something with electronics in the backseat, producing beeps and bleeps and blips. She turned to look over her shoulder; a green CRT light gave her a gargoyle complexion.

"The truck's still parked behind the dry cleaners," he reported. She nodded. "I should be able to tell when they start moving."

"That's excellent. Very good work. Martin, Mr. Jennings visited our friend's dry cleaning establishment today and dropped off some suits. While he was there, he took the liberty of a quick tour of the back rooms, and in one of them there was a large stack of boxes ready to be loaded for shipping. What did you find in the boxes, Bryce?"

"Dallas Cowboys sweatshirts," he said in between bleeps. "Nice thick ones."

"Now, I don't know about you, Mr. Grady, but I

am such a football fan, and sweatshirts like those sell.
And not just in America. They could be sold in Rus-
sia, for instance. In England. To American troops
abroad." Mrs. Womack turned back face-forward.
"I'd guess this is just the first stage of a larger operation."

"But— wait— what about the ones who've already
died? What were they? Accidents?"

Surprisingly, it wasn't Womack who answered, but
Jennings.

"Object lessons. We think he was proving the effec-
tiveness of the process to potential buyers— one of the
buyers, for example, was probably based in Louisiana,
so he picks a Louisiana preacher in Dallas for a religious convention, gives him the special dry cleaning,
and tells the buyer to watch for the preacher's name
in the papers." One of the electronic tones changed
to a higher pitch. "I'm getting movement on the box."

"Bryce put a tracking device in one of the boxes,"
Mrs. Womack said. "Isn't he clever. Where's it moving?"

"South," he said. "Downtown."

Mrs. Womack stopped smiling.

"Drive," she told Martin tightly. "And quickly.
Half-time is over."

Thirty-seven
Ming

They had been quite civil to her in the car, but, of course, there was no point in being cruel to someone about to learn the ultimate lesson. Ming sat at ease in the backseat of the limousine, hands folded in her lap, staring at the eyes of the man who sat across from her.

He had not borne the wait well; for a small man he sweated profusely, and his body odor hung like a dirty cloud between them. He patted his knee and avoided her eyes. His larger partner, seated next to him, stared out the window, pouting.

"She is gone, you know," Ming said. The small man flinched as if she'd slapped him. "There is no use in killing me. I cannot bring her back, if I am dead."

"Look, it isn't for me to say. I told you, eight hours or we take you in. We got to take you in." He rubbed his stubbly chin. "Been a shitty day all around, you know? Want a drink?"

"I thank you, no."

"Okay." He fiddled with the khaki of his pants leg, picked at his thumbnail. "TV? We got TV in here, if you want to watch something. Tapes, too. Mostly sex stuff, but there's a couple of comedies—"

"Thank you, no," she murmured. "I don't laugh."

He tried to offer her a candy bar, then a meal at a fast food restaurant. She politely refused each, though the child inside her wanted to stop, to eat, to drink, to delay what must come.

Paolo had failed her. She had believed, to the last, that he would call, that he would come back.

She had not heard a word from him.

Ahead, the black shadow of a tall building, and over it, the lead gray of clouds. Cold, so cold, and this cold did not freeze her solid but chilled her into brittle pieces. She considered jumping from the limousine, but that might only wound her; they would hardly show mercy if her legs were broken, or her back. It must be as quick as a bullet, as certain as poison, or there was no point in piling one misery atop another.

So focused was she on seeking a way to die that she had almost forgotten the inevitable end of the journey. The dome light went on over her head to remind her. A door seal whispered open and the little man across from her said, not unkindly, "We're here."

She climbed out of the car without assistance, taking each step slowly to be sure she would not fall. The elevator seemed to rise for hours, leaving her weightless and oddly unbalanced, and in the closed metal box, the smell of her captor's sweat seemed as thick as rancid grease.

He held the doors open and gestured for her to go ahead. The carpeted hallway stretched before her, empty. When she took a step into it, the doors of the elevator shut; she looked back and saw that he had not followed. He would be falling now, mopping his brow, breathing a sigh of relief at being rid of the responsibility. Perhaps he would be making plans for a late supper, or an early breakfast. Perhaps he had a woman waiting.

There was no place to run. She continued walking with slow even steps to the door at the end, the plain wood door with no name and not even a lock, only a knob to turn.

She knocked politely and went inside.

The room was dark except for a small lamp burning on the corner of his desk, a circle of warm yellow light on blood red carpet, polished dark wood, the black shine of the toe of his shoe. He was smoking imported cigarettes; the tobacco stank like old leather.

"Sit," he said, voice raspy with smoke. When she had settled herself in the plain chair before his desk, he sat, too. "Maybe it was bad luck. Could have happened to anybody."

She refused to grab the straw and sat in silence, watching the red flare of his cigarette.

"You know you won't be leaving here."

"I know," she said evenly. The fantasy rushed back on her, strong as the smell of his tobacco— a knife in her hand, skin peeling back from muscle, his face. "I'm sorry about your employee. The one who burned."

"He was getting to be a problem. Too bad about the girlfriend, though. She was a competent thief, and they're harder to come by than psychos like Sol. Like you."

He extinguished the cigarette in an ashtray, and now he was only a dark shape in the shadows; he could have been anyone, anywhere, anytime. She closed her eyes and lived the fantasy, felt it rush through her with the force of an orgasm.

"Velvet was never of any importance," she said aloud. "The idea that I will die for her is ludicrous."

"You mistake me," he said. "I'm not killing you because of Velvet. I'm killing you because I'm tired of burying your hobbies, Ming. You're a fucked-up rabid bitch, and it's time somebody put you down."

The noise of his gun cocking was shockingly loud. She found herself gripping the arms of the chair hard enough to break her laquered nails, and could not force herself to relax, not now, not ever again. A childhood prayer came back to her in singsong whispers.

Behind her, the door opened and a square of light spilled in.

"What the fuck— I told you, no interruptions—" He was still searching for words when someone fired from the doorway, six shots, evenly spaced. He lived for several seconds, mouth working, eyes blank and puzzled. He reached out to Ming, where she sat frozen in the chair.

She moved her foot back an inch, out of his grasp.

When he fell sideways to the carpet, Ming turned to look over her shoulder.

"I got here as fast as I could," Paolo said. He looked blankly apologetic as he came toward her. "I'm sorry I took so long."

"That's quite all right," she said. There was something broken in her now, something not even Paolo's violent intervention could fix. All the fear was out now, battering down her defenses, sweeping her screaming with it.

So much fear. She looked at her hands, gripping the arms of the chair, and forced them to let go; they trembled violently and would not stop.

"Paolo, you know they'll never let us leave here alive," she said. "You know that."

"Yes, ma'am, I know."

She looked at him with a sudden quiet feeling of tenderness, her ugly rabid dog, and reached out a hand. He came over to stand next to her.

Outside the window, clouds boiled like gray cotton. It was a long way down, she knew.

She took the gun out of Paolo's hand and calmly shot him three times in the chest. He looked vaguely surprised, but there was no pain. She sat down next to him cross-legged, while the thick carpet swallowed his life, and put the muzzle of the gun under her chin.

With her eyes closed, the cold metal felt like the kiss of a dead man.

Thirty-eight
Velvet

The clothes Parriott had sent were second-rate. Velvet stood in the neon blue bedroom and stared at her image in the mirror, turned right, turned left, and shook her head.

"Just wear them," Robby said wearily from where she sat rubbing her temples. "For god's sake, if you're going to do it, get it over with."

He'd sent over a leather skirt and jacket and a full-body Spandex bodysuit, but the leather was cheap and the jacket was too tight and the Spandex felt scratchy. Velvet stripped it off and tossed the stuff on the bed, fished her own Spandex suit out of her suitcase, and yanked it on. No underwear. This was a no-underwear kind of guy.

If he wanted leather, she'd give him leather. She put on the fringed jacket, the butter-soft skirt, and modeled for the mirror.

"Much better," she said. "First-rate. Worth the money. Hey, Robby, when I get back, you want to go out to lunch or something, just for old times' sake? Kind of a goodbye?"

"I don't think so. I'm going to scrape up a stake tonight if it kills me, and tomorrow Jim and I will be gone." She swallowed hard. "We'll have to leave everything."

"Tonight?" Velvet turned to stare at her. "You've gotta be kidding. It's two-thirty, you've got the shakes, and you're so tired you're ready to go face first in the concrete. You can't go out."

"I'm going. I don't have a choice. They're looking for you, Velvet. They've gotten to Jim, they'll get to me. I have to go." Robby stood and started picking up clothes Velvet had scattered in piles on the floor. "I just have to find something to wear. I'll be fine."

"Oh, yeah, sure you will. You're gonna spend the night in jail, is what you're gonna do." Robby hesitated over the leather Velvet had dumped on the bed. "Want to wear it?"

"What? Oh, no. No. I never— "

"Come on, live a little. Jesus, I never met anybody so fucking restrained. You'll look great, and you'll blend in a hell of a lot better at three in the morning wearing the leather than you will in a damn suit. The Spandex has long sleeves, it'll keep you warm. Put a big coat on top of it, man, you'll be beating off the guys with a club."

"I can't."

She wanted to, though. Velvet leaned over, locked eyes with her, and said, "Can't or won't?"

Robby shook her head and walked away, arms full of clothes. The leather stayed dumped on the bed. Velvet shrugged, wiggled her shoulders, checked her thick makeup, and slid on a pair of dark glasses.

"Fabulous." She fluffed her hair. "Hey. You're gonna be okay. Really."

Robby, gone off down the hallway, didn't answer. Velvet blew one more kiss at the mirror, tugged on her bright technicolor coat, and didn't look back until she was at the front door, unlocking deadbolts.

Robby was crying somewhere in the back, lonely racking sounds. Velvet closed the door quietly and tried to pretend she hadn't heard. As she waited in the hallway for the elevator, she felt her mother's wide, tear-filled eyes on her, heard the quiet sobs.

Oh, honey, why? Why?

The elevator took too long. She jammed the button again, and again, until her finger hurt. When the doors rumbled open, she hurried in, wedged herself in the corner, and watched the hallway. Hoped Robby might—

But she didn't. The elevator doors creaked closed and the world dropped out from under her in slow shuddering jerks.

One more time, Mama. One more, and it's all over.

The street her trick had picked wasn't her idea of a good time, that was for sure— more an alley than a real street, a race track for sanitation engineers. Dark, cold, damp, piled with trash cans and sagging boxes. The wind slashed at her exposed skin like a psycho. There were still a few drunks over in the neon-rainbowed glare of Dallas Alley, mostly wandering around giggling and shouting and laughing; the cops would be clearing it out pretty soon.

She almost wished the cops *would* show; the damned place was a crime scene waiting to happen. She'd been standing for nearly twenty minutes now, hopping up and down for warmth, pacing. Under the layers of coat and leather, she had broken a sweat, but her face and hands and legs were so frozen they felt like putty.

Five more minutes. That was all she was giving him, no matter how much money he claimed he had for her.

Something cold and hard spit in her face. Sleet.

Wonderful. Just what she needed. She pressed herself back against the wall and watched it arrive in a hissing sheet, rattling windowpanes, drawing hoarse delighted screams from drunks running for shelter. She checked her watch. Five minutes hadn't passed.

Watching the cobblestones ice over wasn't quite as much fun as watching mold grow. After three minutes she'd convinced herself that maybe she ought to hail a cab out on the street to get back to Robby's. Robby wouldn't lock her out, would she? Not Robby.

Maybe she ought to hurry.

The sleet had thoroughly rained on the parade; a couple of truly drunk college boys slogged past her, heads down, faces slack, and they were the last. She watched them weave and slip and slide their way across the courtyard. No cops. Nowhere.

Nobody willing to pay her for her wasted time, either.

The wind whipped back in her face, splattering her with ice and rain. Her numbed cheeks hardly felt it, but cold trickled down her neck and made her yelp with disgust. That was *it*, absolutely. She was getting the hell out.

She stepped out of the alley with relief that vanished when her shoes slipped on a patch of ice. She balanced with both arms out, like a wirewalker, and shuffled carefully across the courtyard toward the street where cabs would be waiting, lights on, heaters humming. She didn't have enough money for a cab, but that didn't matter; she'd stiffed cabbies before, or blown them for a fare—

"Hey," a voice said from behind her. A man's voice. She made sure her feet were set, and twisted to look over her shoulder.

A guy stood in the shadows of the alley where she'd been waiting. She couldn't see much of him, but he was kind of short and well dressed. The camel-colored coat looked expensive enough to carry its own insurance policy, and he was wearing a suit underneath.

Not bad. Not bad at all. She pasted a glittery smile on and turned to face him, letting her coat fall open. The wind, delighted, crawled in.

"Hey yourself," she said. Should she try to get back across to him? No, with her luck she'd fall on her ass. "I've been waiting."

He said, "You should be dead by now," and took a step forward into the light; neon from the Alley made his face Easter bunny pink. She knew him, didn't she? Such a wimpy-looking geek; he looked just about ready to cry. "Damn it, nothing's going right. Why aren't you *dead?*"

He had a gun— not a big gun, like Paolo's, just a little .25 automatic. She almost told him she'd seen bigger.

And then he fired. The snap of the shot echoed. Velvet toppled forward to cold stone.

She'd remembered, stupidly, where she'd seen him. At the dry cleaners. Mr. Julian.

Thirty-nine
Martin

It was sleeting outside, a vicious-looking gray slime that coated everything that wasn't moving. Not only that, the windows were fogged over. Martin Grady wiped at the windshield again and squinted.

"This won't do," Mrs. Womack said, and fiddled with the defroster. "My goodness, American cars certainly aren't what they used to be. Go ahead and use the wipers, Marty. This is just dreadful."

The wipers dragged a sullen path over slushy ice and smeared a couple of inches clear. Through it, and the veil of falling sleet, he saw a big white truck across the street in an empty pay parking lot. Its exhaust puffed white smoke in the air like an exhausted runner.

They were just sitting there. Waiting.

"If we lose them—" Agent Jennings said, leaning over the seat to squint out himself. Mrs. Womack finished adjusting the defroster. A blast of cold air whistled through the car.

"We won't lose them," she said. "Did you put on that scarf I gave you, Bryce?"

"Yes ma'am." He only sounded a little sarcastic. Martin adjusted his own scarf— the bright blue one—

tighter around his throat. "We've got to do something, and soon."

"I quite agree. What *is* that noise?"

It was a steady booming sound. Until she mentioned it, Martin had been afraid it was coming from the engine. Agent Jennings pointed off to the right.

"Some kind of dance club. Over there."

"At three o'clock?" Mrs. Womack clucked her tongue. "Don't they shut those things down?"

"Some of them stay open until four," he said, and shrugged when she stared at him. "So I hear. I'm a little old for that kind of thing, myself."

"I should hope so," she sniffed. "Martin, I want you to stay in the car. We have to move quickly."

"What are you going to do?"

She laid the shotgun across her lap, pulled a compact black revolver from a holster on her hip, and checked the rounds.

"Agent Jennings and I are going to ask the driver for his bill of lading."

She opened her car door and stepped out in a rush of wind and ice. Agent Jennings sighed and bailed out after her. The doors slammed and left Martin alone with the wheeze of the heater and the distant boom of the rock club.

He hit the windshield wipers, and in the resulting inch of clear glass watched Mrs. Womack walk quickly across the street in her sensible shoes, head down, shotgun concealed under her billowing coat. Agent Jennings moved in from behind.

The truck continued to idle, windshield wipers madly flapping. Martin tightened his grip on the steering wheel as Mrs. Womack marched right up to the cab's door and knocked on the metal.

The driver's side window rolled down. Mrs. Womack

shouted something that was lost in the wind; the driver cupped his hand around his ear and shook his head.

She flipped the shotgun up from under her coat.

The driver threw himself backward and raised something metal. Mrs. Womack fired, a boom out of sequence with the rock club bass, and he fired back, quick yapping shots.

The windshield fogged over with sleet again.

Martin hit the windshield wipers, but the street was empty, no Mrs. Womack, no nothing. He turned to look over his shoulder. Everything was cloudy with ice or fogged up.

Damn. Damn. Da—

The throaty roar of the truck startled him. They were running for it. Oh, god, he couldn't see anything. He turned on the wipers and put the heater on high, dimly made out the white shape of the truck moving forward.

The passenger-side door opened and Agent Jennings flung himself inside; his gasps shuddered in the air like smoke. Over his shoulder, Martin saw Mrs. Womack's face as white as the ice caught in her hair.

Blood poured from a hole in her leg. She folded into a sitting position on the cold street.

"Drive!" Jennings yelled. Martin pointed wordlessly at Mrs. Womack; Jennings slapped his hand down. "Damn you, drive, don't let him get away! Don't you understand? Go!"

Jennings jammed the accelerator, pinning Martin's foot underneath his. The car leaped forward, and the passenger door slammed shut with enough force to crack the window.

"I can't see!" Martin yelled. Jennings grabbed for the wheel. The car picked up speed, thirty, thirty-five. The tires started a long fast slide.

Something white ahead. The rock club's bass boomed like a giant heart.

"We're going to—"

They slammed head on into the truck.

Cold. Martin tried to sit up, but his head screamed in protest. He felt for it with numbed hands and yelped when his fingers brushed his nose— broken. Bright red blood on the dashboard in front of him, dripping on the steering wheel. It was all over his hands.

Head wound. He had a head wound. They always bled a lot. His arms were okay, his legs hurt like hell, but he could move them. The car was mashed to hell.

There was a limp white balloon hanging from the steering wheel. Air bag.

He turned his head to tell Agent Jennings about the air bag, but Jennings was gone. His door was open, creaking in the wind, and there was blood on the passenger seat.

"Jennings?" he croaked. "Hey, are you okay? Hey?"

He could see through the windshield now, mostly because the windshield was gone. Jagged squares of safety glass hung like fringe here and there; he had a good view of the white truck. It lay on its side like a dying elephant, grille mashed in. One tire was still spinning unevenly. The wind smelled like gas and hot metal.

Somebody opened the driver's-side door. Martin tried to turn his head, but it wouldn't cooperate. He turned it with both hands and blinked.

"Jennings?" No, the face wasn't Jennings. It was a big guy with a blank steroid look. In spite of the cold, he was wearing a sleeveless T-shirt. His arms looked like the Jaws of Life.

"You okay, man?" the Hulk asked. "We called 911.

Shit, there's some old lady shot over there. You do that?"

Martin tried to shake his head.

"I seen you crash. Man. Boom! Lucky you ain't dead, man. You been drinking or what? Hey, if you been drinking, better have one of these." He held up a tin full of what looked like mints. "Altoids. Cops won't smell it on your breath."

"Where's Jennings?"

"Who? The old lady? She's over there. Guy from the club, he used to be an EMT, he's over there with her. Don't worry, he ain't been drinking much."

"What about the truck? Anybody in there?"

The Hulk looked almost cheerful.

"Couple of dead guys, that's all. One of 'em has no face, Randy said. He was pukin' on the sidewalk, so I know he wasn't shitting me."

Over the Hulk's huge shoulder, Martin caught sight of a woman wearing a Dallas Cowboys sweatshirt, brand new. It still had creases. She smoothed it proudly over her hips and modeled it for a weaving leering boyfriend.

Martin held his head together with both hands and peered out at the street.

Chaos. The crash had drawn a crowd out of the club, and now they were at the truck, yanking open boxes, carrying off shirts— a purple-haired woman ran by carrying an armload. A young Hispanic man lifted two large boxes.

"No . . ." Martin's voice sounded slurred and weak. "No, stop . . . hey, stop them, they're taking— "

The Hulk looked where he pointed, and shrugged philosophically.

"Hey, dude, I'm just the bouncer, I ain't the cops. Fact is, I got a couple boxes stashed in my car right now."

Martin gritted his teeth and moved. He got one leg out the door, then the other, but when he tried to stand up, he fell over. The Hulk steadied him.

"Not a genius idea, man."

"I have to stop them," he said. It sounded stupid, and it *was* stupid, but he had to do something, anything. He staggered off toward the looting. The Hulk followed him at a casual distance.

Martin tried to take a sweatshirt out of the hands of a young woman wearing orange leather. By the time he got up again, she was gone, heading for a decrepit Pinto.

He grabbed hold of a middle-aged man in a business suit, and got an elbow in ribs that already felt like confetti. He sat down on the pavement to think about it, head down, and felt a hand on his shoulder.

"It was good of you to try to stop them," said a quiet male voice. The accent sounded English. Martin cradled his head in his hands. The splintering noise wasn't just in his head, after all— sirens, approaching in the distance. The man squeezed his shoulder hard enough to make him wince. "Such a tragedy."

"Had to try," Martin mumbled, and looked up. The man bending over him was about his own age, dressed in a dark sweater and khaki pants, a thick down parka with fur around the hood. He had a smooth Arabic complexion and large soulful eyes. And a smile.

He knew that face. From— where?

"I see you know me," the man said, and it clicked. Fathi el Haddiz. Carling's terrorist. "I'm afraid I don't know you. Were you driving the car? If so, my congratulations. Quite a solid hit. You might even have accomplished your mission, if this hadn't happened. People are so greedy, don't you think?"

He produced a gun from a pocket and pointed it casually at Martin's chest. Martin swallowed hard.

"If you're looking for your coworker, the younger man, I'm afraid he's dead. Head trauma. The old woman is injured, but not seriously, as long as someone keeps pressure on her wound." Haddiz's face went very still. The eyes didn't look soulful anymore. "I'm sure you understand why I can't allow you to live."

He leaned over and put the barrel of the gun to Martin's forehead.

"It's what you might call a Pyrrhic victory, if you had any classical training," el Haddiz said conversationally. "Did you know— "

A shadow flickered at the corner of Martin's eyes, a big shadow. El Haddiz tried to turn to meet the threat.

He met the oncoming piledriver of the Hulk's fist.

El Haddiz's gun fell in between Martin's knees and slid to a stop against his shoes. The Hulk grabbed el Haddiz's collar and yanked him upright.

"No guns on club property, fuckhead," the Hulk grunted, and slammed a fist into his stomach. Several times. When he let the smaller man go, el Haddiz crumpled to the ground and stayed there.

"Thanks," Martin said quite calmly. The Hulk shrugged.

"No sweat."

"Now help me stop these people from taking the shirts."

The Hulk's friendly smile slipped. "Hey, man, I told you, no way. *You* stop 'em."

Martin tried to stand up.

Lights out.

Forty
Robby

Robby hated to admit it, but Velvet had been right. She was so tired it was an effort to walk in a straight line, and her eyes ached from crying. She'd collected only two wallets, and the second had nearly been a fumble; if the guy hadn't been dead drunk, he couldn't have failed to notice. Her throat felt dry and scratchy, her skin uncomfortably warm. Not only exhaustion, though that was part of it— she was coming down with something. A cold. The flu.

She'd had to pay a cover charge to get into the Gearbox, but she was ready to forfeit the five bucks just to get outside where it was cool. God, she felt bad. As she fought her way through the writhing sweating crowd on the dance floor— and collected another wallet, almost against her will— she had to catch her balance against their bodies. Nobody noticed. Half of them were staggering anyway.

She shed her leather coat on the way to the door and folded it over her arm. By the time she'd pushed past the last tight knot of drunks at the door, she'd lost it, dropped somewhere on the dirty floor. A bouncer tried to tell her she couldn't come back in once she'd left, but she shoved past him and made it into the cool blessed air.

The shock of sleet felt wonderful on her overheated skin. She tilted her face up to it and felt some
of the dizziness recede.

Nausea boiled up without any warning at all. She
leaned over and vomited into the gutter, clinging helplessly to the rough oily wood of a telephone pole. *You
look ridiculous,* she thought in between heaves. *Dressed
like a whore, vomiting in the gutter. Just like Velvet.*

She'd worn the leather and Spandex mostly because Velvet had believed she wouldn't; protective
camouflage, that was all. She felt exposed in it,
marked for a victim. She'd never, never do it again.

If I live through it this time, she thought miserably.
Oh, god, I'm sick.

Across the street, a man in a camel brown coat came
walking out of the neon-lit tunnel of Dallas Alley— not
walking, actually, slipping and sliding and trying to
run. He was shouting into a cellular phone. She rested
her cheek against the telephone pole and watched him
come closer; he was expensively dressed, preoccupied.

One last score, and she could go home.

"— Mean, wrecked? How could it wreck? Oh, god,
you're not serious! The whole shipment? Where *were*
you? No, you, where were *you?* This is a disaster! No,
I'm *not* going to give you a *refund—* "

All she had to do was let go of the pole, walk toward him, take his wallet. Easy. So easy.

When she let go of the pole, she almost fell.

"Whoa!" The man in the camel-hair coat snapped
his cell phone shut and grabbed her by the arm.
There. That was better. All she had to do was reach
out— "Are you okay? You look— "

He stopped and stared at her. At her face. At the
outfit she knew she shouldn't have worn. The chilly
slide of icy rain on her skin stopped feeling good
and made her shiver.

"Hey— " he said, and his fingers tightened around her arm. He looked at her face again. "That little bitch wore the wrong clothes. I can't believe it. You're the other one, the thief."

Robby tried to break free, but her muscles felt hot and painful, and her head was spinning. Bile tasted rough on the back of her throat.

"Don't know what you're talking about," she mumbled. Her lips felt numbed, her tongue slow and clumsy. She tried to get his wallet, but it slipped out of her fingers and fell. "Let me go."

"Not a chance." He fumbled in his pocket. His face took on a blank expression of panic. He switched his hold on her to his other hand. "Shit. Shit! I lost it."

"What?"

"The gun. I lost the gun! Oh, never mind, shut up and walk. Just walk. Come on."

He dragged her to a stumble, as fast as his slick-soled shoes could go on the icy sidewalk. Behind them, people and music spilled out of the Gearbox. She tried to break away again but he held tight.

"Faster. Walk faster. Hurry. Are you warm, are you getting warm?" He looked over at her face. "Damn. It's too cold out here."

He let go of her arm and stripped off his coat. Before she could get more than three weaving steps away, he threw it around her shoulders and grabbed her wrist.

"Put it on." He looked almost gray with panic, eyes darting all around on the sidewalk. She tried, but her arm wouldn't cooperate. "Put it on, hurry up! This is the worst day, absolutely the worst day of my life. I know you don't care about that, but it is. Everything was supposed to happen today, and nothing worked, nothing. It's all going up in smoke."

He stopped and a thin panicked giggle worked its

way out of his mouth in a gust of steamy breath. His eyes had a strange shine to them.

"But *you'll* work," he said. He took her arm and threaded it in the sleeve, dressed her like a rag doll. She huddled in the warmth of the coat. "Come on, *walk*. Walk *faster.*"

It seemed to take forever to reach the next corner, a nightmare of uncertain steps and the tight stretch of Spandex over her skin, of dizziness and heat prickling. He was talking to her again, but she hardly understood what he was saying until he shook her hard enough to rattle her teeth.

"Can you feel it?" he asked. "Is it starting yet?"

What boiled up out of her this time wasn't nausea, it was knowledge.

He was talking about burning. He'd put something on the clothes to make Velvet burn. Oh, Jesus, like Arnold, like the man at the hockey game.

She was going to die.

A police car turned a corner and started toward her. She felt the headlights wash over her like sunlight.

The man tightened his grip on her arm.

"Don't," he warned her. "If you run, it'll only happen faster."

She shoved him as hard as she could. He stumbled backward, hit a patch of ice and slid. He grabbed a parking meter to keep from falling. She shrugged his coat off and ran for the police car. Her legs vibrated like rubber bands, her skin flared hot, hotter.

Oh, god, no. No, not like this.

She collided with the hood of the police car with bruising force, stared into the startled faces of two uniformed cops, and hobbled on. There was water flooding out over the sidewalk near Dallas Alley, a wet shimmer in the gleam of neon. A pipe had broken in the cold.

She fell full length in the water and rolled. The shock made her scream, but she kept rolling, back and forth, until she was soaking wet and the cops were pulling her to her knees.

"Drunk," she heard one of them say.

One of the wallets she'd stolen fell out of her skirt. Then the second.

"Stupid," the other one said. "Up, lady. Let's take a little ride."

She was shivering convulsively as they slammed the back door of the squad car, but she was alive. Alive.

The man was gone from across the street. His coat lay discarded on the sidewalk, flapping like a ghost in the wind.

"How much did you have to drink?" one of the cops asked her. She tried to talk past the chattering of her teeth.

"N-n-nothing. H-help me."

"We're going to help you. We're taking you to the station."

"N-no," she said, and took a deep breath. "T-t-take m-my clothes off."

Forty-one
Velvet

Velvet played dead until she was sure he was gone, the asshole, the fucking asshole. At least he was a terrible shot. She didn't even think he'd knicked the leather jacket, though laying on the cold street wasn't doing much for it, either. She eased up to her knees and winced at the ache in her arm. She'd slammed her elbow when she'd dropped, but it was better than breaking her face again.

He'd tried to *kill* her, the asshole. What had he said? *Why aren't you dead yet?*

"Oh, god, the clothes," she said, and got to her feet. "He poisoned the clothes."

She remembered Burt, burning.

It was definitely time to get the hell out of Dodge. Money or no money, it didn't matter. She'd hitch a ride, she'd blow a truck driver, anything, *anything*. She couldn't stay in this town one more minute.

She slogged out to the street, keeping to the shadows and watching carefully for any signs of Mr. Julian, the murderous dry cleaner. She was being so careful that she stepped on something thick and metallic, and it slid under her foot with a screech and almost knocked her on her butt. She reached down and picked up the

gun Mr. Julian had used to shoot her. Not only was
he a lousy shot, he was clumsy, too.

As she came out on the street, she saw him on the
other side, walking with his arm around some woman.

A date? He'd shot her and then went out on a *date*?
The unbelievable fucker.

The woman shoved him back and ran. She was wearing a short black leather skirt, a Spandex bodysuit,
short boots. She ran right into the path of a cruising
cop car.

"Robby," Velvet whispered.

Robby was wearing the poisoned clothes. God,
she'd told her to wear them. Her fault. Again.

Robby fell on the sidewalk in a splash of water.
The cops yanked her up, handcuffed her, and shoved
her in the back of the prowl car. Mr. Julian left his
coat lying on the sidewalk and ran off down the
street. Velvet hid in the shadows and watched him
go, bit her lip and danced from one foot to the other
as the cops secured Robby. God, what could she do?
Follow them? How?

A thin hollow-chested guy came out of the Gearbox
and walked over to a gray rusted-out Camaro. As he
opened the door, she hurried up to lean casually
against the ice-cube cold car fender.

"Hey. I saw you inside," she said. He looked surprised— and dazed. He'd had some chemical altera-
tions. "I just *had* to talk to you."

"Yeah?" He licked his lips and looked around, as if
he wasn't sure she was talking to him. "Well, uh, hi.
So— "

"Wanna party?"

The lights in his head were 10-watt bulbs. She was
beginning to think she'd have to give him the laundry
list, but the switch flipped just as the police car doors
slammed and it pulled away from the curb.

"Sure!" He looked like she'd given him a winning Lotto ticket. "Uh, get in. Sorry, uh, about the mess . . ."

He wasn't kidding. She looked in and saw a mountain of fast food bags in the back, old mail, parking tickets, condom wrappers. She took the gun out of her pocket and pointed it at him. The terror in his eyes scared her.

"Sorry, buddy, I need your car. Give me the keys." When he didn't move, she took a deep breath. "I don't have time to fuck with you. Give me the keys, or I shoot you and take them."

He tossed them over. She caught them one-handed and slid in the driver's seat. He stepped well back from the car, holding his hands in the air.

"Sorry!" she yelled, and slammed the door. It creaked and the whole car rattled. The engine cranked sluggishly, then caught with a roar.

When she looked in the rearview mirror he was running, hands still in the air, toward the Gearbox.

"Sorry," she said again, more softly. "I'm always fucking sorry."

Forty-two
Robby

Robby started to feel warm again after five minutes or so; the blast of the car heater made her sick and dizzy. The cops had given up talking to her, and she'd given up pleading. They didn't understand.

They didn't believe her.

"Oh, hell, what the— " The car slowed; the back tires slid gently, and the cop corrected without even noticing. "Great. Looters. That's just what we need tonight."

The car coasted to a stop. Robby opened her eyes and saw a hissing curtain of ice; it was falling faster now, building to a hard-packed surface on the street. A truck was overturned in the road, its load of boxes spilled out and broken. People scattered at the sight of the police car, arms full of what looked like shirts.

Beyond the truck was a dark blue sedan. It was crushed like a beer can. As she watched, paramedics lifted a man onto a gurney. His face was covered with blood. His blue scarf dragged on the pavement behind him.

"Let me out," she whispered. Her shoulders ached with the strain of the handcuffs. "I'm serious. Lemme out or I'll burn up.

"Yeah, sure, honey. Just sleep it off or something." The older cop didn't even look back at her as he got out. A welcome puff of cold air blew back toward her, but it wasn't enough, she was drying off, she was getting hot again.

The younger cop turned toward her.

"You okay?" he asked. She burst into tears. "We'll be on our way in just a few minutes. Just sit tight."

She lay down on the seat, gasping for breath. So hot. She could feel the fire starting where she'd begun to sweat under the leather.

"Hey!" The younger cop tried to pull her upright. "Hey—"

He got out and opened the back door.

She slammed her feet into the door and threw him out of the way, slithered out onto the pavement and launched into a stumbling weaving run. Her boots slipped and slid on the ice, her lungs ached from the shock of freezing air. Ice crystals stung at her face and neck.

The young cop got up and chased her, shouting. She heard him fall and scream.

"My leg! I broke my leg!"

She made it to the opposite side of the street and into the shadows of an alley, charged past a Dumpster and around another corner, another alley, this one littered with paper sacks of garbage. The air stank of urine and rotting fish.

She stumbled out onto another street, deserted except for a few parked cars. The waving curtain of icy rain swept toward her, and she slumped against a wall and let it soak her.

She had to get out of the clothes. *Had* to.

In the shadow of a boarded-up doorway, three homeless men warmed themselves over a hibachi fueled with old newspapers and magazines. She weaved toward them and stopped, gasping. They didn't even look up.

"Help me," she managed. One of them glanced at

her, then back down in to the fire. He added a curling *TV Guide* to the flames. "Please! Please, you— you— "

"Can't hep you," he said in a high thin voice. "Can't hep nobody. Git."

"I need— do you have— a knife— or— "

The second homeless man looked up, frowning.

"I got a knife," he said, and grinned. His front teeth were worn to thin pegs. "Good knife. Sharp."

"Help me get my clothes off."

The third man added torn-up strips of *USA Today* to the hibachi, as if she hadn't said anything at all.

"Help me take my clothes off!" she screamed. "Don't you understand? Take my clothes off!"

"Been a long time since anybody asked for that," the second man said to the first. The first nodded thoughtfully. "Been, oh, two year. Yeah?"

"Yah. Two year. Maybe two an a haf. 'Member, was over on Ellum— "

She let out a wordless scream of frustration and headed on up the street, into the wind and the bite of the ice.

"You gonna freeze!" the first man yelled after her, and laughed. "Crazy bitch."

A car turned the corner behind her. She tried to run, but her feet couldn't hold on the ice; she slipped off balance and fell heavily on her side. Her head hit the pavement hard enough to make her vision cloud. When she could see again, a rusty Camaro had eased to a stop next to the curb, and the passenger door was open.

Velvet reached down and grabbed her under the arms.

"Help," Robby whispered. "Help."

"What do you think I'm doing?" Velvet asked, and got her in the car. Robby leaned against the door, face against the cold glass, and felt the nausea again.

Still too warm. Soon it wouldn't matter. Nothing could stop it. "Aw, shit, you look like hell."

"Dying," Robby said. Velvet froze in the act of turning the ignition key.

"It's the clothes, right? I knew it. It's the clothes. Listen, it's okay, I'll get you home and we'll get them off—"

"No time," she said. "Going to die."

"Shit." Velvet leaned over her and fumbled open the glove compartment. "Flashlight— oh, great, dead batteries— one glove— what the hell is this? Oh, yeah, ice scraper— uh— condoms—"

She straightened up with a pair of rusty nail scissors.

"Skirt," Robby whispered. Velvet yanked the skirt around and found the zipper, slid the leather down Robby's legs. The bodysuit was the problem— with her hands behind her, she couldn't get it off. Velvet bit her lip and grabbed one sleeve; she sawed at the Spandex with the nail scissors.

"Oh, Jesus, it's like cutting steel or something! Ow!" Velvet wagged her fingers in the cold air. "Hang on, I'm trying—"

Cold white headlights spilled into the car. Velvet stopped working and looked at Robby, wide-eyed.

"Uh, did I mention I stole this car? And you, like, escaped from police custody? Maybe we'd better drive."

She adjusted the rearview mirror and looked behind her. Her face went chalk-white under its thick layer of makeup and bruises.

"That ain't the cops," she said, and started the car. The second the engine caught, she jammed the accelerator and almost spun out on the ice. "Oh, shit, Robby, we're in big fucking trouble here."

Forty-three
Velvet

The car following them was a sky blue Mercedes, and it got close enough for Velvet to see the rabbity sweating face of the driver.

Mr. Julian. Jesus, didn't the guy know when to quit?

The Mercedes spun out on Commerce, whirling around gracefully three times before it broadsided a light pole. Velvet kept driving as fast as she dared, and lost sight of him when she took another left.

"Where're we going?" Robby asked. Velvet risked a look at her. She looked— dead. Pale, sick, sweating. It was the fucking clothes, and she couldn't stop to get them off. Not yet.

"I have absolutely no idea," Velvet answered. "West. I'll know when we get there."

She blasted through a red light and came out on the far side of Interstate 35, hung a left on Industrial. Not a great neighborhood, but deserted. She liked it. She'd just go under I-30 toward the open-all-night adult video place and—

The Camaro died. Just like that. Sputtered and choked and hacked and died on her. It coasted to a stop and slid a little sideways. She pounded on the steering wheel and screamed.

It was out of gas. Trust her to steal a car on empty.

"Velvet?" Robby sounded worse than she looked. "Hot. Help."

"Yeah, okay, sure." Velvet grabbed the nail scissors and got out, ran to Robby's side and dragged her out. She left the Camaro sitting in the street, both doors open, and half-carried, half-guided Robby to the side.

Robby pointed right in front of them, at a chain link fence, a collection of round squatty huts, skeletal machines, and piles of rock and sand.

"There?" Velvet squinted at the rusty sign. "Highway Department. Why the hell not?"

The gates were open, and the lights were on in one of the huts, but it was locked. She banged on the door, kicked it in frustration when nobody answered.

"They're all out icing the roads. Shit. Shit! Here, let's work on this." She wiggled the nail scissors back under Robby's sleeve again and began to cut. It was slow work, and her fingers cramped with cold and pressure. Robby's shivering got worse. "How you doing, kid? You with me?"

"Y-y-yes. F-f-f-eel better." She didn't look better, she looked frostbitten. Velvet cut through the last inch of Spandex on the sleeve and got Robby's arm free.

It was covered with a raw-looking red rash. She transferred the scissors to the other sleeve and started sawing.

There were still a few cars moving— one was coming slowly down Industrial. Velvet watched the approaching lights nervously as she cut. She freed Robby's left arm, grabbed the bodysuit in front and back, and rolled it down.

Robby's skin was flushed red all over, like a terrible sunburn. She'd worn a pair of panties, no bra. Velvet wadded up the Spandex and tossed it in a trash barrel, stripped off her coat, and wrapped it around

Robby's shivering bare shoulders. Nothing she could do about the handcuffs yet.

"It's okay. It's gonna be okay now. You're okay."

Robby sank down on the ground, still shivering.

"Thought I was dying," she said. Velvet sat down next to her and huddled close for warmth.

"Yeah, I'd want to die if I had a rash like that." She watched the car's headlights slow and stop behind the Camaro. "I hope to hell that's not the cops."

It wasn't. It was a Mercedes, sky blue.

Velvet grabbed Robby's elbow and squeezed.

"Stay low and follow me."

The highway guys had driven out every truck except one at the far end of the yard— it had a full load of sand, but one tire was flat. She slithered underneath and pulled Robby after her. She couldn't see Julian anywhere.

"What're you doing?" Robby hissed. Velvet tried the truck's door. It opened. The dome light came on.

"Shit! Get in there!"

She boosted Robby into the cab and climbed in after her, slammed the door, and locked it. Robby twisted and tried to push the button down on her side with her head; the coat slid off her shoulders.

"Could you— "

Velvet readjusted the coat and reached across to press the lock. Outside, everything was quiet, nothing moving. No sign of Mr. Julian, except for the blue Mercedes parked on the road behind the Camaro.

"Now what?" Robby's breath made a thick white cloud in the still cold air.

"I'm thinking!" Velvet slapped herself on the side of the head. "The gun! The gun's in your pocket!"

"Gun . . ." Robby twisted as Velvet dug in the coat's pockets. She came up with the automatic and smiled in triumph. "You can't just— "

"Oh, fuck that. He tried to kill me."

Something slammed into the back window, shattering it into a thousand glittering pieces; Velvet screamed and threw up her hands to cover her head; the gun fell to the floor. She hit some button on the dash, and the engine started up with a grinding roar. Cold air blasted out of the vents. Robby curled into a ball on the seat.

Mr. Julian reached through the ruin of the back window and unlocked the door on Velvet's side. She lunged for the gun on the floorboards, but it skittered away under Robby's feet.

The door jerked open. As Velvet got her fingers on the gun, an iron bar slammed into her arm. She screamed so loud she almost didn't hear the bone break, but she felt it, all right, felt it even more when Julian grabbed a handful of hair and jerked her out of the truck. He hit her again, this time in the side. She fell flat and rolled, and the bar hit gravel instead of her head, where he'd aimed. She rolled under the truck and crawled desperately for the other end of the truck. Where the hell was he? Getting Robby? Beating her? Shit, shit—

She crawled out under the truck's bed and rolled to her knees.

He came around the truck and swung the iron bar again. She overbalanced to avoid it and fell flat on her back. He grabbed her ankle and pulled, grinning. Winning.

"You fucker!" she screamed, and kicked at him. Useless. He stepped back, breathing in deep foggy gasps, and raised the bar over his head.

The truck made a deafening skull-grinding beeping noise. Julian looked up, startled, just as the first wave of sand spilled out.

It didn't seem like much until the second wave hit,

deep enough to come up to Julian's knees, deep enough to cover Velvet's head. She clawed her way to a sitting position and tried to get up. The sand dragged like little hands.

The third wave knocked her flat. She tried to scream, but sand was everywhere, in her mouth, her nose, a dusty flat smell in the back of her throat. The weight crushed her.

Her good hand clawed for the surface and found cold air.

Found warm skin. She grabbed on and pulled blindly.

It was Robby's elbow she'd grabbed. Velvet spat sand and gagged and blinked enough to see Robby sitting spread-eagled on top of the sandpile, naked except for a thin pair of panties, hands still cuffed behind her.

"What— " Velvet choked and coughed, sand spraying in ripples under her chin. "What the fuck did you do?"

"Pulled every lever I could find," Robby said. She looked dazed and apologetic. "I couldn't get the gun. I tried."

A man's foot, still in an expensive leather shoe, poked out of the sand near Velvet's face. It trembled two or three times, then went still.

"Honey," Velvet whispered, "you did just fine. Just fine."

With another tug on Robby's arm, she dragged herself out of the sand and gave the woman a big long one-armed hug, never mind the red lacy rash all over Robby's body. Pain had made her strangely happy. Velvet found her coat near the truck and draped it back over Robby's shoulders and hugged her close for warmth, rocking a little.

The sleet kept coming, steady knives of ice. It didn't matter anymore.

They were still sitting there when the Highway Department supervisor pulled his truck into the lot and said, "That your Mercedes out there on the street?"

Robby laughed. Velvet hugged her closer with her good arm and said, "Absolutely."

Forty-four
Martin

Strangely enough, when he saw the line go flat on Sally's monitor, he didn't feel grief at all, only sadness. He stood while the nurses silently disconnected the monitors and the tubes and left him with her wasted little body.

"I'm sorry, baby," he said, and touched her skin. She still felt warm, still felt alive. She'd been dead for years, but she'd always *felt* alive. "Daddy's so sorry."

He found he didn't want to cry, but he held her limp light hand for a while and watched the sun set behind clouds. The nurses stayed out of his way. When the sun was down, he put her hand back at her side and pulled the sheet over her face. She looked smaller than he remembered.

"Martin?" Adrian Carling's whisper was silk. He didn't turn to look at her, or betray any surprise that she'd come to see him.

It had been two weeks since he'd woken up in the hospital to find that she'd been moved to another, more secure facility. One week since he'd received an arrangement of yellow roses and a card that said *Be patient, Marty*. He'd been patient. He'd had no choice.

"She's gone." It was the only thing he had to say, really. The only thing that meant anything.

"I'm sorry."

He shook his head and stood up. Carling looked pale and thin, but she was okay, getting physically stronger every day. Of course, she'd always been strong in spirit. Not like him.

"Do you want me to help with the arrangements?" she asked.

"What? Oh, no, I made them years ago. They kept thinking . . . it was just a matter of days. But she hung on. She was strong." He met her eyes. "All I have to do is sign a form."

"Will you be okay?" she asked. He noticed she did not ask, *Are you okay*, she knew the answer to that.

"I think so." He sucked in a breath deep enough to ease the tension in his chest. "I've been patient."

"I know. Thank you."

God, so much to say, but he couldn't think of any of it. He settled for information. "Any word on the two women who killed Ed Julian?"

"Gone. They drove his Mercedes to San Antonio and sold it the next morning for cash, hopped a flight to Florida. We lost track of them after that. Oh, and there was a man involved, too. James Patterson, alias Psycho Jim. Professional small-time thief. Other than the fact one of the women boosted him out of the hospital, there's no information so far. I really don't expect there will be."

"Were they yours?" he asked. She looked at him with those secretive eyes, that faint half-smile, and he knew that no matter what, he loved her. He couldn't help it. "Okay. What about the sweatshirts that were looted out of the truck?"

"We've issued a statement that they're contaminated with toxic chemicals."

"True enough."

"We expect to get a ninety percent return." She

shook her head. "It gets warm in this town by March. The other ten percent will probably take care of themselves."

The nurses came in silently to take Sally. He left before he could see it happen, walking too fast for Carling's slow rehabilitating steps to match.

She caught up with him at the elevator.

"I suppose you got the formula," he said to her, as if nothing had happened. *Oh, my baby girl.* She shrugged. "It's what you were sent to do, wasn't it? Get the formula?"

"Among other things."

"What do you think they'll do with it?"

"Not my mission, Marty. I'm in acquisitions, not applications." The tone was just right, casual and careless, but there was a subtle tension around her mouth. *Ah, Adrian, not so tough as you think you are.*

"You might think about stopping them," he said.

"I'm thinking about it. Hypothetically speaking."

She gave him a long serious look. The elevator arrived and a doctor got out, two nurses pushed in. She entered last, turned, held the doors open.

"Coming?"

He shook his head. She reached out and put a hand on his arm.

"Stay cool, Marty," she said. Her fingers squeezed. "Stay out of it. Hypothetically speaking."

He knew, as the elevator doors shut between them, that she knew him better than that.

This book contains flammable materials.

Be careful.